READ BETWEEN THE LIES

OTHER TITLES BY JESSE Q. SUTANTO

Vera Wong's Unsolicited Advice for Murderers

Vera Wong's Guide to Snooping (on a Dead Man)

Next Time Will Be Our Turn

Dial A for Aunties

Four Aunties and a Wedding

The Good, the Bad, and the Aunties

Worth Fighting For

I'm Not Done with You Yet

You Will Never Be Me

The Obsession

The New Girl

Well, That Was Unexpected

Didn't See That Coming

Theo Tan and the Fox Spirit

Theo Tan and the Iron Fan

READ BETWEEN THE LIES

A Novel

JESSE Q. SUTANTO

USA TODAY BESTSELLING AUTHOR

MINDY'S BOOK STUDIO

This is a work of fiction. Names, characters, organizations, places, events, and incidents are either products of the author's imagination or are used fictitiously. Otherwise, any resemblance to actual persons, living or dead, is purely coincidental.

Published by Mindy's Book Studio, New York

www.apub.com

EU product safety contact:
Amazon Media EU S. à r.l.
38, avenue John F. Kennedy, L-1855 Luxembourg
amazonpublishing-gpsr@amazon.com

ISBN-13: 9781662534645 (hardcover)
ISBN-13: 9781662534638 (paperback)
ISBN-13: 9781662534652 (digital)

Cover design by *The*BookDesigners
Cover image: © rustemgurler / Getty; © FamGrafis / Shutterstock

Printed in the United States of America
First edition

To those whose only recourse is self-destruction.
I see you. You are not alone.

A NOTE FROM MINDY KALING

Hi! I'm so glad you've dropped whatever else you were reading and picked up *Read Between the Lies*. If you are fascinated by cancel culture, internet drama, and the surprisingly savage world of publishing, then this is perfect for you! Plus, it's from Jesse Q. Sutanto—the bestselling genius who gave us *Dial A for Aunties* and *Vera Wong's Unsolicited Advice for Murderers*, so you already know it's going to be twisty, funny, and a little unhinged in the best way.

The year is 2018, and Fern Huang is a struggling writer in NYC whose only friend is her sourdough starter, Doughlores. Fern is depressed, broke, and fully obsessed with stalking her childhood-bully-turned-Instagram-famous influencer, Haven Lee.

The good news is by 2020 she's a published author. The bad news? She somehow ends up in the same debut author group as Haven. What follows is pandemic chaos, publishing-world drama, and a social media war so messy I kept switching sides.

This book is twisty, hilarious, and dark in a fun way. Think *Dial A for Aunties* meets *You*, but for people who know what BookTok is. Bring snacks and opinions.

Prologue

The cops arrive in the middle of precalculus. My eyes are riveted on them as they speak to Mrs. Woods at the door. Mrs. Woods turns to look over her shoulder, and her eyes land immediately on mine. My stomach twists painfully. Are they here for me? Then she looks at Haven and nods at her. We have been summoned.

Whispers rake through the classroom as Haven and I stand up and walk toward the door. I keep my eyes down, fear jolting through my veins.

We're led down the hallway, our footsteps painfully loud in the silence. I can hear every single sound—my own breathing, the jangling of the cops' equipment, their heavy footsteps. I sneak glances at them, my terror growing with every detail I take in about them. They're so tall, so large, so present.

Our principal, Ms. James, is waiting outside her office. She nods grimly at the cops, then gestures at me and Haven. "Come inside, girls."

By now, I'm so scared that when I'm offered a chair, I practically collapse into it. In my mind, a single thought repeats itself: What're they going to say? What're they going to say?

The cops settle down across from us. One of them clears her throat. Her gaze is steady as she leans forward and says, "Danielle Wilder was found dead this morning."

Next to me, Haven gasps. My mouth is open, my face frozen.

"We're here to talk to you girls," the officer continues, "because we were told you were her closest friends."

At this, I blurt out, "I'm her best friend." It strikes me, then, what a ridiculous thing it is to say. How childish and stupid. I'm her best friend, as though I were a kid. Then it hits me that Dani and I were best friends when we were kids, and the thought of her back then, her hair always done up in French braids, stabs through my mind, and I burst into tears. "She can't be dead," I sob. It sounds like a whine, a plea.

"I'm so sorry for your loss," the officer says. The kindness in her voice only makes me cry harder.

"What happened?" Haven says. Her voice is shrill, so unlike her.

"Well, that's what we're here to figure out." The officer's gaze ping-pongs back and forth between me and Haven. "Was Danielle struggling with anything? Did she mention to you girls anything to do with her mental health, maybe feelings of depression or anxiety?"

Now, both Haven and I are staring at her with open confusion. "Wait," Haven says slowly. "Are you saying . . . she killed herself?" Her voice breaks then, and she covers her mouth.

"We're trying to determine the cause of death," the officer says. "Is there anything you can tell us that might help us understand how this happened?"

I look down at my hands through a blur of tears. Then I glance at Haven, who is crying, too, now, and a wave of virulent hatred surges through my entire being. It's all her fault. If she hadn't been such a cruel bully, none of this would've happened. I want to jump and scream it out loud, point my finger at Haven and tell everyone what she's really like. But when the officer repeats the question, the words refuse to come out of my mouth. They catch in my throat like a fish bone. And I can't say anything, not even a word, because Haven is right next to me, and I am terrified of what she might do if I tell them the truth.

Chapter 1

The only reason movies and TV shows and books are so obsessed with stories about the underdog triumphing over their bullies is because that kind of thing never happens in real life. In real life, the underdog remains the underdog. The wounds of childhood trauma have broken them, and they are unable to stand up straight and smile convincingly for the camera. Meanwhile, their tormentors carry on as they do, carefree and blissfully ignorant of the permanence of the damage they've wreaked on others. Or maybe they're not ignorant, maybe they know exactly what they've done, and it's a secret knowledge that heightens their sense of power. Maybe it's something they get off on, a dirty little memory that they return to in the darkness of night, to caress lovingly, savoring the ephemeral shot of endorphins that comes with the thought: I did that to that loser, and I got away with it.

Because at the end of the day, isn't that what life is all about? Getting away with things. There is pleasure that comes from that, from having a secret that you know full well isn't quite a good thing, a healthy thing, like sneak-eating ice cream straight from the tub at 2:00 a.m. I don't care what the laws of physics say; ice cream tastes better when you eat it in secret at 2:00 a.m. It just does. Because you're getting away with it, with something naughty. A guilty pleasure, women's magazines call it. And I get it. I may be a mess, but I'm a mess wrought out of low self-esteem and stitched together by thin strands of guilty pleasures.

It is possible I am getting too abstract for my own good. I tend to do that sometimes. It's the effect of having been Haven Lee's target. Growing up, my parents often called me Space Cadet, because I was always floating off into space. Actually, if they took the time to get to know me, they'd know I wasn't so much floating off as I was desperately shutting out the rest of the world because, thanks to Haven, it had gotten too awful for me to exist in. But they never took the time. Nor did they have the energy. I don't blame them.

Meanwhile, Haven Lee maintains the most beautiful relationship with her parents. Every Sunday morning, they meet up for brunch—sometimes at a fancy place with bottomless mimosas; sometimes, when they're feeling nostalgic, at a dim sum place in San Gabriel.

Most Chinese families I know only go to Sunday dim sum together, but Haven and her family are different. Aside from the Sunday brunches, she also drops by for dinners at their house on Wednesdays, where she and her dad make something labor intensive from scratch—dumplings or buns or handmade noodles. Haven's mom makes the cocktails. She goes all out on these cocktails; she has a nifty little device that forms a giant bubble filled with scented smoke, for example, that she blows onto the top of the drink. Haven pops it with the tip of her nose, and the family dissolves into peals of laughter as lavender-or-orange-peel-scented smoke spills out.

The meals are accompanied by good wine, and at the end of it, everyone is red faced and full bellied, and there is so much camaraderie and love in the house I could just die. Meanwhile, the couple of times I see my parents throughout the year are vastly different. I still try to make cheerful conversation, but their sullenness will wear me down after fifteen minutes, and before long, we will accept the silence, our cutlery pinging against our plates with painful clarity while we eat. But, I remind myself, at least my parents are still able to have meals with me. Dani's parents would probably give up everything just to have her back for one meal.

I live as far away from all the painful memories as I can, on the other side of the country, in New York City, but still I can't keep myself from keeping up to date with Haven's life. It's next to impossible not to, especially when she makes her life so readily available for public consumption. Haven is an influencer. Not the type of influencer people love to hate. She's a food influencer. Her food isn't pretentious; there are no acai-and-matcha smoothie bowls with painstakingly arranged flowers on top of them. She cooks hearty meals, high-calorie foods that should stick to her bones but don't. Sometimes they're multistep dishes that take hours of preparation, other times they're ten-minute dishes that she rustles up in her bright and airy kitchen. And they look absolutely delicious. Her followers, over one million of them, have been clamoring for a cookbook for ages. As much as I hate to admit it, if she came out with a cookbook, I would probably end up buying a copy, because her food looks so good. The thing that kills me is that back in school, I was the one who was into baking first. Haven had zero interest in anything involving the kitchen. It feels like yet another thing she's stolen from me.

But unfortunately, I am not an influencer. I have a desk job and a very attentive boss. A fact that I am reminded of when said boss, Annette, barks at me to bring her coffee.

I swipe at my phone, closing Instagram—Haven with her fork midway up to her heart-shaped lips—and hurry to Annette's kitchen. I slide a Nespresso pod out and pause. Today is Tuesday, and on Tuesdays, Annette takes the ristretto. Right. I slide the pod back and spin the tower. After locating the correct pod, I push it into the Nespresso machine as Annette calls out, "Coffee ETA?"

Annette loves saying "ETA" because it makes her sound busy and important. I sometimes wonder why a prewedding photographer needs to sound busy and important, but maybe that's just another thing I haven't quite learned about the wedding industry. When I first started, I was so hopelessly ignorant that I didn't even know what a prewedding photographer was. Then I learned that it's a photographer who takes pretty pictures of couples before their actual wedding day. There is a huge market for it, especially with Asian couples. Ninety percent of Annette's clients are couples from all over Asia who want glamorous pre-wed photos in Manhattan. They come with suitcases stuffed full of gorgeous ballgowns and rented wedding dresses so stunning I often just stop and stare at them.

Annette takes these couples all over the city and photographs them at every iconic New York location. Every single time, she tells the couples that this spot is unique, that very few couples have gone for that spot. Thing is, though, she is lying. I know, because as her assistant, I'm the one who edits the actual photos, and they are all the same, every one of them, down to the poses. Annette believes in being well prepared, in never standing behind the camera at two wide-eyed people and not having a trusted pose to suggest. It's a good strategy, actually, because most people don't like standing in front of a professional-grade DSLR camera. The huge lens and the knowledge of how much they've spent on this photo shoot overwhelms them, and without Annette's gentle guidance, most of them would stand there with frozen, terrified grins.

Annette is all gentle guidance when it comes to her clients, coaxing them into romantic poses ("Look down so we get a good shot of those beautiful lashes of yours, yep, perfect, and meanwhile, you put your arms around her and kiss her shoulder, yes, just like that, oh, you two are naturals!") but with me, she is an army drill sergeant, shouting for ETAs and at me to give her the 35 mm or the 1D lens, and she never does it in a complete sentence, as though she can't even spare the extra words. She never says, "Fern, can I have the thirty-five millimeter, please?" She simply gestures at me and says, "Thirty-five." She doesn't say, "Fern, can you flick the bride's veil up, please?" She cocks her head toward the bride-to-be and says, "Veil."

And—god, I'm embarrassed to share this—but here is the worst part of my job. The most demeaning. I go up to the bride-to-be, my shoulders laden with Annette's massive camera bags, each one weighing at least twenty pounds, and I take the bride's sheer lace veil and wait for Annette's signal. Annette raises her camera and checks the lighting, then she nods. I throw the veil up and scamper as quickly as I can out of the shot. I do it without jostling the precious camera bags too much; each of these lenses costs more than my monthly wages. It's not the weight of the bags that I find demeaning, even though they are brutal and have contributed to my increasingly terrible posture. It's the scampering. The way I am expected to do my job and then disappear as quickly as I can, running like a hamster to hide in the grass so that the real players in life, the Annettes and the Havens, can take their shot.

I have long learned that, just like animals, humans are all born into a hierarchy of predator and prey. Sure, most of us don't go around ripping each other's necks out, but we are all hunting or being hunted in one way or another. And I am one of nature's prey. I've made peace with that.

My patience knows no boundaries. Somehow, even when I think I've had enough, when I think the last shreds of my dignity have been snatched away, I manage to scrounge up an extra tiny bit. Like now, for example. I would've loved to stand up straight, shoulders back, and say in a firm voice, "Annette, you are a brilliant photographer and I admire you deeply, but I don't think making your coffee is part of my job description."

Of course, I don't do any of that. Just the thought of it is enough to make me shiver. An actual tingling going down my spine at the image of me speaking like that to not just Annette but anyone, really.

If I sound like a pathetic loser, it's because I am. My therapist would sigh and shake her head if she heard me referring to myself as a "pathetic loser," but I haven't been able to let go of that label. For now. I have this firm belief that once my book gets published, I will be able to stop seeing myself as a loser.

Annette often jokes about how I'm learning all her trade secrets so that I could replace her one day, but the truth is, I don't want to be a photographer. Dealing with customers terrifies me. No, I want to be an author. It's the whole reason I moved all the way from LA to New York City. Here is the hub of publishing, where every major publisher is and where all the respectable literary agents are. I have dreams of bumping into an editor in chief of some Penguin Random House imprint while buying Annette's kale-and-brussels-sprout salad. Of my manuscript flopping out of my bag (in my daydreams I carry around a printout of my manuscript everywhere I go, even though of course I don't do this in real life) and the editor flipping through the first pages. Her entire expression would light up as she reads my first paragraph. She'd look up at me and say, "Who are you? Let's talk." And my life would change, just like that.

Unfortunately, this isn't how publishing works. The truth is, editors are inundated with manuscripts to read. If one actually fell at their feet at Sweetgreen, they'd probably run away screaming.

But I'm not entirely hopeless; in fact, I have a literary agent. Bet you weren't expecting that. Not Fern! But yup, I do. I signed with her eight months ago (best day of my life), and after three months of revisions, we are now on submission to publishers. Most people outside publishing don't know what a feat it is to even get a literary agent to represent you. My parents definitely don't. They are real estate agents, and when I was querying literary agents, they kept going, "Fern, I don't understand what's the holdup in finding a literary agent to represent you. Our clients come to us with a house and we're like, 'Sure, I'll be your agent.' Why can't you just do that?" I got tired of trying to explain that literary agents get thousands of emails a year from hopeful writers begging for representation and that they can only sign on a handful.

So I know enough to know that my book is actually good. Good enough to get me an offer from a real-life New York literary agent! Her name is Poppy, and she is brilliant. Okay, so she's pretty junior; technically she's an assistant herself, but her boss trusts her enough to start her own list, which is saying something. And everyone says that younger, newer agents are hungry, which is perfect because that's what I am too. Hungry. Starved, really. Like there's a black hole inside me that can never be filled up. It's what I've been for as long as I can remember. But I know that once I get a publishing deal, none of this—not Haven's glossy success or Annette taking advantage of me or even my horrible, painful past—none of it will matter anymore, because that hole inside of me? It'll finally be filled up.

Chapter 2

Age Eighteen

I don't know what I'm doing here. Prom. What a joke. It's not like anyone asked me to come. And Haven left a note in my locker a month ago that said: "If you dare show your disgusting face at prom, you'll regret it."

She hadn't even bothered to type it out. She'd written it in her easily recognizable handwriting, knowing that I don't have the guts to report it to anyone. Every teacher in school absolutely adores Haven. I can just imagine their reaction if I showed them the note and told them I thought it was from Haven. They'd tell me I don't have enough proof, that anyone could imitate someone else's handwriting. They'd give another useless speech about bullying, blah, blah, blah, and at the end of the day, nothing would be achieved aside from me gaining a reputation as a snitch.

So I did nothing, and now it's prom night and I find myself driving to school and selecting the darkest, most secluded spot to park at. I just couldn't stay away. I wanted to go, and, I don't know, I guess torture myself by seeing everyone else there with their friends, all dressed up and looking beautiful and having fun. What a cliché, huh? I guess part of me thought I could be like a character in those YA books where the female main character is way too cool to go to anything as dumb as the school prom. I thought that maybe if I just went in my jeans and shirt and saw everybody else dressed to the nines, I'd be like, "Ha, who wants to go to prom anyway?"

But the truth is, as I sit here in my car watching people arrive, the thought *They look dumb* or anything like that never crosses my mind. They actually look amazing, like models or influencers or whatever. And I'm the one that looks dumb, sitting here in my hoodie and jeans, watching them like a total creep. Tears fill my eyes, and for the hundredth time, I think: Please take me away from this existence. I don't want to exist anymore. It's too painful. Please, universe, please take me away, please just—

Something slams into my window. Holy shit. It's Haven, both of her palms pressed up against my window. Adrenaline surges through my veins, my thoughts a manic scramble of fear and shame and so many other emotions I can't even name. How the hell did I not see Haven approaching my car?

She grins at me, and in the darkness, her face looks grotesque, the mouth stretched painfully wide, her eyes lasered on mine. She looks like a beautiful monster who wouldn't think twice before ripping me apart. As I watch, frozen, she takes her manicured finger and trails it from one side of her neck to the other.

A metallic taste fills the back of my mouth. I am this close to actually peeing myself. In all of my fantasies, I am a courageous heroine eager to face down her enemies. But in reality, I am so scared. So fearful. And so powerless.

Someone in the distance must have called out to Haven, because she turns her head and straightens up, that vicious grin quickly replaced by her usual gentle smile. She shoots me another glare, then stalks off toward the school entrance, her svelte figure sashaying attractively. No one would believe what I'd just seen. The real Haven, unmasked, nothing but sharp claws and fangs. Even I'm questioning it. Did that really happen? Did I imagine it? That's the problem with Haven. Every awful thing she does to me is so quick and fleeting that I end up questioning my own sanity.

I grip my wheel hard and lick my lips, willing myself to calm down. Once the adrenaline starts to ebb, tears rush into my eyes. I spot Dani in the distance, waving at Haven. The two of them skip with excitement and hug each other, and I can no longer stifle the sobs. I wish I could describe the desolation I feel.

They're all going to good colleges. Haven got into Stanford, and Dani's going to Berkeley. I just know they're going to remain friends throughout college while I fade from their memories. I am nothing. Just a blip in their lives that they won't even remember, but I will always remember them. I will always remember my friendship with Dani and how wonderful it was, and how Haven came and ruined everything, and even that wasn't enough—she couldn't stop there, after stealing Dani from me. She had to go and ruin everything else.

I didn't get into any colleges. Miss Jordan, the guidance counselor, had sighed and said, "I did try to warn you, Fern. I told you that you needed extracurriculars. And didn't I tell you to apply to safety schools?"

I told her that I tried, I really did, but that they all rejected me because of Haven. But she wouldn't believe me. No one believes me when I tell them what Haven's done, and maybe that's part of her genius, that she goes to extremes to torture me, to such lengths that it sounds ridiculous. I mean, who's going to believe me when I say that Haven went around bad-mouthing me to every club and every society so that they all rejected me? It sounds crazy. But that's Haven for you.

So now I'm gonna have to go to a community college for a while, and I'm so ashamed of it. I'm such a huge failure. I don't understand why I'm such a loser. I have nothing, and she has everything, and it's not right, because she's so evil. Why can't we live in a world where evil people get what they deserve?

Chapter 3

It's funny how we never know when our lives are about to change. Today, for example, starts out like any other day. In the morning, like usual, I am woken up by Terry's music. Terry is my next-door neighbor, and just like how I'm trying to be an author, Terry is trying to be a musician. But the similarities between us end there. Writing is a quiet endeavor. Terry's vocation, on the other hand, not so much.

He has a keyboard right up against my bedroom wall, which is really not ideal. I once gathered enough courage to ask if he could move it to a different spot in his apartment, and he said, "That room has the best acoustics in the house. You'd understand if you appreciated the arts more." Fair point, I guess.

I admit, after he woke me up at 4:00 the seventh morning in a row, I complained about it to our landlord, who told Terry to turn the volume down. Terry did so, but over the next few days, he turned the volume back up in increments so small that I wondered if I'd imagined it, until it became loud enough to wake me. I didn't bother lodging another complaint. And anyway, I didn't like snitching about Terry behind his back. It felt slimy, the kind of thing Haven might do.

And that is why I spend most of my nights with my pillow pushed down over my head, trying to block out the noise. At six, my phone alarm goes off. I grab my phone, turn off the alarm, and open my Gmail account, hoping to find an email from Poppy.

There is, in fact, an email from Poppy. My heart leaps for a split second before my brain registers the subject line: "Fwd: rejection from Summerhouse Press." My breath releases in a dejected sigh. I scroll through my inbox, taking count of all the rejections that Poppy has forwarded me so far. We are on our second round of submissions. The first round, she sent my book out to ten publishers and received six rejections. The remaining four publishers ghosted her. This round, she sent it to seven publishers, and so far we have received two rejections. I try not to dwell on the fact that Poppy burned through all the major publishers in the first round and we are now left with the midsize publishing houses. Let's face it: I would take a deal from the smallest, least prestigious publishing house if it means that I get to be a published author.

I don't need to go to Annette's studio until later in the day, so after getting up, I go to the kitchen and turn an audiobook on while I make my breakfast. I take out my sourdough starter, Doughlores, from the fridge and pour some of it into a bowl. I'm proud of Doughlores's name. I mean, come on, how cute is that? She's four years old now, so she's pretty mature tasting, and she gives the most amazing depth of flavor to everything I bake with her in it. This morning, I opt to make sourdough chocolate chip oatmeal cookies. I always make way too much to finish on my own, so I set some aside to bring to work with me, and the rest I pack up into various plastic containers.

I go outside of my apartment and knock on Terry's door. When I hear his footsteps coming to the door, I plaster on a sweet smile. Terry grins when he opens the door.

"Morning, neighbor," he drawls. God, I hope he's not flirting with me. I would just die if he did.

"Hi." An awkward second passes, during which he stares at me expectantly. I'm not good with conversations. Blame it on the friendlessness that plagued me all my school years. It's like I've forgotten how to socialize. Sometimes I wonder if this is why Annette hired me: because she knows I'm good at being invisible.

Terry's eyes move downward, to the container I'm holding. His face breaks into a grin. "Did you bake too many cookies again?"

"Oh. Yeah. Do you—" I don't bother finishing the rest of the sentence as he reaches out and grabs the container from me.

"Your cookies are the best," he says in a magnanimous way. "Your muffins, too, and your bread, and those little cakes you make."

I smile shyly. Despite myself, he's actually kind of winning me over a little. Ugh, get a grip, Fern. I take a breath and remind myself to stand straighter. "I was hoping that you could maybe lower the volume on your keyboard?"

Terry frowns. "What do you mean?"

My mind flails. Shouldn't it be obvious what I meant? "Um, the keyboard . . . it's right up against the wall where my bed is, and I can hear you playing—very beautifully, by the way—in the morning . . ."

"Thank you," Terry says. He looks so pleased with my compliment, and there is absolutely no indication that he's absorbed anything else I've said.

I try again. "So anyway, I was wondering if you could lower the volume or maybe move the keyboard away from the wall?" The smile trembles on my lips, begging to slide off. I valiantly fight to keep it on.

"Oh, Felicia, I'm sorry."

"It's Fern, actually, but it's fine," I mumble. "Thank you—"

"But I've tried other spots in the apartment, and none of them feel quite right, you know?" He places a hand on my shoulder, and I gaze down at it, marveling at the wrongness of it, the way I can feel his body heat on mine. He pats me like one would a dog. "The way the sound bounces off the walls and the items in the room—my keyboard belongs right there, in that spot. You understand, don't you?"

"Um . . ."

"How about you move your bed to a different wall?" Terry raises his hands like he's just been hit by a bright idea. "I'll even help you. How does that sound?"

The thought of Terry inside my apartment makes my stomach squeeze like a fist. "That's okay, thank you for the offer," I say hurriedly.

Terry shrugs. "Well, if you ever change your mind, don't hesitate to come to me for help."

"Sure, thank you."

"No worries. Always happy to help out a neighbor."

It's only when I get back inside my apartment that it hits me: How in the world did that conversation end with me thanking him? I smack a palm against my forehead. "Come on, Fern," I mutter out loud. This has always been my problem. I'm not just a pushover, I'm a mat that people feel free to walk all over, and it's no one else's fault but mine.

This, me being a people pleaser, is just one of many of Haven's legacies. Or so I think. I suppose I wouldn't really know, since my torment at her hands started when we were just stepping into our teens, and even before that I'd always been a shy, retiring kid. There's a reason why throughout my childhood, Dani was my only friend. So even without Haven's cruelty, I probably would've still grown into a shy, retiring adult. But maybe not an adult who knocks on her neighbor's door to complain about the noise and then ends up apologizing to him instead. God, sometimes I hate myself.

I give out another couple of containers full of cookies to my other neighbors. They're very grateful, which makes me feel better about myself. See? I want to shout at the world. People like me. I'm a good person.

By the time I get back inside my apartment, I'm smiling. That saying about how spending money on others brings you more happiness than spending money on yourself? So true. Which is why I pack up my remaining cookies for Annette. Karma, I think to myself. If you do good things, good things will happen to you. And if you do bad things, well . . .

Actually, judging from how things are going for Haven, if you do bad things but are good at hiding them, you'll probably go on to flourish. But today is a new day, I remind myself, and we are not going to spare the likes of Haven a second thought.

I smile as I make my way to work, even though there's honestly not much to smile about in my neighborhood and there was one guy who I was pretty sure was jerking off while eating a wheel of Brie on the subway. I'm not sure which disturbed me more: the public masturbation or the sight of him biting into an intact Brie wheel. I clasped my container of cookies like a shield, hoping he wouldn't notice me. He didn't, of course. I don't have the kind of face that anyone notices.

At the studio, I arrange the cookies artfully on a plate at our snack corner and start making Annette's coffee. She arrives ten minutes after I do, and the only indication I get of her appreciating my cookie offering is a single sniff when I bring her in one cookie along with her coffee. Pure Annette. It's okay, though; I don't mind. It brings me genuine pleasure watching people bite into my creations.

The first couple of hours at work fly by as I prepare invoices for Annette's clients and update the books as well as load two sets of edited photos onto the cloud. Honestly, I have no idea what Annette is doing while I perform all these admin tasks for her. Whenever I glance up at her all-glass office, she's clicking away at her computer, though I'm hard pressed to think of what there could possibly be for her to do. I do all the photo editing and the filing and uploading and emailing. She does the . . . You know what? Doesn't matter what she does. It's none of my business.

Ten minutes before my break time, my phone beeps, and my entire body perks up because it's the beep I've assigned to Poppy. *An email!* my mind squeals. Then, immediately following the excited moment of "AH!" is the realistic, sobering thought: *It's probably her forwarding yet another rejection.* I try to temper my excitement as I reach for my phone. *It'll be another rejection,* I remind myself. *Just another—*

But it isn't.

The email merely says: Hi Fern! Okay to call?

In the single second that it takes me to read these five words, my heart rate goes from normal resting rate to high-powered cardio speed.

In fact, my heart thumps so hard I can feel my palm pulsing, can almost see the phone juddering in my hand from the strength of it. "Oh shit," I whisper. I almost drop the phone as I reply: "Yes!" I hit send and stare at the phone, willing it to ring. When it finally does, I stab at the accept button and slap the phone to my ear. "Hi, Poppy? Hi!" My voice comes out slightly breathless.

From inside Annette's office, she glances up, sees me on my phone, then gives a very pointed look at her watch; there are still seven minutes before break time, and she is not happy. Anxiety kicks in, but only for a second. There is no way in hell I am pushing this call back, not even a mere seven minutes back. I give Annette a sheepish smile and mouth "Sorry, I have to take this" to her.

"Hi, Fern, how's your day going?" Poppy says. I swear she has the most beautiful voice in the world, and it's not just because I've put my literary agent on a massive pedestal, the way every other writer in the world has.

"Good, yours?" I say the words so quickly they come out as one single word—*Goodyours?* I don't care, Poppy! I want to scream. I mean, I hope your day is going well, but just tell me why you're calling!

Fortunately, she must have sensed my nervousness, because she cuts right to the chase. "Really good, because . . . we have an offer!" The smile in her voice is palpable.

We have an offer.

An offer.

How many times have I dreamed of hearing these exact words? My breath catches in my throat, and when I blink, I feel something wet slide down my right cheek. A tear. Oh my god, I'm actually crying. I suck in a shaky inhale and manage to say "Hnnh?"

Poppy laughs. "An offer, Fern! From Harvest Press. The editor, Lindsay Tillman, emailed this morning."

My breath releases in a high-pitched whistle. "Oh my god," I quaver. I glance up and see Annette openly frowning at me now and shaking her head. If she notices how emotional I am, she certainly doesn't give a damn. Again, I give her an apologetic grimace. I should get off the phone, but oh god, how can I?

"It's a really good offer for Harvest. Eight thousand dollars per book for a two-book deal. They very rarely break five figures, so this is really strong coming from them."

Key phrases sear themselves into my mind. Really good offer. Rarely break five figures. Really strong. More tears are streaming down my face. I must look a right mess, but I couldn't even care less. My head feels hot and cold at once, and I can barely feel my hands. *The Happiest of Unhappy Days* is my fifth manuscript and has been out on submission for over half a year now, and by now I've been on this journey long enough to know that if it hasn't received an offer after a month, it likely won't receive an offer ever. But guess who's only too happy to be proved wrong? And not just any offer, but a strong one. I could just shriek with the effervescent joy of it, I really could.

But I don't. Instead, I manage to gasp out, "Tha—that's amazing."

"I'm so happy for you, Fern," Poppy says. "All right, so we still have yet to hear from a handful of editors, so what I'm going to do now is email them to let them know there's an offer on the table. And who knows, if someone else is interested, we might even go to auction!"

Auction. That is the magic word that every author dreams of, an all-out fight for their book baby. "Sounds good," I say. Sounds good? Sounds fantastic! Sounds incredible! Sounds utterly magical!

By the time I get off the call, I realize my shirt is damp from sweat. Annette has come out of her office and is lurking at the kitchenette. She clears her throat in a way that has nothing to do with the clearing of phlegm and everything to do with catching one's attention. But you know what? It doesn't scare me. Okay, maybe it scares me a little, but I'm flying so high that nothing can possibly drag me down in this moment, not even Annette. I look up, beaming, my face shining with happy tears.

"Was that a family emergency?" she says snidely.

It clearly was not, unless she thinks I'm some demented soul who would grin at the news of a family emergency. Still, like I said, nothing can possibly get me down in this moment. Her meanness slides off my back effortlessly. "No, it's—I'm going to be a published author," I say, and the moment the words are out of my mouth, a fresh wave of tears spills from my eyes. My god, a published author. A dream I've nursed ever since my middle school years became hell on earth and books became a place of refuge for me. In this moment, everything makes sense. Even that awful saying Dani loved to repeat, "Everything happens for a reason," makes some semblance of sense. Everything did happen for a reason. If Haven hadn't turned everyone against me, if she hadn't bullied me endlessly, I wouldn't have turned to books with such fervent desperation, and I would definitely not be here right now, poised to become a real-life published author. God, if only Dani were still around. She would've loved this for me, I just know it. She would've laughed and clapped her hands and said something like "See? What did I tell you? Everything happens for a reason!" This moment makes all those years I spent eating my lunch in the bathroom worth the while. The best revenge truly is a life best lived, and look at me now, living my best life.

Well, okay. I'm not quite living my best life yet. Especially not right now, with me having to grovel to Annette. She's smiling at me, but I can also see that the smile is fighting her every step of the way. "A published author?" she says, as though the concept of it is alien to her.

"Yes," I say, still beaming. My voice sounds like liquid sunshine to me. Is this what a published author sounds like? Again, the thought of me being a published author sends a shiver down my spine.

"You write?" Annette says, her nose wrinkling as though that's a distasteful thought. Or maybe it's specifically me doing the writing that's distasteful? I have this thing where I'm convinced everyone secretly hates me.

"I do."

"Wow. Well, congratulations." Annette looks half dubious, half calculating, and I realize then she's calculating the likelihood of me quitting.

"Don't worry," I say quickly, "I'm still your assistant first and foremost." It isn't quite true. I have always been a writer first and everything else second. People often say they would be a writer if not for their other priorities, but see, my main priority is writing. Given the choice between spending weekends out with friends or writing, I would choose writing all the way. Of course, I don't have friends, so that's a moot point, but I'm just saying, if I did, I would still prioritize writing. But Annette doesn't need to know that. And the truth is, $16,000 divided over two books is not enough to live off, especially not in New York City, so as much as I would love to quit my job in the most dramatic way possible, I can't. Not yet, at least. But I am tenacious. I will keep writing, I will keep chipping away at my dream of becoming a full-time author, and one day soon, I will get there, I know it.

Because karma exists, and when you're a good person, good things will come your way, I remind myself. And I'm living proof of that, aren't I?

"Well, I hope you're not using your work hours to write your little books," Annette says.

"Of course not," I say brightly, and my smile does not waver, not even a little, as she walks back to her office. Nope, nothing can harsh my buzz right now. I am untouchable. And because I feel invincible, I open up IG, and the first thing I do is tap on the search button. Haven's name comes up as soon as I click on the search bar. Instagram knows me well enough to know that I'm only on here to hate-watch Haven's content. But now, even as I watch her vivaciously happy videos, I don't get that familiar sense of jealousy and sadness that I usually do at the sight of her smiling face. No, this time, all I get is a sense of peace.

Look at me now, Haven, I think. You tried to bury me, but I fought and I crawled and I clawed my way back up to the surface. And now it's my turn to be under the spotlight. And by god, I'm not going to waste this chance. My life is about to begin.

Chapter 4

Over the next few days, my inbox chimes repeatedly with updates from Poppy. The updates are all the same: "Seagull Books has bowed out" and "Appetite Press is backing out" and so on. One by one, the remaining publishers send their congratulations and their well-wishes and tell Poppy in no uncertain terms that they are not interested in my book. I would be lying if I said their mass rejection didn't sting, but the sting is akin to the snap of a rubber band—it hurts for half a second, then the pain dissipates so quickly that you forget it was ever there in the first place. The familiar disappointment, once so harsh that I found it numbing, now washes easily off me. All I have to do is remind myself that one publisher does want me and has given "a really strong offer," words that I carry with me like a talisman.

A week passes, and soon there is only one publisher who has yet to reply. Atherton Publishing. Poppy calls and tells me she has sent them two nudges and isn't expecting a reply from them at this point. "I'm really unimpressed with the editor, Catherine Rudick. We've met in person—we've had lunch! It's so unprofessional of her to ignore my emails like this."

It does seem rude, especially since they have established a relationship. I can't imagine ghosting someone I've lunched with. Still, it sounds like a bullet dodged to me. If an editor can't even be bothered to reply to an agent nudging her with an offer in hand, then it's not like I want to work with that editor. "Oh well," I say lightheartedly. I can afford to be lighthearted now. I could really get used to this version of me. "Bullet dodged, right?"

"Totally," Poppy says. "You have such a good attitude, Fern. You know, that's the number one thing I always tell people they need if they want to make it in publishing. Even more important than actual writing chops," she adds with a laugh. "Though, of course, you have both, so you're golden."

Every word Poppy says, I memorize and tuck away in the far reaches of my mind so I can savor it later. I let her compliment fill me up like sunshine from a goblet, making me warm from the inside out.

"So," Poppy says, "with all the other publishers now out of the running, shall I tell Harvest that you're happy to go with their offer and start negotiating the terms?"

My throat closes up with emotion, and it takes me a second to respond. I start nodding before I realize she can't see me, and through a clot of tears, I manage to choke out "Yes."

Poppy laughs. "Wonderful! I'm going to see if they can increase their advance as well. They probably won't go up much higher, since we're not in a competitive situation, but . . ."

I sag back against my chair, letting her words wash over me. The idea of asking for a higher advance hasn't even occurred to me, because let's face it, at this point, I would've taken a book deal with zero advance, as long as it's from a proper publisher and I can go around telling people I'm a published author. As Poppy continues talking about sub rights—what even are sub rights?—I let my thoughts wander. I'll update my socials to announce my book title and publisher the way that every other author I follow does. Fern Huang, author of *The Happiest of Unhappy Days*, Harvest Press 2020. Come to think of it, I don't know what year my book will be published, so I interrupt Poppy and ask her.

"Publication will likely be in the fall of 2020," Poppy says.

Fall of 2020. A little under two years from now. It feels like forever away, but it also feels magical, like a year that was always going to mean something special, something unique to me. "Sounds perfect," I say. I'm still floating on air when we hang up.

Two years from the time a publishing offer is made leading up to the actual publication of the book may seem like a long time, but it isn't, because of several reasons. For one, publishing is known to be a "hurry up and wait" industry. While the author tears her hair out over editing the manuscript into shape, the publishing team will be working on things like the book cover and sales meetings. I know all of this in theory, of course, though I've never had firsthand experience of it. But I know enough to not be taken aback by how long it will be before my book baby hits the shelves.

I glance up to see Annette glaring at me from her office. When she catches my eye, she makes a gesture that I think is supposed to mean: Get the hell back to work, what am I paying you for? I give her a sheepish smile before morphing my expression into one of fierce concentration and turning my attention back to my computer. I hope it looks like I am furiously editing a batch of photos, but in actuality, I have a tab opened to my Twitter, and I'm scrolling through the meager number of tweets on my profile.

My handle is @FernNotThePlant, and I have a grand total of 112 followers. Most of them are fellow hopeful writers; Publishing Twitter is a huge niche, and people are very active and very friendly on here. I've met up with a couple of them—just one of the many perks of living in New York City. The three of us had met through a pitching event on Twitter and gotten together one rainy afternoon for a coffee. James and Tina were pleasant, but we didn't quite hit it off well enough to make the effort of arranging another meetup. We still regularly talk online, though—or rather, reply to one another's tweets—and that's sufficient for me. I consider them writer friends. My face lights up as I think about telling them my news.

I click on the compose-tweet button, and my fingers hover above the keyboard. I type out: "Guess who's about to become a published author?" I delete it immediately. We're not allowed to announce book deals before they go on Publishers Marketplace, an official publishing website that announces all legit book deals, and the last thing I want to do is jeopardize my deal before it's even happened yet. In fact, I remind myself, I don't technically have a book deal yet. There is no contract. Negotiations haven't even begun. They could still fall through. The thought of it is like a gut punch to me. No way, they couldn't fall through. There is literally nothing that Harvest Press could throw at me that would make me turn down their offer.

I type: "Something good just happened." I lick my lips, then change "good" to "magical" and add "#publishing #writingcommunity." There. That's vague enough not to land me in trouble, but also specific enough to let people know that the magical news has to do with publishing. I hit "Tweet," then I minimize the tab and force myself to go back to the photo editing software.

For the next ten minutes, I busy myself with applying preapproved sets of filters to photos of deliriously happy couples. If I didn't want to stay single before, working for Annette has definitely cemented my decision to stay out of romantic relationships. Just from looking at these pictures, you'd think that these couples are perfect. They can't possibly want for anything. And yet I know what happens behind the scenes, and it's often ugly. This one couple, for example, could not stop arguing throughout the entire half-day shoot. And this other one was even worse—it was obvious the guy didn't want to be there, and the woman felt so nervous that she was dementedly cheerful, shrilly begging her fiancé to smile for just one more picture as he sulked at the camera. The whole time, I felt so sad for her. I wanted to give her a hug. And yet here are their photos, beautiful soft sunlight lining their hair gold, and adoring smiles all around. There is a metaphor for life somewhere here.

I sneak a quick glance at Annette before switching back to Twitter. Seven likes and one comment from a writer friend of mine.

@ChickaDoodle: 👀

Seeing the likes and the comment sends a delicious little shot of endorphins through my system. I reply with a GIF of someone giggling while covering her mouth, then I minimize the tab again and go back to the photos.

The rest of the workday goes this way. Me working in ten-to-fifteen-minute bursts before I give in to my curiosity and check my Twitter. By the end of the day, I have a grand total of eighty-two likes and nine comments. By far the most successful tweet I've ever posted. The whole way home, as I walk down the steps to the subway, as I stand inside the train and hang on to a pole for balance, as I trudge down the street to my apartment, I can't tear my eyes off my phone screen. I know how dangerous it is, especially for a lone woman, to be doing this, but I can't help it. Over and over again, I read the comments.

@TashaRyWrites: Omggg is this what I think it is??

@SammyLL: Fern!!! DMing you RIGHT NOW!!

@Cowcowwo: You can't leave us hanging like this, what is it?!

The rest are just as jubilant, and their joy and excitement is infectious. I have to bite down on my lip to keep from grinning like a total loon. My cheeks are hurting from all the smiling. I did, of course, DM most of them.

@FernNotThePlant: Giiirl! It's AN OFFER.

@SammyLL: OMGGG!! FERN!!! AHHH!

@FernNotThePlant: I KNOW!

@SammyLL: Who from?? How much??!! AHH!!

@FernNotThePlant: I can't say yet, but as soon as I'm allowed to I'll share all the deets!!

I am dying to share the deets, all of them. But then I pause, frowning for a second. Okay, maybe not all of them. The average book advance is around fifteen grand per book. Maybe I don't actually want to tell everyone that I'm getting paid half that. But the rest of it, I am dying to tell. I'm in such a good mood as I climb up the stairs to my apartment that I don't notice Terry until I nearly walk into him.

"Hey, look out," Terry says.

"Sorry!" The apology comes out of me automatically. As soon as I do it, I notice how he's taking up more than half the width of the steps, how it's him and not me who should be looking out. How does he manage to manspread while walking down the stairs? I wonder. Still, even Terry isn't able to wreck my mood.

Negotiations happen surprisingly quickly. Within two days, Poppy tells me they've come to an agreement about all the important details. She somehow even managed to get Harvest to bump up their offered advance by $500, which is a pleasant surprise, given, as she said before, we're not in a competitive situation.

"Poppy, you are a miracle worker," I tell her, and she laughs.

"It's all because of how great your writing is," she says.

I've been represented by Poppy for months now, and our relationship has been cordial so far, but now, in the space of one week, we've gone to multiple emails each day, and the tone of my messages to her have gone from Dear Ms. Tate, I am so sorry to bother you, but I was just wondering . . . to Hiii Poppy! Me again. I was wondering . . . and it is wonderful. Every time I open up my Gmail tab, I get a little bubble of joy as the page loads, because I know there will be an email or two from Poppy waiting for me.

"I gave Lindsay your email address, so you can expect a message from her soon," Poppy says. "She's so excited and so happy to be working with you."

A message from Lindsay Tillman. Lindsay, who is about to become my editor. I have an editor! I want to scream at the world. I bite down on my lip to keep from giggling and thank Poppy. As soon as I hang up the phone, I hurry to the window and fling it open. I take a deep breath of fresh air, savoring this moment. "I have an editor," I say out loud. My voice is so soft that the noises from the street below me drown it out. I can barely hear myself. Oh well. I was never a loud person, and that's okay.

I turn around and pose for a selfie, but I'm not photogenic, and even after five attempts, they all still look weird. I pivot so that I get the most flattering backlight, and the bright morning sunlight diffuses the harder angles on my face and makes me look softer, younger. That'll do. I open up Twitter and upload the picture, then I stop, wondering what to say in the caption. I'm smiling ever so slightly in the picture, one corner of my mouth pushed up, revealing just a small sliver of teeth. "Can't wait to share my story with all of you. xx," I type. Is that cute or is that annoying? There is such a fine line between the two. I mull over the post for a long while before realizing that over fifteen minutes have passed.

Before I got the offer from Harvest, I rarely thought this hard about tweeting. But now, it's like I'm frozen. I realize it's because now, I have something to lose. I'm about to become a published author, which means I would be a public figure, which means people would care about what I say, which means—and the thought arrives with not an insignificant amount of horror—I could get canceled.

This is ridiculous, I tell myself, shaking my head. It's just a selfie, and the caption I wrote for it is perfectly harmless. There is literally no reason I would get canceled over this. I'm just being paranoid. I nod to myself and hit the publish button. There.

I straighten up. Life as an about-to-be-published author is going to take some getting used to. But it's mostly good stuff. It will be mostly good stuff, I correct myself. A positive outlook is all anyone ever needed. I upload the same photo to Instagram and type out the same caption. I'm not as active on Insta; the writing community is much more vocal on Twitter, but since I will, at some point, get a book cover, followed by an actual physical book (squeal!), I will be able to post aesthetically pleasing images of my book. So I should be proactive and try to grow my follower count on Insta as well as Twitter.

With that done, I lower my phone with a satisfied smile. It feels great, doing something I actually care about, something that benefits my career and not just Annette's. It feels like such an achievement. Now, aside from starting to become more active on social media, what else should I be doing to ensure my success as a debut author? I am so determined to be a publisher's dream come true, to be a hardworking author who is talented at social media and does all she can to promote her own book so she doesn't disappoint the rest of the team.

I open up Google and do a search for "2020 debut group." The results are all wrong, so I change the search to "2020 authors debut group." Even typing the word "authors" sends a shiver down my spine. That's me. I am authors. I find a link to a Facebook group. It's a closed group, requiring permission from the admin to join. I click on the FAQ page and begin to read.

> This is a private group for authors who are releasing a debut novel in 2020. Please read the rules before sending a request to join. US Publishers only, and absolutely NO SHARING of anything that is posted inside the group.

There follows an exhaustive list of rules that would normally intimidate me, but reading them now, I feel my spirits lifting. I have never known this kind of joy: the joy of exclusivity. Of course I didn't; I was always the one being excluded. It makes sense now, why bullies like Haven work on the basis of exclusivity. The act of forming a group that you know only a select few people can join in turn makes you feel so unique, so wanted. What a delicious, addictive feeling. I can hardly blame Haven for doing it. No, wait, I lie. I can still blame her. But maybe I also feel slightly less angry toward her? You know what? I definitely feel less angry toward her. Is this what healing feels like? All these years, I have longed to move on from the nightmare that was my middle and high school years but lacked the know-how. I know all the pretty sayings about moving on, but I never understood how one actually moves on. How do you just let go of past hurts, especially when they've gouged wounds so deep into your personality, your memories, your very being? How do you make yourself heal?

Well, here's the answer. You thrive. You focus on what you love and devote all of yourself to it, and the fruits of your labor will heal you. It is only when I blink that I realize my eyes are moist. I utter a small laugh. Can't believe I'm getting teary eyed over joining the debut group. God, I'm ridiculous. If only Dani were still around. If only she and I had the chance to make up, start our friendship over again. She would've squealed out loud like a little kid and hugged me so tight that I'd wheeze for breath. She would've been so happy for me. I shake my head and, smiling, click on the "Join Group" button.

I fill out the form as quickly as I can, my fingers clumsy with excitement. I misspell my name, then the title of my book, and have to go back and retype them. The surge of pride as I fill out the publisher's name is overwhelming. When I'm done, I read over my answers twice before sending the form. A private club. Isn't that what this is? And over the years, what with me being so active in the online writing community, I am well versed in the social norms. Unlike when socializing in real life, at which I am painfully awkward, swinging wildly from being tongue tied to talking too much, online I am thoughtful, funny, witty. I crack people up effortlessly and reveal a vulnerability that makes people comfortable enough to open up to me. I have a handful of close online friends, and I would say these friendships are as meaningful as, if not more meaningful than, real-life ones. Our conversations go deeper, I'm sure, than most people get into with their meatspace friends.

I lean back with a contented sigh. So much has already happened, and yet there is still so much to look forward to. And once I get into the debut group, I know it will be my time to shine. It'll be something I am so much better at than Haven. Haven, who is sunshine personified on the surface, but a monster underneath. In a debut group, it hardly matters what you look like in person; everyone only cares about your personality. They will be able to sense if you are a good person or not, and the knowledge that this is the one space where, even if it were shared between Haven and me, I would shine, brings me much more satisfaction than I would care to admit.

Chapter 5

Age Sixteen

This, I tell myself as I walk down the school hallway to the student kitchen, my arms laden with ingredients, is going to change everything. This is me taking back control of my life. This is me being proactive and setting a new trajectory for myself.

Unbidden, the bitter memories of the past two weeks float up to the surface. The last two weeks have been a nightmare where I've been trying—and failing—to join a club at school. Miss Jordan told me that it is "imperative" that I have at least one extracurricular activity on my school records for college applications. She really likes to use the word *imperative*.

When I told her that every single club rejected me, she narrowed her eyes like I was making it up. I told her it's true. The school magazine rejected me, the debate society rejected me, even chess club. Chess club! I don't even like chess—that's how desperate I was. Then I saw Miss Jordan's face settle into an expression I hate so much. Pity. I don't need her pity. I need her to fix things for me. But how could she, when she didn't even know why I was rejected everywhere? I couldn't tell her it was because of Haven, even though I knew it was. I can totally see her telling them "Don't let Fern into your club, she's such a loser." And they would listen. And it wouldn't even be a hard thing for them to do, because who cares about me? I'm a nobody, thanks to Haven. I have no friends because she's been poisoning the well and everyone looks at me weird. I don't even want to think about the things she's been saying about me.

But none of that matters now, I remind myself. Haven may have knocked me down repeatedly, but I am not giving up. Last week, in a burst of inspiration, I talked to Miss Jordan and asked if I could start my own club. How's that for proactive? She was so pleased when she heard that because she knows how much I love to bake, and she even helped reserve the school's kitchen for me. I made all these flyers and posted them all over the school, and I just know this club is going to change my life.

Outside the kitchen, I take a deep breath and plaster a huge smile onto my face before opening the door, reciting my practiced greeting as I walk in.

"Hi! And welcome to . . ." The rest of my sentence trails off as I take in the vast space before me. There is no one here.

For a second, I stand in the doorway, frozen, then I shake myself out of it. I walk to the kitchen counter and place my heavy bags of flour, eggs, and sugar down. I glance up at the clock. Still five minutes to go before the official start of baking club, so people are probably still on their way here, I tell myself. I start taking out all my ingredients and arrange them nicely on the countertop while reminding myself to keep breathing. My breathing is slightly shaky, though, and I know it won't take much for me to burst into tears. Even though there's no one here, I feel exposed, like I'm being watched.

The door swings open, and my head jerks up eagerly. It's Fia Pereira, an exchange student from Portugal.

"Hi!" I cry out. I wince. My voice came out way too high and excited.

Fia looks at me hesitantly, then says, "Uh . . . is this the baking club?" Her English is so heavily accented that it takes me a beat to understand her. When I do, I immediately nod.

"Yes, yes, it is! Welcome!" Oh my god. I seriously need to tone it down. I clear my throat and say in a more normal voice. "Um, I thought, um, we could bake chocolate cupcakes today?" I kick myself inwardly. Why did that come out as a question? As the founder of this club, I need to be more confident.

Fia nods slowly, still giving me that uncertain look. "Chocolate cupcakes seems like a very simple thing to make."

"Oh!" I say, still in that demented, overexcited voice that makes me want to strangle myself. "Yes, I thought we should, like, start simple, you know? Leave the seven-layer cake for the end of the semester?" I joke.

Fia doesn't laugh. I die a little more inside. Before I can embarrass myself any further, I gesture at the counter and say, "Let's begin!"

The next hour and a half are perhaps the most excruciating ninety minutes of my life. I am so nervous that I keep getting things wrong, then giggling like a complete moron, then apologizing, and the whole time, Fia remains stone faced, not even giving me one single sympathy smile. I try making small talk by asking her about Portugal, but she merely gives me one-to-two-word answers and doesn't reciprocate with any questions of her own, and soon enough, I run out of questions to ask.

"Well," I say as I take out the cupcakes from the oven, "now for the best part!"

There's nothing quite like chocolate cupcakes to break the ice, right? Even Fia cracks a small smile when the cupcakes come out, smelling rich and sweet. We each take a cupcake and unwrap them slowly, blowing on them before taking a small bite.

The smile disappears from Fia's face. A moment later, as I taste the cupcake, I realize why. I swallow quickly, whereas Fia, without any qualms, spits out her mouthful of cake onto a napkin. I look at her in dismay, my face burning with humiliation.

"I'm sorry, I must've mixed up the sugar with salt . . ." I stammer.

"It's okay," Fia says, already grabbing her backpack from the floor. "Thank you. Bye." And without so much as a glance over her shoulder, she pulls open the door and leaves.

My breath comes out in a dejected sigh. I gather the cupcakes and toss them in the trash. How did I mess this up so badly? I've baked chocolate cupcakes at least twenty times in my life, and never have I made such a stupid mistake.

The door swings open again, and I look up, hoping it's Fia coming back to tell me she wants to give baking club another go. But it's not Fia at the doorway. It's Haven, wearing a huge smirk on her face. I wish I could say that I glare her down, but after the painful baking session, I have nothing left in me. I drop my gaze, making myself focus on cleaning up.

"How was the inaugural session of baking club?" Haven says, her voice dripping with contempt.

I refuse to take the bait. Still keeping my eyes on the countertop, I start sweeping eggshells into a trash bag.

Haven leans over the counter, putting her face close enough to mine that I can see each individual strand of her eyelashes. It's impossible to ignore her when she's literally in my face and I am forced to look at her unfairly flawless face.

"No one wants to eat the shit you make, you freak," she says, so softly it's almost a whisper.

"Why do you care?" I say, and hate the whining tone in my voice.

"Because you are a pathetic little shit stain on the underwear of life, and it is my job to scrub you out."

Half a dozen retorts crowd my mind, but none of them come out. I'm frozen, as usual, nothing more than small prey, here for people like Haven to pick on as she likes. Shame burns through my chest. Why am I so useless? Haven is right. I am pathetic. I don't deserve to take up space.

"Trust me, Fern," Haven continues. "Nothing you bake for your pathetic little one-person club is going to turn out well."

My gut sours. It was Haven. I'd thought that I'd switched the salt and the sugar because I was so nervous baking with Fia, but Haven must've done it somehow. Maybe she broke into my locker and switched out my sugar. Maybe she—

As though Haven has read my mind, she smiles. "See, you get it. Took you a while, but you got there. Don't try to start another stupid club. It won't end well for you." Laughing, she saunters out of the kitchen.

I don't know how long I stand there, my face red hot, my stomach knotted. How much more of this torture can I take? And what the hell am I going to do about my college apps? I have nothing to put on them. Absolutely nothing. Haven has seen to it.

Chapter 6

Hi Fern! Has your deal been announced yet? is the response I get from the admin of the Facebook group.

Not yet, I reply. My agent is still awaiting the contract. A stab of anxiety, me wondering if this somehow means I am ineligible.

> Okay, no worries. Usually we only invite authors whose deals have been announced on PM, but once you get your contract, you can send me a screenshot and I'll send you an invite.

Thank you so much! I reply.

The contract takes two long, excruciating weeks to arrive, and by the time Poppy forwards it to me for a signature, I have bitten all my nails into ragged stumps. At night, my dreams have been taken over by nightmares of Poppy calling me to say that Harvest Press has changed its mind about offering me a deal. Each time my Gmail boops with a new message, I get a mini heart attack. Could it be Lindsay? She has yet to email me, though Poppy assures me she remains "so excited" to work with me. I cry again as I sign the contract, and prop my phone up against a tissue box and take a dozen selfies with the document. My smile is tear filled and earnest, making me look like a huge dork, but I don't even care. I post it to Twitter and Insta with the caption "Signing the most important document of my life! #writingcommunity," and the likes and congratulatory comments pour in almost immediately. My Twitter account is at over four hundred followers, and my Insta is at over two hundred, now that I have taken to posting something at least once a day. I'm doing it. I'm really doing it, carving out a space for myself in the publishing industry.

The Facebook debut authors group is amazing. A dream come true. Well, maybe it's not a hundred percent what I was expecting, but honestly, I don't quite know what I was expecting. I've never been part of a debut group, or any other group, really. I'd thought it would be much bigger, but currently we only have fifty-four members, including yours truly. But even so, fifty-four is enough members to make me feel slightly overwhelmed. The first day I get in, I don't post anything, not even an introductory post. I scroll all the way down to the very first post, one that says: Hi everyone! Introduce yourselves in the comments!

I click on the comments and go through every single one. They all follow the same format.

Jessica Sun: Hiii! I'm Jessica, and my book, The Tides We Fight Against, will be coming out from Rose Chapman Books, Penguin, in Spring 2020. It's a story about a mother whose son is diagnosed with autism and how she learns to advocate for him. Twenty-one likes and three comments, all of them about how good the book sounds and how much they would love to read it.

Elsie Crawford: Hi everyone! My book is called Red is the Darkest Color and is being published from Miota Books, Simon & Schuster, Spring 2020. It's set in a world with vampires and—believe it or not—zombies. Thirty-seven likes and nine comments about how they would "literally kill" to read this.

And so on and so forth. Everyone else seems to be with a Big Five publisher, which makes me feel somewhat self-conscious, but then I remind myself that I have a "really strong offer" from Harvest. Who cares that everyone else is at a bigger house? Everything I've read says that in publishing, it's much better to be a big fish in a small pond than a small fish in a big pond. Being a big fish means that your publisher will give you its utmost support and push your book hard. If you're a small fish at a big publisher, you'll get zero promotion; no one will even know about your book, and it'll likely flop. Bestsellers do not happen by chance—they happen because money is poured into the marketing and publicity machine. They're advertised in every possible channel so that when readers log on to sites like Amazon and Goodreads, the first thing they see is a banner for said book.

I scroll through the introductions until I come across one from someone who's with a non–Big Five house.

> **Jenna Duncan:** Hi! My book is called Fighting Words and it's coming from Autumn Books in Spring 2020. It's about two brothers who hate each other and continue on a downward spiral until it ends up with a murder.

Autumn Books is, in fact, not even a midsize house like Harvest Press. It's a small press, and if I remember right, their advance sizes start at three figures and go up to mid-four figures, which means—thank god—mine isn't the smallest deal in the group. Phew. As soon as I think that, I feel like a total asshole. Come on, Fern. Comparison is a thief of joy and all that, and plus, I don't want to be the kind of person who makes others feel small just so I can feel better about myself. I send a mental apology out into the ether. Sorry, Jenna. And also, her book sounds genuinely up my alley.

I click on like and, after a moment's thought, type out: Hi Jenna! Your book sounds insane in the best possible way! I can't wait to read it.

I spend the next hour alternating between working and checking the Facebook group, noting which people are the chattiest, or the most obnoxious, or the ones who sound like they have the biggest deals, and so on. My notifications button lights up, and I open it to find that Jenna Duncan has replied to my comment.

> Thanks, Fern! That means a lot to me. What's your book about?

It takes me way too long to compose my reply. I type: "My book is about . . ." Then my mind goes blank, and I switch back to the Excel sheet I'd been working on for Annette, filling out this month's expenses. Five minutes later, I switch back to Facebook. "About two sisters . . ." I delete what I've written and instead type: "Well, funny you should ask, because your book's about two brothers and mine's about two sisters! Lol!" I read over what I've written and wince. Ugh, I sound so weird. I switch back to the Excel sheet and make myself do a bit more work before switching once more to Facebook. Come on, Fern. You're good at this. Don't overthink it.

But, whispers a little voice in the back of my mind, now you have something to lose. You're no longer just a hopeful writer in the vast #writingcommunity space on Twitter. You're a member of a debut group, a small group of writers whose first books are all coming out in the same year. They're your cohort, your peers, your graduating class. Your second chance. If you mess this one up, too, what's left for you?

And this time, there is no Haven Lee around for me to put the blame on. No one is actively trying to sabotage me, to go around warning people away from me. No excuses. If I bomb this, it's all on my shoulders. No curtain for me to hide behind, nothing to shield me from the fact that it's me, the problem has always been me, and I am foundationally unlikable, that there is something irreparably broken about me, and that's why I have no real-life friends.

I shake my head. Stop it, I think to myself. It's not true. There's nothing wrong with me. I am a good person. My only problem is that after years of abuse from Haven, her words have seeped through the pores of my skin, been absorbed into my flesh, and carved themselves painfully, sharply, onto my bones. I'm a failure. A loser who wasn't able to protect Dani in the end. Even now, ten years after graduating from high school, I carry Haven's words deep in my soul. I feel the weight of them, I hear their whispers in the dark curves of my inner ear, and they shape everything that I do, down to the smallest acts. The way that I can never just strike up a casual conversation with the barista or the nice checkout lady at Trader Joe's, no matter how friendly they're being. The way that the handful of times I find myself at social gatherings, I clam up, scuttling to the quietest corner of the room and holding my drink with two hands, aching for someone to come talk to me while at the same time dreading the possibility of having someone talk to me. And all this I have attributed to Haven, the person who put her elegant fingers around me and squeezed until I was left a misshapen lump marked by her fingers.

But I don't have to let it continue to shape me, I remind myself. I am not the sum of my scars. I am so much more than that, and this book deal is proof. This is what most people don't understand. That for many of us writers, our books aren't just books. They are created through a process that requires us to slice ourselves open so we can bleed all over the page. Our books are proof that we exist, our passports to personhood. And I am good at this, damn it. I may suck at in-person interactions, but online is where I shine.

Bolstered by that thought, I go back to Facebook and type: "My book is about two sisters, one who is seemingly perfect and the other one decidedly not, who discover that upon their parents' deaths, the will they're left with is completely not what they expected. I love that your book is about siblings too, it feels like kismet!" I don't give myself any time to second-guess myself before hitting "Post." Once it's up, I release my breath and lean back in my chair with a small smile, then I go back to the Excel sheet with renewed focus.

At break time, I go back to Facebook and find that not only has Jenna Duncan replied to my comment but another author, Lisa Garcia, has as well.

> **Jenna Duncan:** Oh wooowww I love the sound of that! I am so intrigued, and yes you're right, this definitely feels like kismet!

> **Lisa Garcia:** Can I join in this conversation? My book is about fraternal twins who find out that they might actually be triplets, so they go on a search for the third sibling. It's so tough finding others with books about siblings!

A warm glow pulses deep in my chest and expands to fill my entire body. I'm doing it. I'm actually doing it. I'm making connections, building the foundation of friendship with my peers. What a lovely thought it is, too, to have peers once more. It's a rough realization to have that ever since college, I haven't had much chance to have peers. Annette is my boss and hence definitely not a peer, and—well, that's it, really. Who else am I exposed to on a regular basis? Terry? I want to laugh at the thought of him. He's around my age, but I can barely think of him as a person, never mind a peer. Not being mean; it's just Terry kind of transcends personhood somehow.

> **Fern Huang:** I love this! Hi Lisa, your book sounds amazing! And you're so right that books about siblings are definitely few and far in between, so I'm glad that we've found each other.

Less than two minutes later, a reply comes.

> **Lisa Garcia:** I wonder why that is? Most of us have siblings, right? I have two brothers. Growing up with them was definitely not for the weak of heart, lol!

> **Jenna Duncan:** How funny! I have a sister and I would say the same about growing up with her. 😄

I grimace at my screen. Shoot. How did I get myself into this conversation about siblings? Take a deep breath, I remind myself: Just be yourself. It's all going to be okay.

> **Fern Huang:** I'm actually an only child, but I've always wanted a brother of my own (I figured a sister would just steal all my clothes), which is why I've written a book about siblings. You guys will have to tell me if I got the sibling relationship all wrong!

> **Jenna Duncan:** Omg, you don't have any siblings but you wrote a whole book about them and that book is getting published?? Fern, you are AMAZING! I am in awe! I need to read your book. Actually, Lisa, I need to read your book too. They both sound so good!

The flush of pleasure is almost overwhelming. Look at me, holding my own in this conversation. Our connections are building, budding into proper friendship, and it's so wonderful I could just die.

> **Lisa Garcia:** Agreed! Fern I think it's so cool that you're an only child writing about siblings. I am definitely up for reading each other's manuscripts. Shall we do that? My email address is lgarcia232@gmail.com.

Both Jenna and I share our email addresses, too, and I spend the rest of my break time furiously speed-reading the most recent version of my manuscript, tweaking this word choice and that sentence as the minutes tick down. Then, just as Annette gives an obnoxious clearing of her throat, I get to the end, and—well, I don't know, is it good enough to send to Jenna and Lisa? But so what if it isn't? It's not like I can do anything about that at this point. And if the book is good enough for an editor at Harvest Press to give me actual money for it, then surely it's good enough to share with a couple of other writers that I've just met. But god, it's nerve racking, like stepping outside a changing room naked and asking these two strangers to scrutinize every aspect of my flawed flesh.

Stop that, I scold myself again. This is part of the process. We are writers—what else are we going to bond over if not our writing? I attach the manuscript to an email and type out: I'm so glad that we're doing this! I can't wait to read both of your books! Once again, I hit send without letting myself think twice, then I go back to the Excel sheet and lose myself in numbers.

Minutes later, or maybe hours later—what does time even mean anymore, these days?—my phone beeps with an incoming email. It's from Jenna, with her manuscript attached. Here's mine! I'm going to read yours in alphabetical order so it's Fern's first, lol!

My heart squeezes, half with joy, half with anxiety. Somehow, I refrain from replying right away. I push my phone aside and finish up updating the Excel sheet before moving on to checking the contact-form email on the website. My phone beeps again, and this time, it's from Lisa. That's a good idea, Jenna! Okay, since you're reading Fern's first, I'll read yours first.

This time, I reply immediately. I love this. Okay, I'll read yours first, Lisa. Yaaay! This is perfect!

I can barely concentrate on anything the rest of the day, but fortunately it's a pretty light workload today, with just three general inquiries to reply to. I copy and paste our usual response to the inquiries, then move on to photo editing, something I actually enjoy doing because I can turn my brain off and apply the presets to them before letting Annette know that the folder is ready for her review. By the time I knock off, I'm still buzzing with bubbly energy. I download Lisa's manuscript onto my phone and begin reading as soon as I'm out of the office.

Lisa's book is a family drama, a genre I'm not usually drawn to, but I find myself being sucked in within the first two pages. Her prose is incisive. She doesn't waste any time on flowery phrases, cutting instead straight to the bone. It's a powerful piece, and the more I read, the worse I feel about my own work. Ten pages in, I minimize the document and call up my own manuscript. I compare our opening pages, my heart sinking as I notice how obvious the discrepancy in our skill level is. While I dither about, wasting valuable first-page real estate on introducing my main character, Lisa slices right into the heart of the story. Her opening line is "We find out that we're not twins on a Tuesday afternoon." Mine: "She wakes up to a beautiful morning, with a breeze blowing in through the open window caressing her face."

I thought, when I wrote that first line, that it was beautiful and dreamy, but now I see it for what it is, an author clearing her throat before she begins the actual story. My cheeks blaze with shame. How could I have sent this to Lisa? By now, my stomach is churning, warm acid burning up my chest. I close my manuscript and instead open Jenna's. Please, please, I think to myself, please let hers be bad too. I grimace at how mean that thought was, and correct myself mentally. Not bad, I'm sure it won't be bad at all, but please let it not be so . . . brilliant.

Jenna's book opens with: "For as long as Thomas can remember, he's always hated his brother Kev." Not bad, but definitely not brilliant either. I read on, and the more I take in, the looser the knot in my chest feels. Soon, I feel like I can breathe normally once more. Okay. It's fine. I'm not the worst writer in the group. Plus, I remind myself, Jenna is the one with the smallest deal, and reading her manuscript, I can totally see why. Publishing is a meritocracy, and that's never been clearer than it is now. Again, I feel a stab of shame with that petty thought. Stop thinking like that. That's Haven-talk, that is. I am not this person. I am not someone who judges others, especially my own friends, to make myself feel better. I read another page while making a conscious effort to look for positives. Jenna is great at dialogue. Her characters' speech sounds natural and utterly believable. Jenna is good at pacing. Jenna uses adjectives sparingly.

There. I've proved to myself that I'm not a bitch. I'm a good person.

But it's not enough. I still feel bad, so I open up Gmail and compose a message to just Jenna. Hey Jenna! I couldn't resist taking a peek at your manuscript, and can I just say, OMG! I love it so far! Your dialogues are so realistic. I can totally imagine real people saying them. I find dialogue really hard to write, so kudos to you!

Okay, now finally I stop feeling like an asshole. See? Being a good person isn't hard. It just takes a bit of effort.

With the email out of the way, I go back to Lisa's manuscript, my insides shriveling up once more as I lose myself in her gorgeous story. When I get back to my apartment, I go to my computer and look up Lisa's deal announcement on Publishers Marketplace.

> Lisa Garcia's THEY FALL HARDER IN THREES, a family drama about a pair of twins who find out in adulthood that they may in fact not be twins, but triplets, and go on a hunt for their missing sibling, to Natasha Tory at Paper Machine, in a two-book deal, in a good deal, for publication in spring 2020, by Jasmine Stevens at Stevens Literary Agency (NA).

A "good deal" in publishing speak is anything between $100,000 and $250,000. She is getting paid way more than I am, which stings. I mean, logically, I know it makes sense because the quality of the work is truly staggering, but it still stings, the knowledge that she's so far ahead of me. Still, I remind myself, it's all about the writing, and as long as I keep my head down and keep improving, one day I, too, will get there. And I've had years learning to keep my head down, haven't I? And I should be taking this as my chance to learn. I go back to the beginning of Lisa's manuscript and reread the opening chapter with a critical eye this time, taking apart her writing down to the elements, noting how she achieves certain effects, the cadence and rhythm of her sentences, the succinct elegance of her word choice.

I'm so motivated to improve myself that I could swear my writing skill has leveled up by the end of chapter one. I can identify Lisa's sleight of hand and the conscious decisions she must have made at this paragraph and at that page to make the reader think or feel a certain way. And if I can identify it, that means I can replicate it.

This is what I'm good at. Quiet self-improvement. Watching others, absorbing what they do, how they talk, their hand gestures when they communicate, their facial expressions, and practicing so that I get better at social interactions. And it's just the same with books. This is exactly why I know that my tiny deal is only the beginning, why I know that my publishing journey is going to be a long and fruitful one: because it's quite literally the only thing I have going for me, and I'm not about to let anything get in the way of that.

Chapter 7

The day that my book announcement goes live is the best day of my life, and I'm not even exaggerating. People often say that. "This is the best day ever!" "I am having the best time!" "This is the best night of our lives!" But see, I have kept a meticulous diary ever since I was twelve, so I know, down to the date, that I have never had a day as marvelous as this one. Easy enough to remember even without the diary entries, honestly, since it all went downhill fast after Haven Lee set her sights on me. The only other contender for best day ever is when I was eight and my mom made her first sale and took me and Dad to Disneyland to celebrate. But even so, I remember that among the ups, there were still downs—my parents taking me on Space Mountain because I'd foolishly told them I loved roller coasters when I didn't even know what a roller coaster was, and me scream-crying the entire ride until I lost my voice, me crying again when I dropped my churro and Mom refused to get me a new one, my legs feeling like jelly at the end of the day, and Dad carrying me the entire way back to the parking lot, which led to him being bedbound for three days after doing so pulled his back.

I don't want to sound ungrateful. That Disney trip would remain a core memory of mine as one of the best days a kid could ever dream of. But it wasn't perfect. Even at the happiest place on earth, reality has a way of sneaking in and reminding you that you're not, in fact, in a fantasy world. That you still exist very much within the confines of your own limitations.

But the day of my deal announcement, none of those limitations exist. First of all, it's a true surprise. I haven't been told when the announcement will happen, and so this morning, I wake up just as on any other and unlock my phone while still tucked up nice and cozy in bed. As usual, Twitter is the first app I open, and as soon as I do, the first thing I see is the fact that that notifications icon has the number 20+ over it. I immediately know, of course. I'd been waiting and waiting for it to happen, and what else was it going to be? I click on the notifications, and they're all congratulatory comments. I open up Publishers Marketplace and do a search for my name, and sure enough, there it is.

> Fern Huang's THE HAPPIEST OF UNHAPPY DAYS, the story of two sisters who have to overcome their differences to unearth the mystery of their parents' last will, to Lindsay Tillman at Harvest Press, in a two-book deal, for publication in fall 2020, by Poppy Davidson at Davidson Literary Management (world).

A tiny part of me—a speck, really—realizes that as far as deal announcements go, mine is probably as basic as deal announcements can be. There are no bells and whistles; no mention of deal size, which usually means it's a small deal; no mention of TV or film rights or foreign deals. It's not so much an announcement as it is a whisper in the wind.

But none of it matters because it's mine. It's perfect because it's mine, and I read it thrice over in bed, tears dripping down my chin, before I finally climb out and brush my teeth. Once I'm done with that, I send a message to Annette, telling her that I've woken up with a stomach bug and won't be able to come in today. She replies two minutes later, telling me she's disappointed by the last-minute notification. She doesn't bother telling me she hopes I get well soon, and I am not at all bothered by it.

As I go about making myself coffee and breakfast, I keep picking up my phone to reread the PM announcement. Each time, a shot of pleasure fizzes through me, and I could swear that I'm about to have actual wings sprout out of my shoulder blades, I feel so light and bubbly. Finally, with a hot coffee in one hand and a bowl of cereal in the other, I settle down at my desk. I crop my deal announcement and paste it over a background of a starry night, then I post the image to both Twitter and Instagram with the caption "I am overcome with joy to finally be able to announce my book deal! I am going to be a published author!! #publishing #writingcommunity."

The likes and comments come in almost immediately. I'm grinning at my computer as I go through the comments and reply to every single one. My follower count goes up in real time. I can't quite describe the feeling of watching my notifications blow up while I sit here in front of the computer, seeing the little bell icon shiver and light up every couple of minutes and knowing that it's yet another person reaching out to congratulate me. Me, Fern Huang, outcast, loser, girl who would've been most bullied if not for the fact that everyone simply overlooked her.

"Thank you so much!" I type over and over again. When I next check the time, over an hour has gone by, and still the comments continue to pour in, and I've forgotten to eat my breakfast. My cereal is all soggy, my coffee long gone cold. I take a quick break to stretch and have a couple of bites of cereal before going back to it. I must reply to every single comment, savoring every comment, counting the number of exclamation marks in each one. Who knew I had so many online friends?

The best part is, there are even comments from actual authors. Not debuts like me or hopefuls like most people in the #writingcommunity, but real-life established authors who have published multiple books. Authors whose books I've seen at Barnes and Noble or at Target.

Carla Stevenson: What wonderful news! I'm so happy for you and your book sounds great.

Carla Stevenson has published five books. And here she is, telling me my book sounds *great*. Oh my god. I swallow a mouthful of tepid coffee and read her comment again and again, wondering how to reply.

"Thank you so much, Carla! I love your books so much!" No, too fangirl.

"This means a lot to hear, especially coming from you! I'm such a big fan!" Still too fangirl. She's probably inundated by messages like these ones.

In the end, I settle for a generic "Thank you so much, Carla!" I can't believe I'm calling her by her first name. Whenever I think of published authors, I think of them in the same way that most people think of celebrities, full names only. Come to think of it, this is probably true for most people. You don't often hear people saying "Oh yeah, I got Stephen's latest book." They say, "I got Stephen King's latest book." So for me to call her Carla instead of Carla Stevenson is yet another beautiful reminder of the fact that I've made it. I've successfully separated myself from the masses, elevated past the hordes of hopefuls to become an actual author.

I stay at my computer all the way until past two in the afternoon, when my stomach finally announces it's tired of my preoccupation and demands proper nutrition. Reluctantly, I leave the desk, stretching and being surprised by how stiff my back feels. I've been at the computer for seven whole hours, and it's now 2:00 p.m., and still the likes and comments continue coming. I'm up to 527 likes on Twitter and 112 on Instagram. By far the most successful tweet and Instagram post I have ever made.

I eat standing up in the kitchen, my eyes glued to my phone screen as I make myself a sloppy peanut butter sandwich. Five hundred and forty-one likes on Twitter and two new comments. I can't reply and eat at the same time, so I switch out of the notifications screen, go to my home screen instead, and begin scrolling. My Twitter algorithm has clocked me as a writer, so as always, it pushes writing-related content to me. There are the usual celebratory posts about getting an agent or finishing a manuscript, and the bleak ones about rejections and rants against "gatekeepers" in traditional publishing.

Today, probably because of my own deal announcement, my eyes automatically pick out the deal announcements. I skim through them, feeling happy for the writers whose dreams have come true while at the same time also feeling secretly smug that none of their books sound as intriguing as mine. I know how delusional this sounds, I know. But isn't this a secret thought that every author harbors deep down inside? That their writing is the one that sheds light on a universal truth that every other writer has somehow overlooked, that their characters are the most honest, the most relatable? Of course, I would never say that out loud.

> Helen Nelson of Nelson Books has acquired . . .
>
> . . . the story follows a young woman who . . .
>
> . . . about a magical city that appears only . . .

I like each tweet and congratulate the authors in between bites of sticky PB sandwich. Now that I'm a debut author, I need to get serious about making connections. It pays for me to reach out to my fellow debuts and congratulate them. I continue scrolling.

> . . . Haven Michaela Lee's debut novel, *She Asked for It* . . .

My finger's already swiping up, the announcement halfway off my screen, when my mind catches up to what my eyes have seen. I freeze, every drop of blood in my body clotting, turning jellylike. No, it must've been a mistake. It's a trick of the light, a soupçon of my imagination, a stuttering of my brain, brought about by too much excitement. She was on my mind, that's all. She's always on my mind, that's the problem. The author's name will turn out to be Hazel Lee or Hayley Lee or something like that, and I will dislike her for no other reason than that her name reminds me too much of Haven's.

Every instinct in my body begs me not to scroll down, not to go back to the announcement. I shouldn't even care. I should move on. I should—

My thumb moves of its own accord, swiping down. The announcement returns to the middle of the screen. And there it is, posted by a Twitter account called @HotPublishingNews.

> Haven Michaela Lee's debut SHE ASKED FOR IT, following the media frenzy after a junior associate at a law firm comes forward with an allegation of sexual assault against her employer, a well-respected named partner on the brink of becoming a judge, to Virginia Wallace at Wallace Books, in a nine-house auction, in a major deal, for seven figures, for publication in fall 2020, by Rachel Reed at Reed Literary Management (NA). Rights also to Red Line Books (UK), at auction, in a major deal; Paper Factory, at auction, in a significant deal (Germany); Boucher, in a pre-empt, in a six-figure deal (France); Rossi Publication, in a pre-empt, in a six-figure deal (Italy); Costa Publishing, at auction, in a six-figure deal (Brazil).

My mouthful of peanut butter sandwich turns into a lump of cement and sticks in my throat. I cough, or try to, anyway. It lodges there, refusing to budge. I try to swallow, but that doesn't work either. I realize with sudden, sickening fear, that I am starting to choke. It's a surreal feeling, choking. Because part of me is internally screaming:

Oh my god, I'm choking! But the other part of me is still stuck in normalcy mode, still uncomprehending, still standing there holding my half-eaten sandwich in one hand, wondering where my plate is so I can put it down and resume choking in peace.

Thankfully, the part that's driven by my survival instincts overrides the second part, making me drop the sandwich. I claw at my throat, my eyes tearing up as I wheeze for breath. What do I do? Within the space of a second, my mind whizzes through several different possible solutions: I run out and knock at Terry's door so he can do the Heimlich maneuver on me. I push my fingers down my throat and try to gouge the piece of sandwich out. I—

Too late for any of that. I have never once choked before, and what surprises me about all this is how fast everything is happening, how quickly my body seems to be breaking down. Only two to three seconds have passed, but already my lungs feel like they're on fire, my brain shutting down, my thoughts becoming fuzzy. Random, unimportant thoughts keep stabbing through my head. I'm glad I don't have a cat who'd eat my face after I die, I think. Then another useless thought: I can't die, I'm not wearing cute underwear.

Somehow, in the midst of the cacophony in my head, some tiny part of me, the one that refuses to go down without a fight, manages to grab hold of my body and take charge. Before I know what I'm doing, I rush at my kitchen counter and ram myself into it. The overhang slams into my belly, devastatingly hard, and my entire body convulses at the collision. I hurl, and the next second, the congealed bite of peanut butter sandwich flies up my throat and splats onto the floor with a loud thwack. Air rushes into my lungs, and I collapse onto the kitchen tiles, gasping like a fish out of water.

I don't know how long I remain on the floor, gasping, half crying, half laughing. Dimly, I realize that I've wet myself. I've heard that people who die by strangulation often wet themselves. Does choking on a peanut butter sandwich count as strangulation? The thought makes me laugh-cry again. Sometime later, I manage to get off the floor and trudge into the bathroom to clean myself up. Then I go back out and mop up the kitchen. I can't even look at my half-eaten sandwich, averting eyes as I lift it with the very tips of my fingers, wanting to have as little contact with it as possible. It goes into the trash, along with the blob of chewed-up sandwich that nearly became a murder weapon.

Finally, finally, I am done. My apartment is back to its pristine state, and I am in clean, dry clothes, and there is nothing in my mouth, and I can resume . . .

Right. Reading Haven's deal announcement. The darkness that has whispered at me ever since I read it half an hour ago comes roaring back. The whole reason why I even choked to begin with. How ironic it would've been if I'd survived her attacks all of high school only to die now, at the sight of her announcement. How could I have let her get into my head again, after all these years? I've done the work, gone to therapy, I journal, I meditate, I even did online hypnotherapy for a while. What more do I need to do to exorcise Haven Lee from my life?

But there she is, in the center of my phone screen, a square-cropped photo of her face on the left-hand corner of the deal announcement. How did I miss it before, when I was scrolling? How weird that my eyes glossed over her photo and landed instead on her name. She looks gorgeous, of course. I have known Haven Lee since she was twelve, and she has never once looked less than fashion magazine ready. Her hair falls over her shoulders in loose dark-brown waves, her large eyes beguiling, her nose straight, with the point coming up ever slightly, making her look pixie-like. Her smile is easy and welcoming, with just the right amount of good-natured wickedness to make you look twice. Good-natured wickedness is Haven's trademark humor. I don't know how to describe it, except that talking to her feels like you're being let into a delicious secret, but at the end of the day, you haven't actually learned anything bad about anyone; she never gossiped, or at least not with me, and yet you feel like you've partaken in something delicious and slightly catty, thus forging a strong bond with her. God, her face is so symmetrical, adheres so strongly to the golden rule, that I could die looking at it. How can such a monster look so beautiful?

Unbidden, the memory of Dani stabs into my mind, spearing through every thought. As always, it comes with a dark wave of guilt and fear so strong that it chokes me. I have worked so hard all these years to block the memory of her because whenever she resurfaces in my mind, it is overwhelming. It brings me to my knees, leaving me unable to function the rest of the day. And I can't afford to let that happen again.

I close my eyes. "I am okay," I say out loud, forcing myself to take long, slow breaths. "I am okay. The past is the past, and I am okay."

The mantra works after a while, and when I open my eyes, I feel more grounded. I'm sorry, Dani, but I have to leave you in the past.

Reluctantly, I drag my eyes from Haven's photo to her deal announcement. And somehow, her deal announcement is even worse than her perfect face. Key terms jump out at me. "Nine-house auction." Who the hell has a nine-house auction? What book is so explosively good that nine publishers choose to fight one another over it? In what universe does that happen? Then, of course, the words "seven-figure deal." It's not even a "major deal," which would mean anything over five hundred grand. Oh no, even a major deal isn't good enough for Haven Lee. In the #writingcommunity, we hopeful writers will often list having a six-figure deal as our ultimate dream. I don't think I've ever seen anyone dare hope for a seven-figure deal, it's so unreachable, so rare. And yet here's Haven, striding into the publishing industry with a unicorn deal.

And not just that, but a major deal in the UK? The UK is known for being extremely tight with advances. Last time I checked, the median UK advance size is about half the US's, which puts it at around $15,000. And yet, somehow, Haven has managed to get over $500,000 in the UK. And six figures from other territories: Now, that is definitely a rarity. Most of us would only ever be able to dream of selling to foreign territories, and here's Haven, getting more in foreign countries than we're getting in our home countries. I add up the total amount of money she's gotten just for this one book alone, and it's at least $2 million. Two million for one book. And what's more, the deal report ends with the words "TV/film rights," which means Haven has a film agent.

I stand there for god knows how long, in the middle of my kitchen, staring at my phone, willing the words in front of me to disappear. Maybe this is all a dream. I pinch my arm, and when that doesn't prove shocking enough, I give myself a slap. A sharp one, right across my right cheek, hard enough to make my eyes water. That hurt a lot. This is definitely not a dream.

Haven Lee has a book deal. Haven Lee is debuting in not only the year I am but the exact same season I am. Haven Lee, the girl who single-handedly turned everybody else against me and made my entire high school experience hell on earth and left me a broken husk of a person. The girl whose cruelty ultimately ended up killing the only friend I ever had is back.

Chapter 8

Age Fifteen

Apple maple cinnamon rolls. Who could say no to that? I'm so pleased with how they turned out that I'm practically skipping to school. Even Mom and Dad said they were really good. The school's having its annual bake sale today and everyone only ever brings cookies or brownies, so I just know these rolls are going to be a hit. I can already see people telling me how delicious they are and could I please, please teach them how to make them?

I'm still wearing a dopey grin when I turn the corner and run right into Haven Lee. The tray is knocked out of my hands, and I see the rolls tumbling out in slow motion. I dive after them and manage to catch one, but the others plop onto the sidewalk, and it's only when I feel the squish of cream cheese icing on my palm that I realize there wasn't any point in catching one. It's not like anyone's going to want to eat a cinnamon roll I've held in my bare hand.

Even as I think that, Haven smacks my hand, making me drop the roll. "Oops!" she says, smiling.

I can't stand it. I can't keep my cool. Tears roll down my face as I scream, "Why would you do that!" I crouch down on the sidewalk and gather the cinnamon rolls, sobbing like a little kid.

Haven's foot stomps down onto one of the rolls, then another and another, flattening them. "Oh my god," she laughs, "I am sooo clumsy!"

"Stop it!" I shriek, and lunge at her. I shove her, hard, and she stumbles back and falls onto her butt.

"Freak," she hisses, pushing herself back up.

"Haven!" someone calls out.

Haven and I turn at the same time, and relief floods me when I see Dani. She hurries over to us, her face creased with concern.

"What's going on?" she says, her gaze ping-ponging back and forth from Haven to me.

"She pushed me," Haven says, brushing dirt off her bottom. She lifts her palms up and shows them to Dani. They're bruised, pocked with little marks where gravel dug into the skin.

"She destroyed my cinnamon rolls!" I yell. I'm still crying, my breath coming in and out in short, shuddering gasps, and I sound completely insane.

Haven shakes her head, her eyes wide with innocence. "We bumped into each other. It was an accident, Fern. I can't believe you thought I'd do something like that on purpose."

It takes everything inside me not to scratch her hateful face. "That's not true!" I scream. I turn to Dani. "You've got to believe me. She was waiting for me, she—"

"I saw you push Haven, Fern," Dani says quietly.

"But—" I make myself pause and take a deep breath. "Did you see what happened before that?"

Dani shakes her head. "I'm sorry. I just arrived, and I looked over and saw you pushing Haven."

"But she started it!" I cry.

Dani sighs. "Can you please just—please just be civil to her?"

Haven smirks, just long enough for me to spot, but not Dani. I grit my teeth. "She shoved my tray out of my hands," I growl.

"God, I hate this," Dani groans. "Why can't everyone just freaking be *kind*?" With that, she links her arm through Haven's, and they walk away, leaving me with nothing but a pile of crushed cinnamon rolls.

I want to scream. I don't know how to describe the pain that stabs through me at the sight of Dani linking her arm through Haven's. Dani choosing to believe Haven over me. Dani, the girl I'd known since we were little kids with chronically scraped knees. The friend I had a sleepover with almost every weekend. The friend who, after a trip to Disneyland, came back and gave me a pair of Mickey Mouse earrings that matched hers. I still have those earrings. Sometimes, I put them on at night and think of how Dani and I would grin whenever we wore those earrings together. Her mom would go "Ooh, look at you two with your matching earrings!" and I'd pretend that she was my sister.

I have never felt as alone as I do now, watching Dani walking away from me. Just before they turn the corner and go out of my line of sight, Haven turns her head, and I could swear she's wearing the smallest hint of a smile on her face.

Chapter 9

After that, there is no stopping me. I tried, of course, for a while. I managed to extricate the phone from my hand and paced about my tiny apartment, muttering frantically out loud: "It's okay, Fern. It has nothing to do with you. This is completely separate from you and your book deal. She's all the way back in LA, she can't get to you. She doesn't have a hold over you, it's fine. Just mute her on everything and forget about her. It's fine. It's *fine*!"

This lasted about seven whole minutes. The whole time, my insides churned and boiled, the tension building inside me until the floodgates exploded and I practically pounced at my phone. I do a search for Haven Lee on Twitter but find nothing. She must be on here. A dark feeling claws at my stomach, and I log out of my Twitter profile before logging on to an alternate account. I do the search once more, and this time, her name shows up. I break out into cold sweat. My instincts were right. I haven't come across Haven's Twitter profile all this time because she's blocked me. A tremor goes up my arms, making me shiver. After all these years, she still has it out for me. Why? I give myself a little shake. Doesn't matter. Don't try to come up with an explanation for Haven's wanton cruelty. Focus on this.

Gulping, I tap on Haven's Twitter profile. I can't believe that all this time, I've been stalking her on Facebook and Instagram but never on Twitter. I guess I saw Twitter as a publishing-only space, and there had never been any indication of Haven even being remotely connected to publishing. She's a food influencer, for god's sake! She cooks huge feasts for her adorable parents! And all of a sudden here she is, writing a novel about sexual assault? What the hell?

When Haven's profile opens, the latest tweet she posted is only two hours ago, and it's a link to an article about her UK deal. An actual article, not just a short and sweet deal announcement.

> Margery Lynn at Red Line Books has landed, at a very competitive auction, at a high six-figure deal, the debut adult novel from Haven M. Lee, *She Asked for It*. Film rights have already been optioned, at auction, to Sony Pictures. Pitched as *You* meets the #MeToo movement, the story follows Emma Underwood, a junior associate at a law firm who finds herself caught in a media bloodbath when she comes forward with a sexual assault allegation against her mentor and employer, who is about to obtain judgeship.
>
> Lee graduated with a degree in pre-law from Stanford and is currently based in Los Angeles, California. *She Asked for It* is her debut novel.
>
> Lee said: "I cannot believe what a whirlwind this entire process has been from start to finish. From the moment I spoke to Margery, I knew that this book will be in the best possible hands. She just got it so completely, everything I was trying to achieve with this story. I can't wait to see what she and the team at Red Line Books will do."
>
> Lynn said: "I have never come across a story like *She Asked for It*. I was on the edge of my seat the entire time I read it, and by the time I finished, I had no fingernails left! It's the most tense, heartbreaking, and enraging read you will ever come across. A must-read for every woman in our generation. I cannot wait to introduce everyone to the brilliance that is Haven M. Lee."

Hell, it's such an effective article that by the end of it, I'm wishing I had a copy of *She Asked for It* so I, too, can see what all the fuss is about. I close the tab and go back to Twitter. There is a small node of bitterness in my belly, and I know I'm feeding it with every triumphant post of Haven's that I take in.

@HavenMLee: I am incandescent with joy to announce that I have a book deal!!! I am going to be a published author!!! (Posted along with a screenshot of her PM deal announcement.) Two thousand, seven hundred, and eighty-five likes, and over six hundred comments.

The comments are a riot of celebratory screaming GIFs and equally celebratory screaming words, all caps lock, each one peppered with half a dozen exclamation marks. And how in the world are there almost three thousand likes already? She only posted that this morning.

@HavenMLee: I never thought I had what it takes to write anything remotely approaching a novel, but my dreams have come true, all thanks to my amazing agent Rachel Reed. One thousand, six hundred, and thirty-two likes, and almost three hundred comments.

The fact that her little throwaway tweet thanking her agent got three times more likes than my deal announcement did eats away at my skin like acid. I look at Haven's follower count. She has six thousand followers on Twitter. How in the hell? I continue scrolling, ignoring the way the bitterness is seeping into the rest of my body, tainting me with its darkness.

@HavenMLee: Um, guys? I think I'm going to have some very exciting news soon . . . Over six hundred likes and two hundred comments all begging to know what it could be. Are you serious? I want to snap at the screen. I cannot stand posts like these. Coy, teasing, nothing but bait to get more attention. But look at how effective it was. And isn't that just classic Haven?

@HavenMLee: Signing something utterly magical!!! (Posted along with a photo of her posing with a stack of papers as she smiles up into the camera.) The stack of papers is probably her numerous publishing contracts, I realize as I gaze with growing nausea at her beautiful, flawless face. This one has over a thousand likes. God, how have I missed her presence in the Twitter writing community this whole time? Even on my alternate account, which I sometimes use to trawl through Twitter, I never came across her. How can that be possible?

I scroll down faster and faster, her posts becoming a blur to me. Is it because she rarely uses the writing community hashtag? Yes, I think, that must be it. None of her posts have the hashtag. But why don't they? Every writer I know of wants to connect with other writers. Writing is such a lonely vocation, so isolating, that we all crave connections with like-minded people, peers who know exactly what the struggle of trying to break into publishing is like. But here is Haven, hiding from Publishing Twitter, unlike everyone else. Why?

The answer, when it finally dawns, stops me cold. *Because of you*, a sinister voice in my head whispers. *Because you are intrinsically tied to Dani, and she knows what she did. Because you are so active in the writing community. She would've seen your posts on Twitter. She would've found you. You use your real name on here, unlike on Instagram, where you use a sock puppet account to follow her. She's got you blocked, but that wasn't enough. She's decided to . . . what? To lie low until she can blast out of the water like a great white shark to slice you in half without you even realizing it?* Ridiculous. Even though it's true that ever since high school, Haven and I have largely stayed away from each other, I don't believe that she'd stay out of the writing community just to avoid me.

Who says she stayed away from the writing community? The voice continues whispering.

I scroll through her posts again, this time reading the comments, and it hits me that many of these comments aren't your run-of-the-mill congratulatory messages from random strangers. The way these writers are interacting with Haven makes it clear that they know each other. They call one another "dear friend" or "girlie" or other forms of familiar affectations. The bitterness inside me has grown so thick, so cloying, that it almost chokes me. How is this possible? She's even friends with a lot of the people I know. We have mutuals? What?

I wonder, the voice in my head says, what she's told them about you. What she's told them about Dani.

And now I feel so utterly sick that I think I might actually throw up. No. This can't happen again, not to the only community I have, the only community that I've devoted time and effort into turning into a safe space for myself. I cannot let it turn into another high school experience, with me as a friendless pariah. God, please no. The thought of it is so bleak that my nose starts itching, my eyes filling up with tears. I can't stomach the thought of Haven isolating me from my writing friends with vicious gossip. It would kill me.

The thought strikes with unforgiving clarity. There is no hyperbole here. My high school experience has scarred me so badly that I didn't let myself get close to anyone in college. I have no social life, zero friends, barely a relationship with my own parents. If I lost my online community, I wouldn't have anything else to live for.

I shake my head. Come on, Fern, calm down. Haven Lee has a seven-figure book deal. She doesn't have time for you. She's moved on with her life; she's on to much better things than picking on you. You're not even on her radar. She's probably not actively using the Twitter hashtag because she's above hashtags. Right? She is exactly the sort of person who thinks she's too good for hashtags.

My breath, previously ragged and shallow, starts to even out. Yeah, that's right. Haven probably thinks she's above the writing community hashtag. And she is, objectively. She is above pretty much everyone else in the debut authors group.

Oh god. The debut authors group. Haven is going to be a part of it. It feels as though someone's just kicked me right in the belly. The private Facebook group I'd been so excited to join is going to have my high school bully in it. I close Twitter and check Facebook, and sure enough, there's a new post in the group.

> **Felicity Silver:** Omg my good friend Haven finally got to announce her book deal!! If you think her book

> sounds good, you're wrong; it's a million times better than good, it's AMAZING. Completely mind-blowing. I was lucky enough to read an early draft of it because we're each other's beta readers, and I am telling you, the world is not ready for this brilliance! @ admin, can you send her an invite to join this group? She's definitely in the 2020 debut group, and I've told her to register to join us plenty of times but she's really shy so can we please send her an invite? She is THE nicest person ever, I promise!

There are five comments to this post already, all of them along the lines of: Wow! Yes, we need her in our group! One of the comments is by the admin, who said: Thanks for the heads up, Felicity! I have sent her an invite.

My head swims. Darkness creeps into the edges of my vision. Am I about to faint? I pinch the back of my hand, hard enough to snap me out of whatever this lightheadedness is. This situation is so unreal that it almost makes me laugh. Because isn't that just classic Haven—instead of having to apply to join the group like the rest of us did, to be invited to join? And also, there's the rub—her crony vouching for her, telling us all that she is "THE nicest person ever."

A memory of Haven in middle school, telling me "Stay away from me and my friends, you little freak!" slices through my mind like a scythe. *The* nicest person ever? I beg to differ. Another memory, this one of her shoving me away so roughly that it actually jerks the thoughts out of my head and leaves me momentarily disoriented. Would *the* nicest person ever do that to a helpless kid? Pick on her just because she's a loner? I would be the first to admit that perhaps I'm not like most people, that sure, her calling me a "weirdo" or "loser" isn't completely inaccurate. But Haven being referred to as a nice person is so far off the mark it's not even funny anymore.

Stop this now, I tell myself. I have spent years obsessed with Haven Lee, even after high school ended. She's lived rent-free in my head for so long, and it took so much work for me to evict her. Not fully, obviously, since I spend time now and again to take a look at her Instagram. "Why carry the weight of her ghost on your shoulders?" my old therapist, Aliyah, said. "She's out of your life. Maybe back in school, she had power over you because she was able to bully you, but you're not in school anymore. You moved to the other side of the country, even. So don't continue giving her power over you." I started seeing her the first year I moved here. Getting therapy was the best decision I'd made for myself. It was in Aliyah's office that I took the first steps toward healing myself after the wreckage of high school. Despite the astronomical cost of therapy, I continued seeing Aliyah for eight months before I felt stable enough to end the sessions.

And now, I have carved out a safe space for myself, and there is nothing Haven can do to ruin it. Plus, I have the upper hand; I got into the debut group first. Over the past few weeks, I have established myself as a valuable member of the group. I even have good friends, Lisa and Jenna. We've been emailing each other every day ever since we exchanged manuscripts, and it's been so nice I could cry, thinking about our wonderful connection. They say three is a crowd, but I haven't once felt that way with Lisa and Jenna, and I'm sure they feel the same way about me. Haven can't take that away from me. In fact, I should be leaning on them right now. Isn't that what good friends do?

I open up Gmail and pause, considering my words for a moment before typing: "Hey guys, omg, the craziest thing just happened. My high school bully has a book deal and she's also going to debut in 2020." I press "Send" and lean back in my seat, my heart thudding quickly.

Back in middle school, I'd tried confiding in Dani about Haven picking on me. Dani had wrinkled her nose at me and said, "Haven? Picking on you? Are you sure?" And that had been that. I never told anybody else. If even my friend didn't believe me, who would?

But things are different now, I remind myself. I'm an adult, and so are Lisa and Jenna, and chances are, neither of them knows Haven in person, so they wouldn't be exposed to that irresistible Haven charm. They'll have my back. I lace my fingers together and grip so tightly that my knuckles stick out. They have to have my back. They have to.

My phone beeps with a new email, and I grab it as fast as a striking snake.

> **Jenna:** WHAT?! Omg! No way. That's AWFUL! I'm so sorry to hear that, Fern.

As I read, a bubble pops up with the words 1 New Message.

> **Lisa:** WTF, what are the chances?? Shit, I hate this for you. Is she joining our debut group??

My tensed muscles melt, and I utter a choked sob-laugh. See, they do have my back. They are truly my friends. I feel like a little kid once more, wanting to run home and shout "Mom, Dad, I made new friends!" Sniffling, I straighten up and write a reply.

> **Fern:** She isssss 😩. I know, it is so weird you guys and I have been freaking out about it. This girl made my middle and high school years just about the worst time of my life. She spread ugly rumors about me, when no one was looking she'd shove me and tell me to stay away etc. I had no friends because of her. No one wanted to go against her.

> **Jenna:** Uggghhh, this is the worst. I'm sorry you went through that. Is there anything we can do? Can we talk to the mods and tell them not to let her into the debut group??

My mouth goes dry at the thought of talking to the mods.

Fern: What would we even say to the mods, though? I don't think the fact that she bullied me back in middle and high school is a valid reason to keep her out of the debut group . . . I mean, for me it is, but the mods will see it differently. And it's so long ago, ten years ago now. They're not going to keep her out because of that.

Lisa: Yeah, I hate to say it, but I don't think the mods will keep her out. Even if they wanted to, I don't think they would. I'm sure they'd empathize with you, but she sounds so cunning, if they were to refuse to let her in, she'll surely ask why, and then who knows what they'll tell her?

Fern: Oh god, yeah. I didn't even think of that. I don't want her to know that she didn't get into the debut group because of me. I have no idea what she might do. 😭

Lisa: I had a bully in high school too. I know how these people work. They're always studying the crowd like a predator, and just like a predator, they know to pick on the weakest members of the group. Not saying you're weak, Fern, but she must have seen something in you that left you vulnerable. My guess would be the fact that you're such a sweet, generous person. Like how you're always baking for your neighbors and that awful boss of yours, even now. She must've sensed that. Ugh, this bitch. Who is she? I bet her book sucks.

Lisa's email makes me want to laugh and cry at the same time. I feel so seen by her words. With just one email, Lisa has hit the nail on the head and homed in on the reason Haven picked on me.

> **Fern:** Her name is Haven Lee and I saw that her book got a seven-figure deal, so I doubt it sucks, actually. I bet it's really good.

> **Jenna:** OMG!!! NO WAY!! I saw her announcement on Twitter today and I congratulated her!! ARGH, GROSS!

> **Lisa:** Oh man, I saw it too and I also congratulated her. I'm sorry Fern, I had no idea she's your high school bully. Man, this is the worst. Why do good things happen to bad people?

Why indeed. If there was any justice in this world, Haven Lee would've been outed as the cruel villain she truly is a long time ago. But that kind of poetic justice, while it makes for a great ending to a movie, rarely happens in real life. The Haven Lees of the world will continue strutting confidently into a future so bright it blinds the rest of us, while the Ferns of the world will be left behind to pick up the broken pieces of themselves.

> **Fern:** Yeah, it really sucks. I didn't even know she was into writing. She never once showed any interest in it back at school. Anyway, it doesn't matter. All that matters is I have you guys. It means the world to me to be able to open up to you. I love our little club. It's my safe space.

> **Jenna:** Awww Fern!! Of course! It's my safe space too. I'm soooo glad I found you guys too. The debut

group is getting too big and overwhelming anyway. Every week there are like ten new people joining and so many new posts I can barely keep up. And now we're about to switch over to Slack??

Wait, what? Switch to Slack? I've heard of Slack a couple of times here and there, and it sounds like the dumbest thing. Why do we need yet another messaging app?

Fern: Ugh, do we have to switch over to Slack? God I hate having to get used to yet another different app.

Lisa: Actually, my workplace uses Slack and it's pretty cool. You'll love it. We'll be able to chat in real time!

Aren't we already chatting in real time? I whine to myself. But I would never say that to them. That's something that old Fern would say. Old, pathetic Fern who let herself shrink smaller and smaller to stay out of Haven's growing light. But I am grown up now, and I refuse to be left behind in the dark again. If the group is switching over from Facebook to Slack, then I am going with them. In fact, I'm going to download Slack right freaking now and familiarize myself with it so I won't be lost once we make the move. How's that for proactive?

Speaking of proactive, I need to get ahead of Haven. She's caught me off guard with her stupid book announcement, and I can't let anything like that happen again. My inner Aliyah says, "Are you letting Haven live rent-free inside your head again?" No, I am not. There is a difference between obsessing over her without an aim and therefore with no end in sight, and obsessing about her to watch my back. Whether I like it or not, Haven Lee is back in my life, but this time, I am not going to let her ruin me.

Chapter 10

There are a few people who voted against moving to Slack, but they were by far the minority, and by the next day, there is a new post pinned to the top of the Facebook group with a link to the Slack group. The move comes at the perfect time; Haven has just joined the Facebook group the night before and made an introductory post.

> Hi everyone! I can't believe I'm in a debut group, oh my gosh! How cool is this? I am so intimidated by all of y'all! My name is Haven and my book title is She Asked for It. It's about a woman who defies all odds to stand up for herself and was inspired by the #MeToo movement. I can't wait for 2020 to get here!

I read her introductory post with a scowl on my face. To everyone else, it'll come off as a perfectly nice message, but I know better. This is Fake Nice Haven. Haven who is trying to fit in. Why is she saying *y'all*? She's not Texan, she's—

I stop myself. I'm being petty, and I hate it. I hate that she has this effect on me. You know when people who are in love say "I love who I am when I'm with them"? Well, Haven has the opposite effect on me. I hate who I am when I come across Haven. I know I'm a good person. I like doing nice things for others. But something about Haven just reaches through all the layers of goodness I have worked so hard to build around myself and seeks out the strands of darkness inside me, yanking it out, writhing, onto the surface.

I snap myself out of it and scroll back up to the pinned post. "Bye, Haven, hope I won't see you on the other side," I mutter, and click on the Slack link.

I promised myself to become familiarized with Slack, but all I've done is download the app. I created a Slack group, then clicked around in the empty space. I typed out a message, "Hi," and then "Hello," then got tired of talking to myself and quit the program.

The debut group Slack is a completely different affair from my solo Slack. First off, as soon as I join, I see five channels have already been created by the mods. There is a #general channel, a #celebrations channel, a #commiserations channel, a #questions channel, and a #random channel. The #general channel is moving in real time, with messages popping up on the screen at a furious pace. Over sixty people have joined the Slack group, and thirty-two of us are currently online. I scroll down the list of names of people who are online and breathe a sigh of relief when I don't spot Haven's name on it, then I turn my attention to the general chat.

Kelly: Omg this is so much better than the FB group! Thanks for creating this chat group, @Anna!

Mariana: Agreed, this is so cool! I love the fact that we're just . . . chatting with one another! Thank you @Anna!

Others are chiming in, thanking Anna as well. I quickly type out: "Yes, I love that we took the plunge here, great idea, @Anna!" and hit Enter. Moments later, Anna, who also happens to be online, reacts to all our messages with the heart emoji. I breathe a sigh of relief. See? I'm a member of this group. I belong here, unlike Haven.

Having established my presence in the #general channel, I peruse the other channels. The #questions channel has just one post in there.

> **Yuna:** How long after you folks signed your contract did you get your edit letter? It's been three months since I signed my contract and I still haven't received my letter yet, and I'm starting to get antsy!

No replies yet. Good question, though. I type out: "I signed mine two weeks ago and still no edit letter either. 🤷‍♀️" But as soon as I hit Enter, I regret my reply. Did that come off as callous? I didn't mean for it to be. I right-click on my message and delete it from the chat. It disappears without a trace. I release a small sigh and start typing a new response. "I have no idea, but I'm sure it'll appear soon!" No, that sounds stupid. Never mind. I switch out of the #questions channel and go to the #commiserations channel instead.

> **Alaina:** My book JUST got announced and it somehow has a one-star review on Goodreads already?!! WTF??

Her post has two replies.

> **Becca:** OMG what!? You should report it to your publisher!

> **Stacey:** Yesss srsly, wtf it's obviously a troll since none of our books are even out yet! Report to Goodreads!

I've always been an avid reader, so I'm a total GR junkie, but from years of experience on Twitter's #writingcommunity, I know that Goodreads, the largest book review site, is a source of sleepless nights and stomach ulcers for authors. The more experienced authors always tweet about how authors should block Goodreads from their web browsers, but of course no debut author is going to listen to that. In the whirlwind since my announcement happened—god, was that only yesterday? I've been so distracted by the nightmare that is Haven Lee and her announcement that I have forgotten all about my own book. I haven't even checked to see if it's up on Goodreads yet.

I switch from Slack to Goodreads and type my name into the search box. Oh my god. It's there. It actually is there. *The Happiest of Unhappy Days*, by Fern Huang. I stare at the computer screen for a long while. There is no cover, of course, and zero ratings and reviews, but it's my book. My book is actually listed on Goodreads! For a few moments, I merely sit, reading the title and the synopsis of the book over and over, marveling at the unreal sensation of seeing my book online like this. I try to savor the joy, but it doesn't last long before a certain curiosity uncurls from the edges of my brain. I try to ignore it, but it grows like an itch, subtle at first, then increasing in intensity until it becomes unbearable and I must scratch it. I watch in mute agony as my fingers fly across the keyboard of their own accord, ignoring my silent protest. Don't do it, my mind begs, it's not good for you, this is not healthy. But they type "Haven Lee" and hit Enter.

There's her book. *She Asked for It.* An average rating of five stars, from four reviewers.

How is that even possible? It was only announced yesterday, for goodness' sake. Who are these people—these losers—who are so quick to review books as soon as they appear on Goodreads? Get a life! I want to scream at them. Haven's book doesn't have a cover yet either—of course it doesn't—but somehow, her page looks fuller than mine. Which is probably because her publisher has spent the extra time and effort on making sure her book has all the descriptions it needed to stand out on Goodreads. I scroll down to the ratings and reviews. There are four ratings and two reviews.

> **Amyreads:** If you buy just one book in 2020, let it be this one. Seriously you guys, this is without a doubt the most important book you will ever read. Inspired by the #MeToo movement, Lee has written a book with such complexity, so many layers, and just when you think you've figured it out, there are more surprises and twists to come that will blow your mind. It's going to haunt me for the rest of my life and I LOVE IT.

The other review is only one line long, but somehow it leaves me feeling even worse.

> **Shelby's Bookshelf:** YOU MUST BUY THIS BOOK JUST TRUST ME YOU NEED THIS BOOK IN YOUR LIFE.

Two five-star reviews. Not just five stars but absolutely rabid, passionate reviews. Reviews that you just know came from people who will be talking about the book nonstop to their friends and families until they, too, go out and purchase the book. I once read a Twitter thread about the kind of book that publishers and agents dream of getting. They look for good books, but they dream of books that make people want to make others read them too. The one-in-a-million book that catches fire and spreads like a piece of hot gossip because after reading it, it would be impossible to keep such a delicious thing to yourself and you need your friend to read it, too, so that you can meet over coffee or wine and go "Isn't that book so freaking good?"

From the look of everything I've come across, Haven's book is poised to set the world on fire. I pick up my cup of tea to sip, but my hand slips and I nearly drop it on top of my keyboard. With a start, I realize that my palms have gone clammy, my chest tight like my rib cage has just shrunk and is now squeezing my lungs. I force myself to step away from the computer and pace around the apartment once more, counting to five while doing some deep breathing exercises. Back in high school, thanks to Haven's bullying, I started having mini panic attacks. Aliyah worked with me tirelessly to come up with a good technique to stop these attacks, and it's been years since I had one, but now here it is again, my old friend rearing its ugly head. I force myself to focus on my five senses, noticing objects I can see, smell, and feel, until the grip around my chest loosens.

Okay, I tell myself when my breathing is no longer labored, I need to stop this. It's not good for me. I need to set boundaries for myself. No more looking up Haven or her book. Mind your own business.

I return to the computer and close the Goodreads tab. There, I huff, relieved. See? I can do the right thing. The mature thing. I go back to Slack. And this time, I find that Haven is, indeed, online, and not only that, but she's started replying to the other authors.

On the #commiserations channel, she replied to Alaina's post about the one-star review on Goodreads, saying: Ugh, Alaina, I'm sorry to hear that, how sucky! But my mentor told me it's best to ignore Goodreads completely. I actually have it blocked on my browser because I just know I'd obsess non-stop over it, and GR is such a cesspool of trolls, you can't trust any reviews on there. Your book is beautiful and I have no doubt that you'll get many five-star reviews which will drown out the haters!

Immediately, my chest tightens up again. It's her. And on the sidebar, I can see the green dot next to her name, which means she's online. She's online right this very second, existing in the same place as me, and it hits me then. *She can see that I'm online too.* Trepidation overwhelms me, and I scramble to close the Slack window. I hunch over, my arms hugging my stomach as guilt, grief, and fear roil inside me. I can't help but think of Dani. As much as I try to leave Dani behind, there are times when the memory of her comes roaring back with such strength that it threatens to crush me.

I'm breathing hard now, as though I've just sprinted. I have a strong urge to crouch down and hide from the computer, which is crazy, I know. Haven can't see me; logically, I know that. I know. But I feel her eyes on me, watching me with that knowing gaze of hers. Her gaze feels like an insect crawling across my skin, its legs brushing against the little hairs on the back of my neck, its pincers poised to pierce through the sensitive parts of my skin. I shudder and stand up so abruptly that my chair clatters back.

"She's not here, Fern," I mutter out loud. "It's okay, you're okay. This is not high school. You're free of her. She has no hold over you. She can't see you. She can't. You need to go back in there. You can't let her take this space away from you, otherwise you lose."

God, I know it's true. I know that if I walk away from the debut group Slack, then Haven will win. Again. And she wouldn't have to do anything to win this time. I throw my head back, blinking at the ceiling to keep the tears from falling. It feels so wrong, but I have to go back to the Slack group. Plus, I tell myself, it's not like she can tell me to fuck off like she did back in school. Because if she does, if she sends me a mean message online, then I can screenshot it and show it to everyone. Then the rest of the world will finally know the truth about Haven Lee.

The thought of it calms me. Yes. Haven no longer has dark corners to trap me in. She can no longer whisper threats to me. If she's going to be her vile self, she'll have to do it online, leaving behind a trail of evidence that can be used to out her. I am as protected as I can be from Haven. I can do this.

Taking a deep breath, I sit back down and open the Slack once more. The #commiserations channel has even more replies.

Alaina: You are so right @Haven! Ughhh I really shouldn't have let it get to me, I feel so dumb now, lol.

Haven: Omg, you are not in the least bit dumb! The only reason I blocked GR is precisely because I know the slightest bit of negativity will cause me to spiral! #TheEmotionalMaturityOfAToddler. 😄

FelicityDao: LOL tell me about it! Haven is right, she got me to block GR ages ago and #noregrets!

Alaina: I love you guys! What would I do without you? I've blocked GR now and I feel sooo much better already.

I'm scowling as I read the chat. Alaina loves them? You don't even know these people! I scream silently at them. I raise my hands to type something, but I hesitate. The knowledge that Haven will be able to see the words "FernHuang is typing . . ." pop up on the screen makes me feel lightheaded. And anyway, what would I say? What can I possibly add to this conversation? Haven's already swooped in and saved the day.

I switch to the #questions channel and to my dismay, find that Haven's also been in here.

Yuna: How long after you folks signed your contract did you get your edit letter? It's been three months since I signed my contract and I still haven't received my letter yet, and I'm starting to get antsy!

Haven: So much of this industry is "hurry up and wait", isn't it!

Yuna: Girl, tell me about it.

Haven: I got mine two weeks after signing my contract, but I know it differs from editor to editor and I really wouldn't read too much into it. Have you asked your agent? She should nudge your editor for you.

Yuna: Idk, I don't wanna bother my agent.

Haven: I don't think it's bothering your agent at all! It's not like you're asking her to do something every week, and you've waited three months, I think a check-in is understandable.

Felicity: Agreed! I would've checked in a lot sooner honestly.

Yuna: Hmm. Okay you're right.

Haven: Yeah, it won't hurt! If your agent doesn't think it's reasonable to nudge your editor, she'll tell you. It'll be fine! That's why we have agents, right?

Yuna: Thank you for the much-needed kick in the butt. I don't know why I've just been sitting here questioning myself endlessly. Ok, I'm going to message my agent right now! Aaah, wish me luck!

Haven: Good luck! You got this!

It seems as though in every freaking channel, Haven has made a new fan. I scroll up and reread the whole exchange between Yuna and Haven again. How does Haven do this? My reply to Yuna's original question now seems so stupid in comparison that I thank the universe that I deleted it as soon as I posted it. And isn't it just typical Haven to drop a subtle mention about how much better she's being treated ("*My* editor sent *my* notes within two weeks, unlike *your* editor!") before she gives actual useful advice? Also, is her advice actually good? Should Yuna be reaching out to her agent asking her to nudge her editor? I for one would definitely not do any such thing. I have this thing about not being a bother, ever, so the thought of reaching out to Poppy and asking her "Hiiii Poppy, do you think you could possibly nudge Lindsay and ask her when she'll have my edit letter ready?" actually makes me do a whole-body shudder.

No, that is terrible advice. There is nothing worse than an irritating, high-maintenance client. If Poppy is ever asked about me, I want her to say, "Oh, Fern Huang? She is the easiest client to work with! I'm so happy I'm her agent!"

Right. I know I'm right. The question is: Does Haven know that she's setting Yuna up for failure? Is she secretly hoping that Yuna would become known to her agent as a difficult client? As soon as I think this, the answer becomes obvious. Because of course Haven knows what she's doing. Haven always knows; she always has an ulterior motive. She believes that everything is a zero-sum game and that in order for her to get ahead, others need to fall back. Maybe—a dark, sly thought surfaces—maybe she's doing this because they've got the same agent? And she wants to be the favorite, so she's making Yuna look bad.

I do a quick Google search to see who Yuna's agent is, and aha! Yuna isn't represented by Haven's agent, but she is represented by Haven's agent's colleague. They're repped by the same agency. Close enough for poor Yuna to find herself Haven's next target.

I feel the familiar sensations of my chest tightening at witnessing some unfortunate soul become Haven's next victim, while at the same time a pathetic sense of relief courses through me because hey, if Haven's picking on someone else, she's not picking on me. But as soon as I think that, I seethe with self-hatred. I refuse to give in to that selfish thought. I can't think like that. I need to stand up for others. Back in middle and high school, when Haven first set her sights on me, I prayed countless times to the universe to send me someone, just one person, who'd be willing to stand up for me. I foolishly thought that Dani was that person for me, the one who'd take my hand and tell me it's okay, we've always got each other. It took me a while to realize that happy endings only happen in movies. I was on my own, only because nobody else was brave enough to stand up to Haven. But now, I can be that person for someone else.

I click on Yuna's name and start up a private conversation with her. An eternity passes before I decide on what to say.

> **Fern:** Hi, Yuna! How's it going?

I watch, my mouth dry, as Yuna starts typing a reply.

> **Yuna:** Hey, good, good! I'm just getting used to the Slack group. How are you?

> **Fern:** Good, thanks! Yeah, me too. It takes a beat to get used to.

There follows a long, painful silence. I can sense Yuna behind her screen, waiting and wondering why the hell I've reached out. It's not too late. I could just say "Anyway, just wanted to say hi!" and then run away. But as I type "Anyway, just wanted . . ." I get a flash of myself in middle school, watching from afar as everyone hangs out together. An image of Haven whispering something behind her hand to the others, then all of them glancing at me for a quick second before bursting into peals of laughter. No. I can't let it happen again.

> **Fern:** So anyway, I saw your question about the edit letter . . .

> **Yuna:** Oh?

> **Fern:** Yeah, and I saw the suggestion to ask your agent to nudge.

Yuna: Yeah, I feel so stupid for not thinking of doing that sooner. So glad that Haven talked some sense into me.

No, no, I want to shout at Yuna. Haven does not talk sense into anyone. She only whispers poison.

Fern: Well, I actually don't think it's a good idea. I mean, I think it's pretty normal not to have an edit letter after three months and I also don't have my edit letter yet. I think that's pretty normal, actually.

Yuna: OH. Really?? Omg. Aaaah! Now I'm so torn.

Fern: It's just, idk if asking your agent to nudge would come off as like, high maintenance or something, you know?

Yuna: Oh man. You're right. That IS pretty demanding, isn't it? But I am getting nervous about the lack of an edit letter . . . I don't want things to start running late and then because of that my book ends up getting pushed back a season or something, argh!

Publishing is notorious for running slow. Unless it's a book by a celebrity author or a book whose topic is super timely, many books get delayed because of various reasons—for example, an editor who is tardy with sending her edit notes. In theory, I know this. But of course I have no idea if that's what's actually happening with Yuna's book. Is her editor late? Or maybe three months to write an edit letter is normal? Who the hell knows? We're debut authors, we know nothing, we're babies in this industry! But I know one thing, and that's to be suspicious of anything Haven says, and this becomes my touchstone, my guide that tells me what's right and wrong. Trust your gut, Fern. And my gut is telling me that Haven is up to her old tricks.

> **Fern:** I totally get that. I wouldn't want my book to get pushed back either, but I think you should trust that your agent has things under control and that if she thinks your editor is running late, she will absolutely check in with her and make sure everything's running smoothly.

> **Yuna:** Whew. Okay, that is such a good point. I do trust my agent, she's the best! You're right, I should just lay off her and let her do her job in peace. Ugh, this whole industry is such a minefield, I swear!

> **Fern:** It really is!

I hesitate, then continue typing.

> **Fern:** And also, I would be extra careful about any advice that Haven Lee gives . . .

As soon as I hit Enter, all my senses scream at me. What have I done? I right-click on the message to delete it, but it's too late. Already, I can see that Yuna is typing something. She's seen my message.

> **Yuna:** Oh my gosh, what do you mean? Why??

For a second, I am frozen, wondering what to say. Then I think: Screw it. I might as well tell her the truth.

> **Fern:** I just don't think that she has other people's best interests at heart. I mean, she asked you to

nudge your agent and that would've made you seem like a difficult client. Idk if you know this, but she's represented by your agency too.

Yuna: OMG IS SHE??!! We're agency siblings?? Wait, is she repped by Leanne too??

Fern: No, her agent is Rachel. But I'm just saying, she might feel competitive because you guys are at the same agency . . . IDK, I'm just guessing here. I'm sorry, I feel like an asshole, I don't want to gossip about her.

Yuna: Of course not!

Fern: I'm just saying this to warn you so you don't fall into the trap of listening to Haven's advice because sometimes it doesn't come from a good place.

Yuna: That makes sense. Wait, do you know her from before?

Fern: Yeah. That's why I know what she can be like.

Yuna: Wowwww, that's wild! Thank you so much for reaching out and letting me know!

Fern: Of course. Cone of silence please! I'm honestly kind of terrified of her, LOL!

Yuna: Omg of course! Cone of silence! Omg now I'm so scared of her, hahaha AAHH. I can't believe I'm her agency sibling. Dude, her deal sounds INSANE.

Fern: Doesn't it?? I'm happy for her, really. I just wish that her having a huge deal like that would occupy her time enough so that she'd stop doing her usual shit.

Yuna: Yeah. Oh man, I mean, why bother sabotaging someone else's career when hers is going so well??

Fern: I don't know, but that's pretty par for the course with the Haven I know.

Yuna: Wow, okay. OKAY. I'm sooo glad I haven't sent that email to my agent. Now I know. Thank you again!!

There. I've saved someone from Haven's clutches. Something I've wished for myself countless times, and I've managed to start the ball rolling. Is it cliché to say that I feel proud of myself? Oh, to hell with it. I absolutely do. I want to give myself a pat on the head, actually.

"And now," I say out loud, "I am closing my laptop and going to enjoy the real world."

This was something Aliyah drilled into me. The value of a good walk, using all my senses and noticing everything around me to help ground me in the space outside of my own head. I've had to work hard at it because after so many years of bullying, I developed a habit of escaping reality and burrowing into myself, curling my consciousness into a tight ball and pretending that nothing else existed. It's taken years to pull me out of my shell, and now I relish my daily walks.

I leave the apartment with a sense of, if not peace, then something approaching it. I'm no longer a passive observer, lying back and letting Haven trample people over in her rush to the top. And I'm stopping myself from obsessing over her again by indulging in a self-care session. I've grown so much as a person, and I am so proud of myself for it.

Chapter 11

Jenna: You need to be more active in the general channels, Fern! You can't let Haven's presence intimidate you into staying silent

Lisa: ☝ What she said

Fern: Uggghhh I know but I'm so scared of becoming a target again

Jenna: Omg, you know we have your back!

Lisa: Right. And if you keep on staying quiet, you're only punishing yourself by not letting yourself have this

Jenna: Yeah, it's part of our debut experience! We've earned the right to be members of this debut group, so you shouldn't let Haven make you miss out on this too

Fern: I knowww. Okay, I'll say something in one of the general channels . . . can you guys reply to it though?? I know it's stupid but if no one replies I'm going to feel awful

Lisa: Yes, of course!

I switch from our private channel and check out the general channels, wondering which conversation I can join. It's been three days now since the Slack was created, and aside from my first day, I haven't said anything in the general channels. I told Lisa and Jenna it's because of Haven, and they've been trying to get me to partake in the conversations ever since. It's a refreshing change. I can't help but compare their reactions to Dani's when I first told her that Haven was picking on me. But then I feel guilty comparing their reactions to Dani's because these are grown women and Dani was just a kid back then. My best friend who has haunted me for the last ten years.

Lisa and Jenna have my best interests at heart, and I know it, but the thought of saying something where Haven can see it also makes me want to shrivel up and hide in a dark corner, lest I attract Haven's attention. In my mind right now, Haven is like that huge girl robot with laser eyes in *Squid Game*. If she catches me moving, her eyes will lock on mine, and then she'll kill me.

No, it's different this time. I'm no longer a loner with no one on my side. I have Lisa and Jenna, and I also have Yuna and also Alexis, yet another debut I reached out to privately after seeing her interaction with Haven. I will be okay.

I click on the #commiserations channel and check the latest post, which was only posted two minutes ago.

Kristin: Ugh, does anyone else's editor want to change your book title? My title is YOU'RE MINE FOR GOOD and I know it's not the best title, but my editor is suggesting changing it to FOR BETTER OR WORSE and I'm just not feeling it.

Haven hasn't replied to this one; no one has, probably because they haven't had a chance to. I have a very tight window during which I can send a quick reply before Haven does. She's not currently online, but I have noticed that sometimes she replies even when it doesn't seem like she's here. I wonder if she's turned on some kind of privacy setting so people can't tell when she's online. I wonder if it's because of me. I consider what to say before I begin typing, and even then, I delete and rewrite my message many times over.

> **Fern:** My editor mentioned a possible title change, but she hasn't sent any actual suggestions yet. It's stressful, isn't it! But I really love FOR BETTER OR WORSE, it's so ominous and catchy! I already know from the title that it's going to be a super suspenseful thriller!

There, that's a good response, right? I empathized with her, acknowledged her feelings, and ended on a positive note. And honestly? Her original title sucks. *You're Mine for Good*? It's too on the nose.

I smile when I see the words "Jenna is typing . . ." at the bottom of the chat window. Jenna really does have my back.

> **Jenna:** Agree with Fern, FOR BETTER OR WORSE is an awesome title! I bet the change in titles can feel really jarring at first, but I looove the new title!

> **Lisa:** Yeah, it's a super intriguing title for sure! It's so disturbing in the best way, like I seriously would pick up the book just based on the title alone

I nearly cheer in my seat. Is this what it's like to have an actual supportive group of friends? Friends who care and have your back? It feels like drinking pure honey, every part of my body coming to life. I luxuriate in the glow of it like a cat stretching in the sun. God, it feels so good, and I have waited so long to have this. I smile when I see that Kristin, the OP, is typing a reply. I bet she's going to thank us for making her realize that the new title is a better one.

> **Kristin:** It's not a suspense. It's a romance novel.

Oh.

Okay, so maybe she's not about to thank us. I scramble to the private chat with Lisa and Jenna and type: "OMG IT IS NOT A SUSPENSE NOVEL."

> **Jenna:** LOLOLOL OOPS!!

> **Lisa:** BAHAHAHA! I mean, to be fair, who the fuck would've known?? Both titles sounded like suspense novels!

> **Fern:** Especially her original one! YOU'RE MINE FOR GOOD?? WTF? How is that a romance novel title?? That sounds so toxic and creepy??

I'm actually grinning in real life, whisper-laughing to myself. From inside her office, Annette glances up, her mouth turning into a thin line when she sees my barely repressed smile. I quickly school my face into a serious I'm-editing-photos expression, but it's too late. It's obvious Annette has caught me slacking—ha! literally Slacking—off.

Lisa and Jenna are still laughing over the faux pas, their messages coming in at rapid-fire pace. I force myself to close the Slack window and go back to actually editing photos. When Annette barges out of her office, making her every move loud to attract my attention, I keep my eyes glued firmly to my computer screen. I hope I'm exuding model employee vibes as I furiously color-correct backgrounds and remove blemishes from smiling faces. It's only when Annette goes back into her office with a huff that I allow myself to switch over from Photoshop to Slack. I check the #commiserations channel, and well, well. Guess who's inserted herself into the conversation.

> **Haven:** I think FOR BETTER OR WORSE works for a romance novel too. I can just imagine it in a beautiful typesetting, set against a cover with lots of flowers and colors on it. I think that would really pop. But I know what you mean, titles are stressful, not to mention a real pain to come up with. Have you talked to your agent about this? At the end of the day, if you're not happy with it, then you should have the final say.

The familiar sickening feeling rises up inside me, souring my stomach. I'd thought that my reply had been a good one. My heart was in the right place. I really did think that, based on those two titles, Kristin's book was suspense. I didn't mean to make fun of it or anything. But now, it looks like I was a mean-girl bully making fun of her title, and worse still, Haven's response really highlighted that. On the face of it, Haven's message is innocuous. It doesn't refer to me or Lisa and Jenna at all, but even without that, it makes us look awful, while of course Haven comes out of it smelling as fresh as flowers.

I quickly switch to the private channel.

> **Fern:** UGH have you guys seen Haven's reply??
>
> **Lisa:** Yeah. Ugh is right.
>
> **Jenna:** Is she always like this?
>
> **Fern:** Yep. Now you see what I had to deal with all of middle and high school

Jenna: She is good. Very good.

Fern: Yup. When it comes to making herself look like the good guy and me like a villain, there is no one better than Haven

Jenna: It's not just you, now I feel really bad as well!! We need to fix this

I release a frustrated breath through my teeth. My phone beeps with an email. I glance at the screen, and my breath catches in my throat. The sender is Lindsay Tillman. As in Lindsay, my editor. Finally! As I swipe at my phone to open the email, I notice the #commiserations channel name lighting up with a new message. I click on that.

Lisa: Sorry Kristin, we didn't mean to make it sound like your titles were confusing or anything. Totally agree with Haven that FOR BETTER OR WORSE works beautifully with a romance novel too!

"Totally agree with Haven"?? I feel physically sick, like I actually might throw up right now. The private chat lights up with a new message.

Lisa: There. Now you two need to say something along those lines too. We need to salvage this.

The vise around my chest loosens, just a little. Lisa isn't turning her back on me like Dani did. She's being smart. Strategic. And she's asking me to be a part of her plan, because she and Jenna are my friends. Right.

With Lindsay's email burning a hole in my mind, I quickly thank Lisa and tell her she's right before typing out a message in the #commiserations channel.

Fern: Yes, agree with Lisa and Haven. I'm so sorry about the suspense novel comment! A romance novel titled FOR BETTER OR WORSE sounds heart-achingly beautiful and I can't wait to read it!

It's a kind of blessing to have Lindsay's email coming in now, actually, because it means I don't have the luxury of doing my usual habit of hemming and hawing and second-guessing myself and self-editing a million times before hitting send. Once my reply is posted, I switch to my phone and read Lindsay's message.

Dear Fern,

Greetings and welcome to the Harvest family! I am so happy to be working with you on your beautiful book. This story moved me so much, and I can't wait to be part of the process of releasing it to the world.

I'm sorry it took me a while to send you a welcome email. I am delighted to introduce myself to you now, and guess what? I was so excited to work on your book that I started early and I have my editorial letter ready for you! It's attached to this email. I hope you find it helpful, and let's set up a time to chat on the phone once you've read it and had time to digest it. I would love to be able to brainstorm ideas and answer any questions you might have.

Everyone here at Harvest is so delighted to have you on board!

Best,

Lindsay

With slightly trembling hands, I tap on the document to open it. When it does, my heart sinks. Without even reading it yet, I already know it's going to be bad, because first of all, it's twelve pages single spaced, and second of all, it starts with "What really grabbed me about this book is the beautiful writing, along with the really interesting concept." Already, I know this isn't going to be a quick and easy editing round. In fact, it sounds more like Lindsay is expecting a rewrite. I scan the rest of the document, my despair growing as certain sentences leap out at me.

"I think we can cut the first four chapters . . ."

"How about moving Chapter 17 forward, so the timing of the incident . . ."

"I'm not sure about the direction of the story from the midway point onwards. It seems to switch from one genre to the next. I wonder if we could . . ."

By the time I get to the end of the letter, I am questioning why Lindsay wanted to buy the book in the first place. Why bother acquiring a whole novel if you're just going to ask the author to completely gut it? The changes she's asking for are not just significant, they will require me to delete about 70 percent of my manuscript before hacking and slashing apart the remaining 30 percent to fit into a whole new manuscript. At this point, it might actually be easier for me to write a whole new manuscript.

Despair engulfs me. It really feels like I just slid down a rocky path and found myself at the bottom of a pit. Never mind my stomach; my entire body is knotted up, my palms sweaty and my throat dry. When I glance up, I find Annette openly glaring at me from her glass office, and I duck my head and go back to working on the latest batch of photos. But now, the grinning faces feel personal, like they're rubbing their intense happiness in my face. Why is everybody allowed to be happy except me? Haven't I gone through enough? Don't I deserve just a moment of peace? I click and swipe furiously at their faces, overexposing their skin until it's nothing but a pale blur. Then, sighing, I click "Undo" and start over. An hour later, I'm finally done uploading the folder to the cloud. I let Annette know that the file is done and ready for her to review, and her response is a scoff. I'm so wrapped up in my own misery that her rudeness barely stings, but I do make a mental note to bake something for her so she's less mad at me. Admittedly, I have been a pretty crappy employee lately.

When I finally knock off, I grab all my things and rush out. I message Lisa and Jenna as I walk to the subway.

Fern: My edit letter just came in and it is HORRIBLE 😭

Jenna: Oh no! What did your editor say??

Fern: She basically wants me to rewrite the book, and I'm not even exaggerating

Jenna: 😭😭

Lisa: WTF?? Have you spoken to your agent??

Fern: No, I literally JUST got the edit letter and you guys were the first people I told!

Jenna: I'm so sorry to hear that! That is soooo shitty!!

Lisa's and Jenna's empathy is a strange experience for me. On one hand, I love it, savoring the sympathy and kindness flowing from them, lapping it up greedily because I've had so little of it my whole life. But on the other hand, it's also surprisingly firing me up. I find myself feeling even more upset about the whole thing. I always thought that venting about your troubles to your friends would calm you down, but it's interesting to see that it's having the exact opposite effect on me. And Lisa is right to bring up my agent. Poppy would definitely have something to say about this. People jostle me as they briskly walk down into the subway station. It's a warm day, and the back of my neck is hot and itchy, but I was so upset at the office that I forgot to grab my hair claw before I left.

> **Lisa:** I don't think it's right for an editor to buy a book, only to ask the author to change the entire thing! Wtf?? If you wanted a different story, then buy a different book!
>
> **Jenna:** Riiiight? I totally agree!

They're right. It's total bullshit that Lindsay is asking me to change my whole story. Why did she even buy it in the first place? Oh right, the beautiful writing or whatever. My train screeches to a stop at the station, and I shove my way in. Just my luck, of course, that in addition to the shit show that is Lindsay's edit letter, I'm now having to deal with subway rush hour. I make it into the train just in time before the doors close. It smells so bad in here. It always smells bad in these trains, but when the weather gets warm, it becomes almost unbearable. I breathe through my mouth, trying my best to ignore my surroundings as I stare at my phone. Lisa and Jenna are still ranting, though now they've moved on to how shitty publishing treats authors in general.

I open up Gmail and compose a message to Poppy.

> Hi Poppy!
>
> I hope you're doing well . . .

The train sways, and I bump against a man, who shoots me a dirty look. I grimace apologetically and stuff my phone into my pocket so I can hold on to the handrail. I'll just compose it in my head first. I don't want to be a huge burden on Poppy. I have to make sure my email is diplomatic, but also not wishy-washy. But what am I asking her in the first place? Am I asking her to intervene on my behalf and tell Lindsay that no, I am not doing all those edits because they're too major? Am I just emailing her to whine at her so she can empathize with me? What is it that agents do when their clients are in this situation? God, why does it smell so bad in here? Doesn't everyone know of the existence of deodorant by now?

By the time the train arrives at my spot, I stumble out and take huge gulps of warm subway-station air. It's not the best air, but it's still miles better than that stuffy subway odor I've just had to deal with for the last forty minutes. My head is pounding, and I feel nauseated. I can't get inside my apartment fast enough. Once I'm in, I scramble to the kitchen and pour myself a cold glass of water. I chug it with the relief one might feel after a strenuous cardio session and then stand there for a moment, breathing hard. It takes a while for my breathing to slow down, and even then, when I try to go back to writing an email to Poppy, all my mind does is come up with a scrambled mess. I am barely coherent, and I sure as hell have no clue what to say to her.

Instead, I open the Slack and go to #commiserations. This is exactly what this channel is for, isn't it? And sharing something like this, opening up about my vulnerability, will help me connect with others.

> **Fern:** Guys, my editor just sent me her notes and it is so overwhelming. She basically wants me to rewrite most of the book. Sent me a TWELVE-PAGE edit letter! 😭 I don't know what to do.

I hit Enter. Since it's after work hours, there are quite a few people online, and to my relief, the words "Several people are typing . . ." pop up. Moments later, I get my first reply.

> **Yuna:** Whaaaat? That really stinks! I hate that for you.

> **Alicia:** Omg worst nightmare. What did your agent say about it?

I quickly type back: I haven't told my agent yet. I will, but I don't really know what to say to her? What should I say?

Several people are typing again. Then it comes, a reply from the last person I expected to hear from.

> **Haven:** How do you feel about her edits? Are they completely wrong or are they actually valid?

I stand in the middle of my kitchen, unmoving, staring at her message. A snort of disbelief escapes me. Is she serious? "Are they *actually* valid?" Is she really showing her passive-aggressive side on a general chat right now? Not to mention that this, after all these years of no contact, is our first communication with each other. Well, never mind, it's going to backfire on her. Everyone will see now what a bully she truly is. But then the next reply is:

> **Felicity:** Oh that's a good point! Will the changes make the book better, Fern?

A pit opens up deep in my belly, dark and endless. No. Not Haven's friend chiming in and making it seem like what Haven said is reasonable instead of subtly mean. Where are Lisa and Jenna? Just as I think that, Lisa pipes up.

> **Lisa:** I mean, I feel like regardless of whether the changes are good or not, the editor should've warned Fern that she expects extensive changes when she made her offer! She's put you in such a difficult position.

Haven: That's such a good point, Lisa! I totally agree. Did she not mention anything during the call?

I wince. I appreciate Lisa sticking up for me, but she doesn't realize that she's just made things more awkward for me because I didn't have a call with Lindsay when she offered. I grimace as I type.

Fern: I didn't have a call with her before she bought the book.

Lisa: What?! Why not?

Whose side is Lisa on here? I want to cry out. The truth is so embarrassing that I want to shrivel up and hide, but it's too late now.

Fern: Well, she was the only editor who offered on the book, and my agent didn't mention having a call or anything.

For a moment, there's silence. I am so painfully aware that I am surrounded by writers who had multiple editors fighting over their books. Writers like Haven and Lisa, who have had to get on many, many phone calls where editors raved about their books and tried to win them over by offering this and that to them on a silver plate. Meanwhile, I, of course, had to take whatever I could get.

Haven: Oh okay. I see. I would have a call with her now to discuss her notes in depth. And honestly I think this is a good sign, she cares so much about the book that she wrote twelve pages of notes for it . . . that's not something an editor would do for just any book.

Anxiety claws at my chest. This is the thing with Haven. Her replies are so well crafted that a casual observer wouldn't notice anything off about them. But I see right through her. She's making herself out to be a good person, trying to be kind to me about my shitty situation, but there are always ulterior motives with her. Already she's made me look bad, painted me as ungrateful for the immense work my editor has devoted to my manuscript. I need to remedy this, and quick. I can't afford to let Haven outmaneuver me like she did before. I know what she's doing: She's laying the groundwork to push me out of the group and turn me into an outcast once more.

> **Fern:** Thank you for the advice. You're right, I really appreciate the amount of effort my editor put into the book. I think I'm just overwhelmed by the amount of changes she wants me to make to it. 😅
>
> **Lisa:** It is totally overwhelming for sure! I don't blame you, I would have the same exact reaction. But yeah, looking at it in that perspective is helpful. It sounds like she's super invested in your book!
>
> **Felicity:** Oh totally! In fact, I kind of wish my editor would do the same!!

Do you, Felicity? I think snidely. Then I immediately feel guilty for thinking that. I hate having mean thoughts. I don't want to be like Haven, thinking the worst of everyone. I've worked so long and hard on myself to get rid of awful thoughts like these. I have established healthy coping mechanisms to avoid this negativity, but this entire interaction with Haven is so triggering. This is the real problem I have with Haven. It's not just that she's a bad person. It's that I hate who I am when I'm with her. I need to end this conversation.

But before I can do so, there's another reply from Haven.

> **Haven:** I think that's the right thing to do, Fern! And who knows, you might end up loving the changes. Publishing works in mysterious ways.

My mouth turns into a desert. Dani's voice rings through my mind. That was her thing, and Haven knows it. She was always saying that various things work in mysterious ways. When we were kids, it used to be a running joke between us. She'd say something like "Life works in mysterious ways," and I'd go "Algebra works in mysterious ways." I can't believe Haven just did that.

> **Fern:** I'm going to email her now. Thanks everyone!

It's only after I shut down Slack that I notice that my shirt's sticking to my skin with sweat. I put the phone down on the kitchen counter and guzzle another glass of water. I literally feel as though I've just sprinted down several blocks after not having eaten anything the entire day. I'm shaky and lightheaded, and my breath is coming out in shallow, rapid gasps. A panic attack? I used to get them all the time back in high school. I go through the usual motions of grounding myself in the present moment, looking around at my surroundings and naming things I can see, smell, hear, and feel. My shakiness ebbs away slowly, leaving me utterly spent. I go to the bathroom and strip down, avoiding looking in the mirror, full of self-hatred. I stand under the shower until I run out of hot water, then I am forced to come out.

After I've dressed myself, I pad into the kitchen and take out Doughlores. The only thing that is sure to bring me peace on days like this is baking. I look up my saved recipes and decide on sourdough raspberry and white chocolate muffins. For the next half hour, I lose myself in the act of measuring out the ingredients and then mixing them together. There's just something about thick batter or pliant dough that helps me leave behind whatever is bothering me, and I thank the universe every day that no matter how bad things get, I will always have this outlet.

It is only when the muffins are in the oven that I let myself check my Slack again. There are new messages in the #commiserations channel, but I go straight to the private chat with Lisa and Jenna. They're talking about something else completely unrelated, and for a second, I wonder if I should just move on and try to forget what happened. But then what are friends for if not to obsess over the little details?

> **Fern:** Ugh, I hate that Haven replied to my thing in #commiserations. I'm not imagining it, right? She was being . . . ugh?

> **Jenna:** Wait, what happened in #commiserations? I haven't checked that channel yet! BRB going to catch up.

> **Lisa:** Hmm, I'm not sure I got any bad vibes from her? Which part of what she said was bad?

Shit. I can't tell Lisa that Haven saying "Publishing works in mysterious ways" is a pointed, cruel threat. I see now, belatedly, that from an outsider's perspective, everything that Haven said is perfectly innocent.

> **Fern:** It's just she's reminding me a bit about some stuff she did back in high school.

> **Lisa:** Ah, right. That really sucks. I'm sorry you have to deal with that. But anyway, I still think you should talk to your agent first

I sigh with frustration. That's not the point, I want to wail. I mean, yes, sure I'll talk to Poppy first. But the point is, Haven made me look bad in front of everyone, and she did it so smoothly, so subtly, that no one even realized she was doing it. It feels like high school all over again. What can I do to stop it from happening? I'm not crazy, I know I'm not. I'm not imagining it. Everyone else just—

A new private message pops up, and all my thoughts screech to a sudden stop. Because the name that's appeared in bold is Haven's.

> **Haven:** Hey, Fern. It's been a while. How're you doing? Congratulations on your book deal!

For the longest time, my mind remains blank. No, that's not quite right. It's actually whizzing around at such a fast rate that I can't make out any thoughts, it's just a blur of blinding white. How can she just pop back into my life like this? So casually, as though nothing terrible happened in our past. As though Dani were still alive. I give a small shake of the head and blink furiously. My fingers hover over the keyboard and move of their own accord, bypassing the mess in my head.

> **Fern:** Hi. Yes it's been a while. Thanks, and congrats on your deal too

I add an exclamation mark at the end of the last sentence to be friendly, then find that I can't bear it. I delete it, reread the message, and hit send.

> **Haven:** I just wanted to reach out and say I hope there are no hard feelings. That was a million years ago, huh? I'm sure we've both grown a lot as people.

My entire body feels hot, as though the blood in my veins has been replaced by liquid flames. No hard feelings? A million years ago? We've *both* grown a lot? How dare she? It was ten years ago, and I still remember everything she did to me, to Dani, down to the smallest details. It was ten years ago, but Dani is still dead. She will forever be gone. But of course, to Haven, none of it truly mattered. It was all just a game to her, and now here she is, trying to play the role of the bigger person. What do I say to her? Should I tell her she's full of shit and I know exactly what's behind that beautiful mask of hers? Should I pretend like I don't know what she's talking about, so she has to spell it out?

Of course, in the end, my cowardly ass doesn't do either of those things. I can't even do passive aggression; I'm more of a straight-up passive kind of person. One might call me a doormat. I would call myself a survivalist.

> **Fern:** God, no, of course no hard feelings. High school was a whole different life. So glad we're in the same debut group

As soon as I hit Enter, I feel so slimy, so unbearably uncomfortable, that I immediately follow up with Gtg, I'm meeting a friend for dinner. Bye!

I close the window and bury my face in my hands. I squeeze my eyes shut and focus on my ragged breathing. I'm okay I'm okay I'm okay I'm . . .

Eventually, I calm down enough to look on the bright side of things. I'm still on the other side of the country, far, far away from Haven. Haven reached out with a peace offering. Sure, it's probably a calculated move, but she has no incentive to target me again, right? I'm a nobody. She has better things to focus on, and like she said, we've both grown into different people. She might've changed. She might've found peace, her vicious edges sanded down by maturity. And all her messages in the Slack group aren't that bad. Yeah, she's different. She's no longer the Haven who made my life hell for seven years. And now that she's reached out, we can put everything behind us.

Maybe she and I can even become friends one day.

Chapter 12

Despite my initial despair over Lindsay's notes, I do hop on a call with her after a week of licking my wounds, and the call helps me see that Lindsay's vision for my book is in fact really good. I end the call excited to work on my book, to take it apart and sew it back together all better. I spend the next four months toiling over it, deleting entire chapters, erasing beloved characters, and rewriting the bulk of the story over again. When I finally get done, the book is altogether a different story. The only thing that made the cut was my main character, and even then, she's very much changed. I send the new draft to Lindsay with not a little apprehension, and proceed to go on vicious evening runs in the hopes of outrunning my anxiety while I wait for Lindsay to read it.

By the time she replies a month later, I've lost five pounds thanks to all the extra running I've been doing. The first line of her email says: Fern! I can't believe how well you've tackled this draft.

I burst into tears. I made it. I was handed a seemingly insurmountable obstacle, and I managed to overcome it. Lindsay continues to tell me how proud she is of me, and I think: You know what, Lindsay? I totally agree with you there.

And in this way, the following year alternates between plodding along and whizzing by. Haven and I don't become friends, but we are generally cordial toward each other, and I have gotten really good at carving out my own space away from hers. Lisa and Jenna and I chat throughout the day, every day. On weekends, our chat channel is generally quieter, since they're both married with kids, but on weekdays we rack up hundreds, if not thousands, of messages to each other. The general Slack channels have settled into a comfortable rhythm, and you know what? Some days, I don't even really think about Haven as much. Thanks to a combination of meditation, my evening runs, and my incessant baking, I have trained myself into an almost peaceful online coexistence with my nemesis. I am so proud of myself.

There are moments when I backslide. For example, at some point, someone in the debut group suggests exchanging manuscripts with one another so we can read everyone's books and then provide them with a review on Goodreads. The unspoken agreement is, of course, that you should only give other authors positive reviews, though no one would actually say this out loud. "Honest reviews" is what we actually said. We created a shared folder on Google Drive and uploaded our manuscripts into the folder.

Of course, I immediately open up Haven's manuscript. When it loads, I see that there are twenty-seven other people currently reading it. I go back to the shared folder and open up my manuscript. There are only three other people currently reading it. Then, as I stare, one of the bubbles disappear, followed by another. Now there is only one person reading my book. I would be lying if I said that didn't hurt. They didn't even stay that long, only long enough to read the first page. Is it really that bad? I've hacked and slashed at my manuscript, thanks to Lindsay, and I think it's in amazing shape now. I may have whined endlessly while I edited it, but looking at the new draft, I am glad that Lindsay suggested all these changes. And yet here it is, still unable to retain anyone's attention. What is it that I'm missing?

I go back to Haven's manuscript with a sigh. I read the first sentence, frowning. Then the next, and the next, and before I know it, I've just raced through three whole chapters. When I finally tear my eyes away from the screen, I'm confused for a split second, feeling that disorientation that comes with resurfacing after a deep nap. I glance back at the screen, my mouth dry. Holy shit. Haven's book is so good.

Unbearably so. When I first started it, I'd read with a critical eye, hoping to catch weaknesses to bitch about to myself, but instead, it grabbed me by the throat and yanked me into its dark, seductive world, and I forgot everything else and fully immersed myself in it.

Shame overwhelms me. Is this what it feels like to be truly humbled? I'd assumed all this time that the reason Haven got her massive seven-figure deals is because of, well, the same reasons she always got the best of everything—because she's beautiful, because she's charming, because she has this thing about her that makes people fall in love with her and want to give her the world. But now, reading her manuscript, it becomes clear that the reason Haven got these huge deals is simply because she's a brilliant writer, and this is somehow so much worse.

For years, I've clung to the thought of writing as my own special, unique thing. No one else at my high school had the same passion for it that I did, and even in college, when I studied creative writing, I held this secret thought in the deepest folds of my mind that no one else wanted this quite as badly as I did. I knew it wasn't true, of course, I wasn't completely delusional, but it was a thought I liked to hold on to, just to give myself a sense of hope, a sense of purpose from the universe that tells me: Fern, you are not just another drop in the ocean. You are unique. You have something that is so distinct to you, something that makes you special.

But now, it's clear that this isn't the case. I have to accept the painful truth, that there's nothing about me that's special, not even my writing. No, it's Haven that's special. Haven who's been blessed with everything: beauty, brains, and heaps and heaps of talent. I wish I could take apart whoever made her, dig my fingers in and rip everything apart and try to find the why of everything. Why does someone like Haven get the entire world and someone like me get nothing? She even got Dani, and look what happened to Dani in the end. Tears rush into my eyes as the memory of Dani threatens to overwhelm me once more, and I shake my head furiously, trying to literally shake it off.

So suffice to say I spun out for a bit there. Okay, for a couple of weeks. I would keep myself away from Haven's manuscript, swearing off it for the sake of my mental health, then within a couple of hours my resolve would crumble like a sandcastle, and I'd click on the document and devour more chapters. I did this until about halfway through her book, then I abandoned all pretense of not reading it and gulped the rest of the story down in a single night. The next day, I stumbled into the office like a zombie. I hadn't even bothered to hide the dark circles hugging my eyes. Annette looked up from her desk, glanced at me, then turned her gaze very meaningfully to the clock before rolling her eyes. But I'd spent the rest of the night in a baking frenzy, and Annette brightened up a little when she saw the container of donuts I'd brought in.

But I am doing well now. Reading Haven's book was a hiccup, but eventually I did get over it. Eventually. I slowly wrenched my focus, kicking and screaming, back to my own work. Eyes on the prize, I reminded myself, and now here I am. I've got a good routine going. I bake, I go to work, I come home, I go for a run, then I spend the rest of the evenings writing reviews for my fellow debuts. In bed, the thought that puts me to bed is: Just one more year before I become a published author. It's a thought I take out of a drawer in my mind as I pull my duvet over me and burrow into my bed, a lovely, sweet thought that brings with it a slow, gentle joy. I go to sleep nowadays with a small smile on my lips. 2020 is going to be the year that my life will finally begin.

When articles about a strange virus start circulating in the news, I pay them very little attention. There's nothing new about a strange virus in a faraway country; it's a familiar story to me, one that has a predictable end—the government will find some way of shutting down the spread of the virus, and all's well that ends well. I remain focused. How can I not? My book is coming out this year, this beautiful, glorious year.

I only start paying attention when COVID-19 starts going viral (hah!) on Twitter. Seemingly overnight, my Twitter feed goes from publishing news to COVID-19 news, with people tweeting about how they know a friend of a friend who traveled to here or there and came back with it. Still, the many years I have spent learning to put blinders on and ignore the world around me and focus on my own shit kick in, and I'm able to ignore these tweets, shutting them down mentally. It doesn't matter, I tell myself. The government—or governments, rather, since the virus is now in multiple countries—will come up with a way of dealing with it. It'll be fine. I need to focus on my book, which is due to come out in just six months' time.

Based on the size of my advance, I already knew not to expect much marketing and publicity from Harvest, so, in an effort to be proactive, I shelled out twelve grand to hire an independent publicist. Sarah Clarke came highly recommended, and she told me she would get me interviews in magazines and also pitch me to events like book festivals and conferences for me to speak at. Twelve grand is a lot of money, but I don't have college debt, since I went to a community college for two years before transferring to a cheap in-state school, and I'm a single woman with a full-time job and no social life. I don't have friends that I have to go out for dinner and drinks with. I don't travel. My hobbies, baking and running, are about as cheap as hobbies get. I figure I've been so responsible with my money that I deserve this one thing—to be able to ensure that my book doesn't fade into obscurity as soon as it comes out. I did have to empty out most of my savings for it, but it'll pay off when my book takes off and starts earning royalties.

When I told Lindsay that I was hiring an independent publicist, all she'd said was "Sounds good! Just let me know once you find one so we can collaborate with them." I'd been half hoping for her to pat me on the back and tell me how happy she was that I was being so proactive and that she wished all her authors could be like me, but oh well. In time, she'll come to appreciate how on the ball I am, I'm sure. After all, what says "I'm invested in this book doing well" louder than me actually investing money in it?

But the news about COVID-19 doesn't fade away as I had expected. In fact, it starts ramping up. It's in the US now, apparently. When I go outside, I start seeing people wearing surgical masks, which creeps me out a little. The debut group #commiserations channel is full of unfortunate authors who have just debuted early in the year and are wailing about how all this news about COVID is drowning out their debuting news. More and more people are choosing not to come to events like book launches because they're scared of crowds. I send replies telling them how sorry I am about it but that I'm sure their books will do well nevertheless, before privately thanking the universe that I'm not debuting just yet, when our government hasn't figured out how to stop this strange new virus. But, I reassure myself, I'm sure that by the time September comes around, this will be long gone, just another news cycle we've forgotten about.

A couple of Annette's clients cancel their photo shoots, saying that they're worried about this new virus. Annette doesn't show up for work one day, and stupidly, I wonder for a second if she has COVID, but when she does message me, of course it turns out to just be a stomach bug. I sigh and settle back in my seat with relief.

The relief turns out to be short lived. Things become worse; more cancellations come in, many of them asking for a refund. Then, before I can even worry about Annette's business, I see an announcement that schools in New York are going to be shut down for a while. It is this piece of news, more than anything else I've read about COVID, that really hits home for me. I think it's because New York City is one of the most competitive places in the world to live in, and I know how crazy it drives some parents. School is one of the most vital components of the city, something that New Yorkers are obnoxiously proud of, and for it to be shut down is unthinkable.

I'm not sure why, but I still go into work the next morning. An asinine decision, I realize, as soon as I step into my train and find it deserted. But I'm so used to this routine that the thought of stepping back out and simply returning home doesn't even cross my mind. I continue with my commute, and when I get out of the subway station, I take in the largely empty streets as I walk to the office. Annette isn't there when I arrive, but I go about setting everything up, making coffee and laying out the bagels that I made this morning. I fire up my computer and take a sip of coffee as I call up Annette's calendar. My coffee cup pauses halfway down to the coaster. Annette's calendar is empty, save for one measly shoot left in this month.

Do not panic, I tell myself. I click through to the work email and cross-check all our bookings alongside the messages of cancellations. And it all checks out. All our clients for the months of March and April really have canceled on us. Well, all except one couple. Melanie and Alex. I quickly compose an email.

> Dear Melanie and Alex,
>
> I hope you're doing well! I'm just sending this email to confirm your photoshoot on the twenty-fourth of this month. If you need to discuss locations and outfits, please don't hesitate to reach out to me. We're so excited for this session!
>
> Best wishes,
>
> Fern

There. I'm being proactive. Proactive is my word for the year. I'm proud of myself. I could've slid back into my old, unhealthy ways, obsessing over Haven and bemoaning the fact that I don't have a deal like hers. But I didn't. I took charge of my publishing journey, hiring Sarah and making connections in the debut group, and I'm doing the same at my day job, making sure Annette's clients are taken care of despite this—whatever this virus is. I send a quick email to Annette to let her know I'm at the office and that I will stay here until closing time. Never hurts to remind her what a dedicated employee I am. Then I settle down and open up Google Docs.

They say that the best time to work on your second book is before your first one comes out, and I've taken this piece of advice to heart. I'm twenty thousand words into my second novel, and it's chugging along nicely. My extremely healthy routine has been good for both my mental health and my creative energy, and I can't wait to finish this draft and send it to Lindsay.

I'm happily tapping away at the keyboard when a new email pops up. It's from Annette.

> Fern, what in the world are you doing at the office? Have you not been keeping up with the news? There are no shoots going on, we've caught up with all of the editing work, so there's nothing left to do at the office. Go home.

My mouth goes dry, and I read the message again. It's brusque, which sounds very much like typical Annette, but there's also an undercurrent of concern, which is not at all like her. A note of fear begins to keen softly, an annoying little pitch that I can't quite shake off. I get up and throw away the bagels even though I have yet to have one myself, then I dump the rest of the coffee and lock up the office. On the commute home, it strikes me again how deserted the streets and subway stations are. Where is everybody?

I can't get into my apartment fast enough. Inside, I lean against my door and force myself to take a few deep breaths before taking off my shoes and putting down my bags. I fire up my computer and check the group Slack. The mods have created a #covid channel, and it's the most active channel now.

> **Felicity:** They've shut down schools here, it's crazy, what the hell am I supposed to do with my kids??
>
> **Yuna:** Same. I have a 6yo boy, FML. I've just been sitting here guzzling wine and crying tbh
>
> **Haven:** I'm so sorry to hear that, that is awful. My heart goes out to all the parents out there! Yall are heroes!

My own little group chat is also obsessively talking about it.

> **Lisa:** Kill me now, my 7yo and my 3yo are fighting and James is pretending not to hear anything. He's just shut himself in the home office but I bet he's not really working, I don't even know WTF is going on
>
> **Jenna:** Girl, I hear you. The twins have been on each other's throats the whole morning. How do teachers deal with it?? They're not even allowed to hit them. HOW DO THEY DO ITTT?
>
> **Fern:** Omg sounds so stressful! I can't even imagine!

My little platitudes feel so pathetic. Usually when people say things like "I can't even imagine," they're just saying it to seem to convey sympathy. But I truly cannot imagine the stress that parents of small children must be going through to have the schools be shut down like that, and because I can't imagine it, I feel like I'm walking through a minefield, unsure if I'm about to say something wrong. And it also feels like I'm not allowed to talk about how scared I feel, how shaky the future feels and how I don't know what to do with myself. Oh god, I definitely can't complain about not knowing what to do with myself to Lisa and Jenna, who currently have their hands full with their tiny kids.

It's fine, I tell myself. The schools are only shut down for a little while, right? In a few weeks' time, this will all be over, and everything will be back to normal. In a few months' time, I won't even remember that this happened. It'll all be a weird memory we'll laugh about. In the meanwhile, I should make good use of this time and work on book two.

Somehow, I manage to write a few hundred words, though they're not very good words at all, then I hop on over to Twitter for a short break. When I next glance at the clock, I realize I've just been doom-scrolling for the last ninety minutes. I get up from the computer and do a few stretches. The rest of the day crawls by, the hours stretching like taffy. I stare out the window and am struck once more by how empty the streets are. The sight is so disturbing that I close the curtains even though it's still light outside. I make myself an early dinner, settle down in front of the TV for some Netflix, and end up ignoring the show and doomscrolling on Twitter until way past two in the morning.

I jerk awake the next morning on the sofa and scramble up, breathless. Judging from the angle of the sunlight streaming in through the gap in the curtains, I know it's late morning. Possibly even noon. I'm going to be late to work, Annette is going to—

Reality catches up with me. Right. Annette has asked me to stay home until . . . until things go back to normal. I look around blearily, locate my phone, and pounce on it. Maybe things are looking up. Maybe they've reversed the school shutdown.

Instead, things are looking even worse. Now there's talk about a larger-scale shutdown. Nonessential businesses should prepare to be shut down. I'm not too sure what an "essential business" would be, exactly, but I know that prewedding photography is nowhere near essential. I look around my empty, silent apartment, and it hits me then how woefully unprepared I am in case of a quarantine. The last time I went to the supermarket was four days ago, and I only grabbed my usual stuff; I didn't think to stock up on anything because I was so wrapped up in publishing and so in denial about COVID. With this realization sinking in, I rush to the bathroom to wash up and throw on some fresh clothes before rushing out the door.

The trip down to the neighborhood supermarket is surreal. The whole time, I feel as though I'm in some dystopian movie. But when I turn the corner, there is a long line snaking out of the supermarket. My heart sinks. I join the back, and the tension is so thick in the air that it's nearly electric.

Nobody in this line is happy. We glare at one another, painfully aware of how limited resources are at this moment in time and wondering how far we would go to ensure we get what we need. I haven't even thought to wear a mask, and as I wait in line, I kick myself for the thousandth time for having buried my head in the sand when it comes to COVID. Now I look like one of those COVID deniers.

Inside the store, I swipe things without really thinking. My mind is a mess—I can hardly make a single coherent thought out—so I just grab whatever I see that I think I might vaguely need: flour, rice, a six-roll pack of toilet paper, eggs. Then I stand there for a few seconds, wondering what else it is I might need. Someone shouts out, "Hurry up please! There's a long line waiting outside!" I startle, my face burning. God, I'm so stupid. I look around frantically and grab more things. Eggs. A pathetic avocado. I should get canned food. Right. I hurry to the canned food aisle, which is mostly empty, and grab whatever's remaining. On second thought, I snatch up another bag of flour and two bags of sugar, and now I have way too many things to carry, but somehow I still feel like I'm woefully unprepared for whatever is coming next.

I struggle with the bags all the way home, panting, the sacks so heavy I feel like my fingers are about to be yanked right off. As I unlock my apartment, Terry's door opens, and he pops his head out.

"Hey, neighbor," he says.

"Hey." I push my door open and am about to say bye, but he continues talking.

"Just stocked up on the essentials, huh?" he says.

I look down at the bulging bags, which are killing my neck and shoulders. "Yep. Anyway—"

"I was laid off," he says, his expression wide open, like he's expecting me to give him a hug.

"Oh. I—I'm sorry to hear that." Should I say more? I'm bad at social interactions in general, and even worse when it comes to awkward situations like this.

Terry shrugs. "Well, what're you gonna do, right? It's a pandemic, baby!"

I wonder if he's high. "Yeah," I say.

"Do you need help with that?"

"No," I say, so quickly that it makes the thick atmosphere unbearable. "Sorry, I should—we shouldn't be talking in such close quarters. 'Cause of the, uh, the virus."

"No, yeah, of course. Just thought I'd be neighborly and say hi. Anyway. Take care."

"Bye." I rush inside and lock the door before letting my head thump against the wall, my throat dry. I don't know why I was so nervous talking to Terry. I mean, sure, I've never liked the guy, but the anxiety I felt earlier is something new altogether. With a sickening feeling, I realize it's because of the virus. The sight of his unmasked mouth and nose in such close proximity made me want to wash my hands sixteen million times. I'd thought that I'd largely kept my head out of this whole pandemic thing, but I guess in the end, all that news did seep into my pores, turning me paranoid.

Paranoia is a feeling I am very familiar with, and I hate this about myself, hate how quickly I recognize the dark edges of it, hate how easily it calls out to me. I turn on an audiobook while I put away the stuff I'd bought, trying to keep my mind off the fact that there is a literal pandemic unfolding around me right now. Whenever I think about the word *pandemic*, it appears in my mind as a shriek, harsh and jagged, the letters flashing in fire alarm red. I exhale and push the word out of my mind. When I'm done putting everything away, I make myself a cup of chamomile tea and take it with me to the computer. Feeling intensely lonely all of a sudden, I open up the Slack group. But every channel now seems to be talking about nothing but COVID.

#General channel:

> **Anna:** Welp, our offices just issued the WFH mandate, so I guess I'll be around a lot more often in the coming days!
>
> **Yuna:** Happy to have you here, I'm the same, I'll be bored out of my mind the next two weeks, lol.

#Covid channel:

> **Felicity:** You guys, I was just informed that my launch event is going to be canceled because of the pandemic 😭
>
> **Haven:** Oh my god, Fel, noooo! I'm so so sorry, is there anything I can do??

#Questions channel:

> **Christine:** Does anyone know of a good publicist? My in-house publicist is sick, and poor thing has enough on her plate so I'm looking to hire an external one . . .

Of course, the channels that are properly hopping are #commiserations and #covid. Everyone is miserable, and some of us even know people who have contracted the virus. I sit there sipping my tea and catching up with the messages with a growing sense of dread. When did all this happen? Why do I feel so out of the loop?

The thought of it makes me want to laugh—I am having FOMO over a pandemic. God, that's pathetic. I check on the group chat.

> **Jenna:** I don't even know what's going on with my launch event 😭. Did you see what Felicity said? Hers has been canceled. Mine's only three weeks after hers. I bet it'll end up being canceled too 😭
>
> **Lisa:** Oh my gosh, that would be heartbreaking, but Jenn I really doubt it would be! I mean, the stay home order is only going to last for a month, right?? We just sit tight at home for two weeks and it'll all be over and things will go back to normal!!

I hadn't even thought of Jenna's launch event. I'd known it was happening, of course, Lisa and I had even discussed going to Boston and surprising her at her event. I hadn't booked flights for it yet since it's still about a month away, and I find myself being relieved that I'd procrastinated booking flight tickets for it. That's a shitty thought to have, I chide myself.

> **Fern:** Omg Jenna, that SUCKS! I agree with Lisa though, there's still plenty of time to go and I'm sure things will be fine by then. I can't imagine this thing lasting too long.
>
> **Jenna:** IDK honestly, it feels like it's going to last a while, but maybe that's just my pessimism talking . . .

I'm about to reply when the sound of a sharp keyboard note pierces through the wall. My head jerks up, my whole body tensing. It's Terry, banging on his keyboard with what sounds like even more vengeance than usual. I scramble to find my headphones, but even with the noise-canceling feature turned on, I can still hear the vague sounds of his keyboard. God, am I really going to be stuck in this apartment, with a neighbor who thinks he's the next Beethoven? I bury my face in my hands and pray to the universe that the virus will be cured soon and that before I know it, things will go back to normal. They have to. Right?

Chapter 13

The first day that New York City officially goes into shutdown, I wake up to three irate voice messages, two emails, and five texts from Annette. I scroll through her texts, each one angrier than the last, and with my stomach twisted into painful knots, I call her back. She picks up on the first ring—my god, has she just been sitting there fuming, waiting for me to call back? She doesn't bother saying hi.

"You messaged my clients?" Annette hisses.

It takes a long while for me to realize what she's talking about. I have to sift through the fug of sleep, the daze of the past few days, and my anxiety-ridden brain, and even then, what I manage to come up with is a confused "Uh . . ."

"Melanie and Alex," Annette snaps. "You emailed them?"

"Oh!" I sit up, shaking my head, trying to clear it. "Yeah, I did. I thought I'd send them an email to reconfirm their booking. I thought it might be a good thing to do because we'd gotten so many cancellations because of, uh . . ."

"Because of the pandemic?" Annette says sarcastically. "Oh yeah, you bet I know. Do *you* know there's a pandemic going on right now? Why would you ask them to reconfirm? The entire city is shut down!"

"But it should only be for a month—" I warble, my voice coming out pathetically thin and high.

Annette laughs, and it sounds so nasty, so unhappy, that I pull the phone away from my ear while she cackles. "Oh, just a month, huh? God, have you always been such an idiot or did the virus affect your brain?"

"I don't—"

"Melanie's dad passed away from COVID the day you emailed her."

Everything around me screeches to a stop. My lungs stop working, the air catching midway down my windpipe. "I—"

"Yeah. She is livid. Heartbroken. Every awful emotion you can think of, she is that. And she's taking it out on me, because my idiot assistant sent her an email asking to reconfirm in the middle of the pandemic which killed her father. She's talking about a lawsuit, she—"

"A lawsuit?" I squawk. "On what grounds? She can't just—"

"Don't tell me what she can or can't do. She's grieving, Fern! She just lost her dad. She's lashing out, and sure, yeah, she might not have actual grounds to sue me, but who cares right now? She could post about it on social media. It would destroy my reputation. I built my business on client referrals. Do you know what this is going to do to my company?"

Shame is no longer running through me in waves. It's completely engulfed me, swallowed me whole into its dark mouth where there is no light, no sips of air for me to take. I'm suffocating with it. "I'm so sorry, I didn't think—"

"Exactly. You didn't think. Maybe you thought I wouldn't notice, but this isn't the first time you've done something careless. Ever since you got that publishing deal of yours, your head's been in the clouds. You swan into the office late. Your work has become sloppy—I often have to retouch the photos you edited. Not to mention the numerous complaints I've received about you."

"Wait, complaints?" I feel like a hunted rabbit, all my senses dialed up to a hundred. I feel like the entire world is looking at me. Judging. Annette's received complaints about me? But how is that possible? Memories of all the photo shoots I've assisted in rush through my mind like a machine gun, *rat-tat-tat*. No, nothing has happened that would make anyone lodge a complaint about me.

"Yes. I've received a handful of messages from prospective clients who said that you were rude to them and that's why they're not hiring me as their photographer," Annette says.

"What?" I cry. "That's impossible. I was never—"

"I kept you on because I liked you, Fern. Despite all these problems. But it's clear to me now that your head isn't in this business, so I'm going to let you go."

I don't say anything. I can't. There are no words. I sit there, phone clutched in a sweaty hand, staring into my lap as Annette fires me.

"And if Melanie does end up suing me, I won't protect you," Annette says by way of goodbye. Then she hangs up.

I lower the phone slowly. I stare at it, cradled in my hands. I look at the camera, and it seems to be laughing at me, spying, knowing every wrong I've done. With a shudder, I shove it under my duvet. Complaints from prospective clients? I haven't been rude to anyone, I know it. Whenever we receive an inquiry, I've always responded with my usual canned response—a hyper, cheerful reply with information regarding the numerous packages we offer. It has five exclamation marks peppered throughout the message and ends with: "Again, congratulations on such an exciting time, and we look forward to working with you to making your engagement shoot as unique and beautiful as your love story!" Nobody can possibly be mad about that. Unless . . .

No. Surely not.

But now that the thought has surfaced, I can't push it back down. Could this be Haven's doing? Unbidden, an image of Haven sitting in front of her laptop, typing out the words "I'm writing to lodge a complaint about your assistant, Fern Huang. Fern was extremely rude when I emailed asking for more information, and . . ." It is so vivid that I can imagine the smirk that she would have worn while composing this email. The smug glee that must have felt like a shot of joy as she clicked "Send." Yes, I can imagine it all too easily. This is right up Haven's alley.

Rage leaps like a fire in my stomach, licking all my insides. After all these years, Haven hasn't changed one bit. I need to do something. I need to—

Stop, a small voice in my mind says. You don't know for sure that it was Haven. Haven doesn't even know what your day job is. Annette's website doesn't mention your name at all. Figuring out what you do for a living would be tricky for most people. You're just spiraling because you feel guilty over what you did do.

I cover my face with my hands. My cheeks are burning hot, and is that any wonder, given how intensely stupid I've been? Annette was right. What was I thinking when I sent that email to Melanie and Alex? Why did I send it? I recall now, with another stab of shame, how I felt so proud when I sent it off, like a little child who's found a dead frog and is proudly showing it off to her parents.

Hot on the heels of the shame is dread. It doesn't wait for the shame to ebb away. It pounces, claws out, before I even have a chance to catch my breath. I'm out of a job. No more pay. It's okay, I squeak silently at it, I have savings. I—

No, I don't. I've spent the bulk of my money on the down payment for my publicist. The realization knocks me over like a punch straight to the gut. I feel sick. I think I might actually vomit. My mind skitters back to the past once more, and I'm floating, watching myself make the transfer with such confidence, no unease whatsoever, just complete and utter joy at the knowledge that I'm investing in myself. "Investing in myself"! What a joke. I want to pounce on my old self and punch her over and over in the face, tell her what a dumb bitch she was and that she needs to save her money because there's a freaking pandemic on its way.

Maybe Sarah will give me a refund. Right. She should, because she hasn't started working on my book. That money I transferred to her was a down payment to reserve her time. She said she only starts actively promoting the book three months prior to publication. It's not too late. I grab my phone and tap frantically at it. I delete my first three tries at a message, then finally write: Hi Sarah, I'm so sorry to disturb you, but a financial crisis came up and I can no longer afford your services. Would it be possible to have the down payment that I made six weeks ago back as a refund? Thank you so much.

There. That's reasonable. Of course, my heart cracks as I hit send, crying out: What about my book?

I unsend the message, plucking it back from the ether. My breath comes out in ragged sips. There's a reason I hired a publicist, and that is because I want—no, I need—my book to do well. It is the only good thing I have going on in my life, and am I really so ready to give up on it just because of Annette?

No, there's no "just" about it, the sensible voice in my head hisses. You don't have a job, you don't have any money. What are you going to live off?

But, I argue with it, I'm an author. My books are my job. The photography thing was merely a side hustle to get to publishing.

A "side hustle" that was paying you a living wage! the voice shouts. Publishing is all fine and good, but how are you going to live off that? Your advance, after taxes and agent fees, will barely cover two months' rent, *and* you get paid over the course of two years. It is not sustainable. Send that email. You need the money now.

I squeeze my eyes shut, my thumb hovering over the send button. No, I can't do it. I can't justify giving up on my book, my dreams, like that. And anyway, who's to say that I won't be okay? I might find a new job. This is New York, after all, the city where dreams come true, as long as you work hard enough. Actually, come to think of it, chances are Annette will come to her senses and ask me to come back and work for her again. After all, I've been responsible for basically running her business for the past few years. How is she going to survive without me doing everything—making her schedules, sending out all her correspondence, keeping the books, not to mention the artistic side of things, like helping her out during shoots, carrying her backbreakingly heavy gear, and editing the photos? Annette may be the woman behind the camera, but I am the woman behind the scenes, and I would love to see her try to replace me. She'll be back in no time, I'm sure.

I get another vision of Haven sending anonymous complaints to Annette, and I swat the thought down with ferocity. I don't have any proof that Haven was the one who did this, I remind myself. My therapist, Aliyah, pointed out that I often jump to the worst possible conclusion in any given scenario, and it was something she and I worked hard to minimize. I take a few deep breaths and do a grounding exercise by looking around me and listing five objects I can see in my room. I'm okay. I'm safe. Everything will be okay.

Somehow, I manage to make myself climb out of bed. I take my time washing up in the bathroom before padding out into the kitchen. As I make myself some coffee, I open up my Slack app. It's become a habit now—it's the first thing I check most mornings. The debut group channels are all full of unread messages. They are mostly about the pandemic and how they can't believe that they're going into lockdown. The group has members from all over the world, and it's very weird to know that countries like Singapore and England are heading into lockdown mode. In a way, it's making me feel both lonely and connected.

I sip my coffee and mull over what I'm going to bake today. Now that I don't have a job, I have all the time in the world to bake, so I might as well go full hog and make the most time-consuming thing I can think of. I decide to make puff pastry. I made it once before, and the process was so labor intensive that I decided frozen store-bought puff pastry was good enough for me. But hey, nothing's stopping me now! In fact, I come up with yet another way of keeping me even more connected to the Slack group. I create a new channel. #Culinary.

> **Fern:** Now that we're in full lockdown mode, I'm going to have a hell of a lot of time to cook and bake, so I thought this channel would be a great way for us to show off our culinary skills just for fun!

There are quite a few people online this morning, probably because everybody is either working from home or laid off like myself, and immediately I see a few people typing at once.

> **Yuna:** I love this channel! I'm actually about to make a batch of radish kimchi. I'll upload pics later!

> **Jenna:** Yasss I can already tell this is going to be my favorite channel. What a great idea, Fern! And here is this morning's coffee: A dirty chai latte!

Attached to Jenna's message is a photo of a delicious-looking drink. It has layers of colors—brown and white—and it looks so rich and creamy I could practically taste it.

> **Fern:** Omg that looks AMAZING Jenna!

> **Alicia:** WOW, Jenna! That looks sooo yummy. Definitely puts my shitty instant coffee to shame, lol!

More messages come in, and I set aside my phone with a smile, take out Doughlores, and begin working on my dough. I'm so proud of myself for starting this channel. Talk about making lemonade out of lemons. I'm kneading the dough when Terry starts banging on his keyboard—and I really do mean banging; he's no longer even pretending to play it properly. I fantasize about marching over to his place and kicking him in the shins, but let's face it, there isn't a version of me in any multiverse that would do that, so I force myself to focus on kneading the dough. I might have kneaded it a little harder than necessary. Baking bread is definitely right up there with running on my Top Five Healthy Coping Mechanisms.

By the time I'm done, I'm perspiring ever so slightly, and I feel better. I give the dough an affectionate little pat and set it in the fridge before moving on to making the filling. I've decided to make some

Danish pastries today, so I get to work making a cream cheese filling, along with some homemade blueberry compote. It's only when I'm rolling out the dough and cutting it that I realize I'm actually smiling. Despite everything—getting fired and having to deal with Terry's noise in addition to an actual pandemic, I like that I've started something worthwhile in the debut Slack group. The #culinary channel is something I think is going to help a lot of us in the coming weeks, and I'm so proud of being its creator. I can't wait to post my pastries on there.

It takes me much longer than usual to get the pastries done; I find myself spending a lot of time and effort to make them as pretty as possible, making sure the cream cheese is piped into the little pastry boats just so. When they're out of the oven, I put a dollop of blueberry compote on each one and finish them off with a dusting of icing sugar before arranging three of them carefully on my prettiest plate. I take the plate over to a window to get the best possible lighting and take dozens of photos of them from various angles. I end up with two beautiful photos, which I edit to really bring out the colors and textures, then, unable to wait another second, I post them both to #culinary with the caption: "Whipped these up today! They smell gorgeous." The replies come in almost immediately. I guess everyone is glued to their screens.

> **Jenna:** Oh my GOD, did you really make them yourself?? They look perfect! Omg I want!!

> **Yuna:** WOW Fern! Are you a professional baker?

I don't bother trying to stop the huge grin from taking over my face. A professional baker? I giggle to myself as I put the pastries into a plastic container. No, I am not a professional baker, but maybe I should be. Maybe I could be one of those home bakers who sell their goodies on Instagram. That could be a good way of earning money, especially now that Annette's fired me.

I check Slack again to see how many people have responded to my Danish pastries post. There are twelve hearts and five more comments about how good my pastries look, but then I scroll farther down and find that Haven has posted too. And she's made a beautiful rustic loaf of sourdough bread. She's posted two photos, one where the loaf is whole and you can see the prettiest leaf scoring pattern on the top of the perfectly browned crust, and in the other picture, she's sliced it open, revealing the airy, soft crumb, which is a surprising shade of blue. Her caption reads: I made sourdough today! It's blue because I used pea flower water, isn't it just the most beautiful thing ever??

Her post has thirty-two hearts, twenty-seven head explosions, and twenty-four heart eyes. There are over twenty comments, and more still being typed, all of them gushing over how stunning her loaf of sourdough is.

No, this can't be happening. I created this channel. I'm the one with the sourdough starter I've kept alive for years. Haven is—well, I've never seen her so much as even mention sourdough on her social media accounts, and yet here she is with a picture-perfect loaf of bread. Peevishly, I wonder if she's lying, if she actually bought the bread from somewhere and then posted about it to get attention. I can see her doing that.

Stop it, I scold myself. It doesn't matter. So what if she did? It's none of your business.

But still, I can't stop myself from scrolling through the comments, my head feeling feverish with jealousy as I read the adoration from other group members.

> **Haven:** Wanna know something really sad? I named my starter. Meet Breadley Cooper.
>
> **Yuna:** BREADLEY COOPER!! 😂 That is the best name ever!

Nooo! I want to scream. Breadley Cooper has nothing on Doughlores!

I know, I know how stupid it is to be jealous over someone's name. No, not someone. A sourdough starter. Well, technically they're alive, so they count as someone, right?

Okay, time to distance myself from the computer and go for a run.

But as I push the chair back and stand up, the realization hits me. We're in lockdown. I can't go out for a run. I go to the window and stare outside, looking down on the streets. There are a few cars driving past, but aside from that, it's completely deserted. No pedestrians, and definitely no runners. I return to the computer and fire up Twitter. The news is more dire than before. New York City is inundated with cases of COVID, with people dying faster than ever. Fear stabs into my chest, cold and sharp. Again, I'm struck with how strangely removed I've been feeling from this entire thing, when the reality is that I am just as susceptible as everyone else. I need to be much more careful. I go to the kitchen and give my hands a good wash, then I go online and order a bunch of antibacterial wipes. Or try to, anyway. They're sold out everywhere.

I pace the living room. It's only noon, so it's way too early to—I don't know, watch TV or go to bed. I pinch the bridge of my nose. I won't allow myself to do either of those things. Back in school, when Dani's death made me spiral into the dark depths of depression, I spent many an afternoon mindlessly watching TV or napping the day away. When I finally clawed myself out of that dank hole, I made myself a promise that I would never go back to that state. I will keep fighting to stay present, to stay alive. I won't be defeated like this. I know, I think to myself, I'll work on my second book.

I open my manuscript and refresh my memory by reading the last page I've written. And it's shit. It's awful; it's nearly incomprehensible. What the hell was I thinking when I wrote it? I delete three paragraphs. Then I delete the entire page. I scroll up, take a deep breath, and start reading the previous page. It's as bad as the one I've just deleted. I scroll farther up, my chest tightening as my eyes scan the pages and find nothing but trash. "No, no . . ." I mumble to myself. This can't be right. I felt, if not happy, then perfectly content the past few weeks as I steadily chugged away at the keyboard.

I'd been so proud of myself for getting to work on the sophomore novel early: I was right on time to get it sent to Lindsay before my debut came out. And now, halfway through the manuscript, I'm realizing that it stinks.

I switch over to Slack and open up the private group chat.

Fern: Omg guys I am freaking out. I'm reading what I've written for book 2 so far and IT IS SO BAD. 😭 What do I do??

Lisa: What do you mean bad? Like in what way?

Jenna: Girl, I feel you! I'm in the middle of my second book right now and it is SOOO hard. I totally get you, but don't worry, I bet it's not bad at all! It's just the pressure of book 1 getting in the way and making us all crazy.

Fern: No, it's sooo bad. Everything about it! The writing is awkward, the plot is super lame, and the characters are so flimsy and their dialogue is so painful!

Jenna: I don't think we're the most accurate gauge of our own work

Lisa: Yeah, I totally agree with Jenna! I cannot be trusted to judge my own writing for sure

Jenna: Why don't you send us like the first three chapters or something and we'll let you know if it's good? I'm sure it's great!

Lisa: I love that idea! Yeah, send it our way Fern!

Gratitude floods through me, and I can practically feel my knotted muscles loosening up. What would I do without Lisa and Jenna? I don't deserve them. They are so good to me.

Fern: Oh my gosh, would you really do that for me?

Jenna: Duh! I know you two would do the same for me

Lisa: Yup

Fern: Thank you thank you thank you!!!

I send them the first three chapters immediately, then I putter around the other channels, noting with not a small amount of bitterness that Haven's sourdough has received even more love while my Danish pastries lie forgotten. What's the likelihood that Haven would've baked something at the same time I did? And then posted it mere minutes after I posted about my pastries? Fern, a small voice says, this way lies madness. But I bat the voice away, continuing to stare at Haven's magazine-worthy photos of her bread. No, I mean, really now, what are the chances of it happening? Or, and this is more likely, is it that Haven has a stash of pretty photos of her food and she was just waiting for me to post mine before she posted hers to upstage me? She wouldn't, would she? Because that'd be . . .

"Crazy!" Haven's voice follows me down the hallway, tinged with her high, girlish giggle. "There goes Little Miss Crazypants!"

I shake off the memory. No, Haven wouldn't do that. Why bother? She has everything going for her. This pandemic isn't even touching her. She works from home and for herself, so obviously no one is laying her off. She works as an influencer, so I bet her views are through the roof, so actually, this pandemic isn't just not touching her, it is in fact good for her. So she really has no reason to go out of her way to sabotage me.

Except that's just the sort of person she is. Hasn't she proved time and again that she will absolutely go out of her way to harm me for no reason other than because she enjoys tormenting me? And posting pretty photos of her bread a few minutes after I posted my pastries isn't exactly going out of her way, is it? It takes nothing for her to bake some bread, which she was going to do anyway, and then wait for me to post something before posting it. After all, she knows I created the #culinary channel, so it was inevitable that I would post there.

My phone beeps with a new message on our private channel. Great timing, stopping myself from going into a spiral. Maybe Lisa or Jenna has scanned through my chapters and is raving about them?

But when I read the message, my blood goes cold.

> **Lisa:** Omg girl, have you read Haven's new manuscript? It is SO GOOD?? Like, how does she do it?? I know I'm supposed to be reading Fern's chapters but I srsly can't stop reading Haven's thing.

I've never fainted ever in my life, but I damn near do so right then. It feels as though all the strength has poured out of me, sucked out by Lisa's message. It becomes clear to me that Lisa and Jenna talk to each other privately, behind my back. As I stare blankly at the screen, the message suddenly disappears. Lisa must have realized she'd posted it in the wrong channel. How long have Lisa and Jenna been chatting without me? What else do they talk about? Why did they feel the need to talk privately? I thought our chat group was the only private group we needed. Do they secretly hate me?

"No, no, no," I moan to myself. Don't go there, Fern. That way lies madness. How long did it take for me to crawl out of that darkness the last time I found myself buried in it? Doing nothing but staying in bed and hiding from reality by binge-watching TV shows while feeling increasingly worse about my life. Come on, use your healthy coping methods. But my healthy coping methods are (1) baking, which Haven has ruined, and (2) running, which the pandemic has ruined.

What the hell am I going to do?

Chapter 14

Age Twelve

"Guess what?" I say to Dani as we walk out of the school building. Our friends stream out alongside us, and we call out goodbyes to all of them.

"What?" Dani says. She passes me her can of Coke. She's allowed one soda every three days, and because she's my best friend, she shares them with me.

I take a sip and savor the way the bubbles pop in the back of my mouth. "There's going to be a new kid at school. A girl."

"How'd you know?"

"I overheard Mrs. Rawlins talking about it. Apparently she's going to be in our homeroom."

Dani shrugs as I pass the Coke can back to her. "Cool," she says, in a meh tone of voice. I can't believe she's not more excited about it.

"I can't wait to meet the new girl," I say. "I bet she's going to be really awesome."

Dani doesn't reply, and for a second, I wonder if she didn't hear me. Then she says, "Why are you so excited about it?"

"I don't know, I guess because it's a new thing and it would be fun to have a new friend?"

"I guess," Dani says. "Oh hey, check out the new earrings my aunt gave me. They're from Japan!"

All thoughts of the new kid flee my mind, and the rest of the way to Dani's, we chat about everything from the latest lip gloss to which boy has the strongest body odor. I love these afternoons when I walk home with Dani and spend the rest of the day at hers, doing homework and eating cookies. I usually stay there until half past five, then Dani's mom drives me home in time for dinner.

But that day, in the middle of writing our compositions for English, Dani suddenly looks up and pokes me in the arm. "Fern," she says, and there's something in her voice that makes my instincts prick up.

"Yeah?"

She looks at me with wide eyes, as though she is almost scared. "Um, about that new kid . . ." She chews on her bottom lip for a bit, then says, "I know you're super excited about her, but do you promise you and I will be best friends no matter what?"

Warmth spreads across my body, and I laugh. "Oh my god, Dani! Duh, obviously! I can't believe you were worried about that!"

Dani giggles. "Well, I mean, you were just so excited about her! And you know what they say, life happens—"

"In mysterious ways," I say at the same time as she does. Dani says that so often that it's become an inside joke between us. "You know no one's ever going to replace you. We're Dani and Fern. We're besties forever."

We grin at each other, our smiles equally wide.

"Besties forever," Dani agrees.

Chapter 15

I manage to hold on to my apartment for exactly two more weeks before it becomes clear that I will not be able to make the coming month's rent. I emailed my landlord, asking if an extension was possible (There's a pandemic, I whined in my message), and his answer was a flat no (I realize that, sweetheart, he replied, but rent's still due). I then emailed Sarah, begging for my deposit back (There's a pandemic, I whined in my message), and she reminded me that deposits are, on the whole, nonrefundable (It's the entire purpose of a deposit, she said, it's a down payment to ensure that the vendor's time isn't wasted. Stay safe!). With that, I was shit out of luck.

There are more humiliating things than moving back into your parents' home more than a decade after moving out, but not much more. Especially since my parents aren't the kind who'd welcome me home with bright smiles and open arms. In fact, when I finally pull up in my car, the first thing that Mom says when she opens the front door is "You're home" in the same tone of voice one might use to say "We need more milk." A toneless, emotionless statement. Is it strange to say that I would've preferred her to show some disappointment? At least it would be an emotion of some kind, something I could've bounced off. Unbidden, a flash of Haven's parents dart through my mind—her mom and dad happily puttering around her as she cooks, her dad telling her that the noodle soup she made for dinner reminded him of how it felt when he was a little boy coming home to his mom's cooking.

My dad turns up at the doorway and says, "Oh, Fern," like he hasn't been expecting me all along, like I haven't called in advance to tell them that I need to come back here. And again, there isn't so much an inflection of emotion in his voice as there is an uninterested pointing out of fact. Not "Oh, Fern!" but "Oh, it's just Fern."

It's because you were home for Christmas, I tell myself, trying my best to cement over the hurt. And it's only April now, so obviously they're not going to make a big deal of seeing you after only four months apart.

But Haven's parents make such a fuss over her when she visits them twice a week. She posts her homecoming all the time. Both her mom and her dad and their two dogs will be waiting at the door, and as she slides into the driveway, they wave at her excitedly, their eyes aglow with joy at the sight of her. The dogs wag their tails. While her mom embraces her, her dad insists on taking her bags so she doesn't have to carry them to the house. The dogs dance on their hind legs, begging Haven for a cuddle.

The first thing I notice as I walk inside my parents' house is the smell. It's not an unpleasant smell, per se—a mix of laundry and cleaning fluid—but it's so ascetic, not at all the scent one would associate with a home. It's clean; I'll give them that. That's one thing my parents have going for them. There are no pictures hung up on the wall, no decorations. They have always said "Don't do anything that would bring the house's value down in case we decide to move." They've lived here for over thirty years now, but still they insist on never sprouting roots, never letting themselves get attached to it. They haven't changed a single thing about the house since moving in. It still has the same light fixtures and everything. If my parents were to die, it would be as though they were never here. As though they were just ghosts passing through.

I know that this is part of their immigrant identity. They are so scared of making waves because it might upend the little ship they're forever on. Whenever anything happens, their reaction is: Keep your head down and stay out of trouble. Pretend not to see the fire until it engulfs you, and when it does, try to burn as quietly as possible. Do not make a fuss.

Sometimes I wonder if this is my future I see before me. That I might end up like them, afraid to leave my mark in the world. It's probably one of the reasons why I write. Writing is my quiet little way of leaving something behind, so I know that all this isn't just a dream. So I know that I've existed.

The second thing I notice about Mom and Dad's house is the silence. There is never any music playing in here because we might disturb the neighbors. In the evenings, they watch TV while they have dinner, but they do so with subtitles on and with very low volume, so low that I always have to strain my ears to hear what the actors are saying. Even when Mom and Dad fight, they do so in hisses, like snakes warning predators away but never striking, always saving their venom for another day. Their lives are like a held breath, everything hanging in stasis. Growing up, I sometimes found myself randomly holding my breath when my parents were around, as though my body was waiting for something to happen. Then I'd notice and think: What the hell? Why was I holding my breath? And I'd have to consciously tell myself to breathe normally.

"How was the drive?" Dad says under his breath, like he's half hoping I wouldn't hear.

"It's good. Long." I lug my bags across the living room and notice Mom wincing as they drag across the polished floor, but she doesn't offer to help me with them.

"I've prepared your old room," Mom says. Coming from her, this is as close as it gets to a tight hug.

I acknowledge the effort with a smile. "Thanks, Mom."

She hesitates for a split second before nodding. She's never gotten used to me calling her "Mom." When I was little, she'd asked me once to call her "Mama," but I'd said, "What if the other kids hear and make fun of me?" and she'd backed down immediately. "You're right," she'd said, "it would call too much attention to us." I still think back on that moment and wonder what our relationship would've been like if I'd just agreed to call her Mama. I still haven't forgiven myself for not doing it. She so rarely asks me for anything. But I didn't know, I want to tell her: I was too young, I didn't understand what it meant. And anyway, if I brought it up now, she'd probably feign ignorance and tell me she's forgotten about the whole thing.

My old bedroom is the only space in the house that has some semblance of personality. As a teen, I saved up and splurged on removable wall hooks so I could hang all sorts of posters. They're mostly of Green Day and other emo rock bands from the early 2000s, like My Chemical Romance, because, like every other teen, I really thought I was something different and unique and so I couldn't possibly like the mainstream stuff. Not me, misunderstood Fern Huang. I smile at the memory of my high school self. God, I was insufferable.

I'd planned to take a shower as soon as I got home, but once I drop my bags, I immediately feel so incredibly exhausted. I flop onto my bed and breathe out slowly. It's as though my entire being is deflating, admitting defeat. Here I am, after all these years of working my ass off, back at square one. I stare at the popcorn ceiling for god knows how long before I take out my phone and unlock it.

I avoid opening Slack. Ever since I found out that Lisa and Jenna talk behind my back, the sight of the Slack app icon makes me feel nauseated. I still participate in our three-person channel, but every time I do, I get so self-conscious that I end up second-guessing everything I write. Instead, I open Instagram. Thanks to my efforts in the past one and a half years, I've grown my follower count from three hundred to over two thousand now. Every time I look at the number of followers, my heart does a tiny skip of joy. That's all my efforts, I want to crow to the world. I've been posting diligently, once a day at least, and my page is a beautiful mix of scrumptious-looking baked goods, me holding up books I've read and loved, and little snippets of my own upcoming book. And over two thousand people have seen it and thought: She seems cool, I'll follow her! Isn't that amazing? For once, I am grateful for all the crap I've had to go through with Annette, because it means I now know how to edit photos to get the best possible lighting and colors to catch the eye.

But then I go to my alternate profile's feed, and the top post that gets pushed to me is Haven's content. It's Haven's mom, sitting on a comfortable lounge chair and saying to the camera, "Reading my baby's AR—wait, what is this called?"

Off-screen, Haven says, "Mooom, I told you, just call it a book."

Haven's mom: "Aiya, what is the proper name?"

Haven: "ARC. Advance reader copy."

Haven's mom: "Oooh, so fancy."

Haven giggles.

Haven's mom: "Okay, reading from my baby's advance reader copy. This is an advance copy because the book is not out yet. So this is a very special copy."

Haven: "Mom, just read it!"

The video is so cute I could just die watching it. Their love and adoration for each other is palpable, even when they're bickering, and it's not even real bickering, it's the type where you can hear the good-natured smile behind the words. It's impossible to watch it without smiling. And when Mrs. Lee starts reading, it is impossible to tear my eyes off the screen. I watch it all the way through, and when it replays automatically, I don't scroll up. I watch it again. Then I tap on Haven's name, and my stomach drops because Haven has been busy too.

Like me, she's been posting on her account diligently. Except while I was growing at a steady pace of a handful of followers a week, she's basically blown up. She's started a new account for her writing and now has 1.2 million followers. A proper book influencer. And every post has hundreds of comments along the lines of Who do I have to kill to get an ARC of this book!!! I cannot wait to read it!!! Her followers, unlike mine, are passionate—rabid, almost. I know that people exaggerate online, that emotions become overblown on social media, but it's still so jarring to see.

I tap on her previous post. It's of Haven holding up a fellow debut's book, her beautiful face grinning into the camera. The caption reads: Happy book birthday to this gorgeous creature! You guys, if you buy just one book this month, let it be this one. Ugh, how do I describe the brilliance that is @Yunawriteseverything?? I cannot! My babe Yuna is so talented that if we weren't such good friends, I would be writhing on the floor with jealousy. Seriously, do yourselves a favor and get this book. Get it now. You can thank me later!!

The pinned comment is from Yuna, and it says: YOU ARE THE BEST 😭

I know it's utterly ridiculous to feel jealous or weird about this in any way, and yet part of me still feels like Yuna and I have a special connection because of how we first interacted with each other on Slack. I was her friend first, I want to whine at the universe. I click on my profile and look at the photo I posted about Yuna's book. I'm not as photogenic as Haven, so I'd taken the time to arrange Yuna's book artfully, with a plate of homemade jam thumbprint cookies on one side and a cup of milky tea on the other and flowers here and there. It's altogether a beautiful image, both calming and inviting. My caption reads: Happiest of publication day to my dear friend @Yunawriteseverything! I'm so proud of you and your book. Secrets of the Blind Mouse is a beautiful story about a scam artist who falls in love with her mark, and after a decade of marriage, slowly comes to learn that all is not what it seems within their relationship.

The post garnered only three comments. The one from Yuna says: Thank you so much, Fern! It's perfectly nice, but it's nowhere near the same level as YOU ARE THE BEST 😭

I switch back and forth from my post to Haven's until they blur together in my mind. I see now, how compared to mine, Haven's comes across as more genuine. Mine is a well-thought-out book review. Hers is pure word of mouth, someone grabbing you by the shoulders and going, "Trust me, you are going to *love* this!"

How does Haven do it? How does she convey closeness and familiarity with everyone? How is she everybody's bestie? She is the type to greet people she's just met with a heartfelt hug, and you can just tell from her posts. I've always envied those people, the ones who greet unfamiliarity with open arms. So many times I've told myself, Greet them with a hug. Greet them with a hug. Greet them—and then I meet them, whoever they happen to be, and my arms stick to my sides, and I end up giving them an awkward wave instead.

I look at Haven's other recent posts—there seems to be a lot more involving her parents—then I make myself close Instagram for my own sake and open up Slack instead. I remind myself that Lisa hadn't said anything mean about me to Jenna. She was probably just feeling weird about reading Haven's new manuscript and didn't want to hurt my feelings. Everything is okay. I should stay active in the private group chat. There is no good reason for me to lose my two closest friends over this. Taking a deep breath, I click on the private channel and send a message.

Fern: I'm back in Cali. (Sad face)

Jenna: Awww. Are you back at your parents' place now? How is everything?

Fern: Same as it was when I left ten years ago. Literally nothing has changed. It's like going back in time.

Lisa: Oof, I hear ya. I can't imagine having to stomach my parents' house now. Doesn't help that they're uber religious people and I'm not.

Fern: I'm sorry to hear that. My parents aren't too bad, they're just . . . not affectionate, you know? Like, standoffish. It's always a little awkward to be around them, and I'm their kid!

Jenna: Speaking of kids, mine are driving me craaazy! Just this morning, Emily was like, "Mommy, I don't want French toast for breakfast." What kid doesn't want French toast for breakfast??!

Lisa: That's hilarious! I totally get what you mean. Jameson threw a huge tantrum this morning because, and I quote, "I don't like the way the sun looks this morning." Like, sorry kid, if I had the power to control the sun, I would change it up for you, but unfortunately, I don't!

Jenna: 😂😂😂

I reply with laughing emojis as well but don't add anything to the conversation. Ever since schools went into lockdown, our chats have shifted from publishing-oriented topics, tightening around parenting topics. Logically, I know this makes sense. Jenna's and Lisa's kids are home and demanding all their attention, so of course they would be hyperfocused on them. But still. It makes me feel excluded. I never know what to say when kids are brought up, aside from a polite chuckle and a benign virtual nod. I never know if it's okay to be like, "Yeah, kids are terrible," or if that would be crossing a line. Jenna, Lisa, and the other parents in the debut group are often saying stuff that implies that kids are a nightmare, but somehow it's not okay if a childless person like me is the one saying that. I would just come out of it looking like a monster.

Instead, I check the general channels. #Commiserations is my favorite one to check because it makes me feel better to know that I'm not the only person having a tough time, so I save that one for last. I click on the other channels, sighing when I get to #culinary and see that Haven has been posting her culinary wonders nonstop every day, while I've spent the last week or so driving cross-country. Her creations include Taiwanese beef noodle soup, dumplings from scratch, pain au chocolat, and an Italian pastry I've never seen before but is apparently called a sfogliatella and looks like something out of a Michelin-starred pastry shop. Everyone oohed and aahed about her photos, and I don't blame them. They really are stunning, even without the professional-level photography. Meanwhile, I've been stuck in my car, stopping at sad roadside motels and eating instant ramen. It seems highly ironic that the channel I created to give myself an outlet to get out of Haven's shadow and shine has become yet another place for Haven to bask in compliments. Well, never mind. I'm home now, and I've been steadfast with feeding Doughlores every day so she's still healthy and alive, and once I feel less floppy I will resume my daily baking.

Finally, I open #commiserations. People who have debuted earlier this year are sharing their sales numbers. Most of their books have tanked, unsurprisingly, and some are reporting sales as low as twenty copies in a week, which is truly abysmal. I don't know why whenever I say I'm an author, people automatically think Stephen King or Rick Riordan, but most authors don't sell anywhere near the numbers that these star authors do. They're selling hundreds of millions of books, but the average author would count themselves lucky if they sell over ten thousand books in their lifetime. And, from the looks of the #commiserations channel, none of us are on our way to selling anything even approaching ten thousand copies. Someone has sold six hundred copies in the first week, and that's the best number we've got so far.

I allow myself a few moments of petty reverie. This is why I like the #commiserations channel. No matter how differently we're faring outside of publishing—some of these debut authors are high-powered lawyers; there's even a doctor or two among us—within publishing, the playing field is leveled, and we're all given the same starting line. I, an unemployed nobody, have as good a chance as everyone else to start over and make my mark in the publishing world. I comfort myself, too, with the knowledge that this applies to Haven. She might've gotten the seven-figure book deal, but like the rest of us, she will also be debuting during the pandemic. There's no escaping that harsh reality. COVID, a terrifying leveler, has pounded its fist down onto all of us, and we are all in the same boat. There is something strangely comforting in that.

But just as I think that, the #celebrations channel lights up. Something inside me twists, as though even without opening the channel, some strange instinct has perked up and is telling me it's going to be about Haven. I shrug it off. For a moment, I tell myself not to open the #celebrations channel. To stay here in #commiserations and pretend that all is not well with everybody else, and therefore all is well with me. But my thumb moves of its own accord and taps on the screen. The #celebrations channel loads, and somehow, it's worse than anything I could've imagined.

> **Haven:** GUYS! I can finally announce this!! I have been sitting on this for months and it's been KILLING ME!!! MY BOOK IS GOOD MORNING AMERICA'S BOOK CLUB PICK!!!

Chapter 16

The darkness doesn't swallow me whole in one gulp. No, it starts slowly, sucking my toes in so gently that I don't feel it happening until it's up to my ankles, and by then it feels like so much effort to try to walk away. I sit there and lose myself in the endless scroll. I scroll up, and up, and up, reading and rereading Haven's old posts, seeing them in a whole new light now.

In the #covid channel: This pandemic has taken so much from all of us. I refuse to let it take away the joy of debuting too. I'm choosing to focus on all of the good that's still happening!!

In the #random channel: This might be a really stupid question, but does anyone know what is a good number of copies to sell within the first week of publication?

In the #writing channel, in response to someone talking about how tough they're finding book two, she said: Forget everything about book one! My debut is so raw and so unpolished and honestly, not even very good because it was just me thought-vomiting onto the page! You know, it's like I opened up the floodgates and let everything out without caring about stuff like pacing and character development and all that. But having written it, I've learned so much and I know my second book will be less messy, and I'm sure that's true for you too!

Back when Haven posted all these messages, I'd read them as her being genuine, or well, as genuine as Haven is capable of being, I suppose. But now, with the newfound information that she's known all this time that she's *Good Morning America*'s book of the month, I'm seeing all her messages in a more sinister light.

For example, when she said that the pandemic has taken so much from us all and how she's valiantly refusing to let it take her publishing joy, well, that's easy for her to say because she already knows that despite the pandemic, her book will still be a massive bestseller. People are devouring more content than ever, so *Good Morning America* is still going strong—well, stronger than ever, even, and so when her book drops on the show, people are going to be buying it in droves. The pandemic hasn't taken away anything from her; in fact, it's giving her even more than she already has. Was she smiling when she posted that in #covid, secretly laughing at the rest of us, whose debuts, unlike hers, are being pummeled by the pandemic?

Then, the question in #randombookquestions about how many copies one can expect to sell. Surely she must know that the number of copies a *Good Morning America* book pick sells is going to be wildly different from the rest of us plebs' books? It's not even going to be close. We're talking a sale of two hundred books versus twenty thousand books. And now I see Haven in my mind's eye, typing the question with a smug, gleeful look on her flawless face. A few people answered her question with a range of numbers from a hundred to one thousand. How she must've laughed at them. Pathetic, she would've thought to herself. I will probably sell over forty thousand copies.

And the third post, where she'd reassured someone about their sophomore book by telling the world that her debut book is shit. Hah! The cruelty is so obvious now. How did I miss it before? She's saying that even her worst effort deserves seven figures and an endorsement from one of the biggest book clubs in the world. Stupid wannabe writers, she must've thought, your best efforts are still nothing compared to my worst effort.

What galls me is that nobody else seems to be able to discern this. Everyone reacted nicely to Haven's veiled posts, thanking her for her "wisdom" and "kind words" and telling her she's so "supportive" and "the best hype woman." And when I go back to the #celebrations channel, I see that her post about being *Good Morning America*'s pick already has over thirty hearts and a ton of comments screaming congratulations and telling her no one else deserves this as much as she does. Really? No one else deserves this? I could think of plenty of people more deserving.

"No," I say out loud. I squeeze my eyes shut. That's such a mean, petty thought to have. I slam my fists into my temples. Stop it, stop it. I don't want to turn into that person again. I am a good person. I have only good thoughts in my mind and goodwill in my heart. I won't let Haven turn me into this jealous, petty cretin. I'm different now. I promised myself this, at Dani's funeral, that I wouldn't let Haven's cruelty turn me jagged. It's the best thing I can do to honor Dani's memory. She always strove hard to be good, and I will do the same. I've come such a long way. I'm not a kid any longer, for one. For another, I have healthy coping mechanisms. That's right. I can bake. And maybe out here in SoCal, where things are so sprawled out and the sidewalks are extra wide, I can actually go out for a run. But the thought of getting up and changing into my running gear right now, after such a long drive, leaves me winded. Another healthy coping method, my mind whispers: Lean on your friends. You have them now, remember? It's not like how things were back then, where you only had Dani, and then Haven took her away . . .

Oh yes. My friends! I quickly switch over to the private channel. Lisa and Jenna are both online. I look at our previous chats, mulling over how to phrase what I'm about to say in the least bitchy way possible.

Fern: Did you guys see Haven's announcement?

Lisa: About the GMA book club pick?

Fern: Yeah

Jenna: Oh man, yeah! How crazy is that??

I lick my lips and cock my head to one side. "Crazy" could be either positive or negative here. Which one did Jenna mean? The thing is, I want to vent at them about all my messy feelings, but at the same time, I don't want to come off as too jealous. There is such a fine line to walk here.

Fern: Yeah. I kind of have feelings about it . . .

Jenna: Girl, you are not the only one. I am hella jealous right now!!

Lisa: Me toooo. I would literally kill to be a GMA book club pick omg

My heart sings. They get me. They are my people. My tribe.

Fern: I'm so glad you said that! I don't want to be a horrible person, but I am DYING with jealousy 😭

Jenna: Saaaame! It doesn't make you a bad person at all! I think it's human nature

Fern: It's just, out of all people, why HER, you know?

Lisa: What do you mean?

I stop typing. What does Lisa mean what do I mean? Isn't it obvious? I literally meant what I said: Why Haven?

Fern: Oh it's just like, it feels like everything good only ever happens to Haven . . . IDK, I'm probably just being dumb

Jenna: You're not being dumb at all!

Lisa: I wouldn't say that everything good only ever happens to her. So . . . I'm not supposed to tell anyone this, but she's had to move back to her parents' house because her dad got COVID and it was touch and go for a while back there

Fern: WHAT?!

I am literally gaping at my phone, and here's the thing: What I'm really shocked about isn't the fact that Haven's dad got COVID—I mean, I am shocked about that because, of course, it's shocking news—it's the fact that Lisa, my friend Lisa, knew about it.

Fern: How do you know?

Lisa: She told me. Listen you guys, she told me in confidence so pleaaaase do not tell anyone!

Haven told Lisa? Lisa, *my friend* Lisa? A dirty, ugly feeling has awakened deep in my belly and is gnawing away at my flesh. I feel sick. Have they been chatting with each other behind my back all this while? From how long ago? What do they talk about with each other? And why have they been talking? Who started it?

A million questions buzz through my head, leaving me frozen. I don't even know what to say to her right now. Luckily, Jenna seems to have read my mind.

Jenna: Wait, she told you in confidence? You guys talk to each other?

Yes, go Jenna! I want to cheer at her. A surge of goodwill washes over me as I look at Jenna's name. Jenna is my rock. She's always had my back, at every instance she's been there to prop me up, to lend me a voice of support.

> **Lisa:** Yeah. Remember about a month ago I posted in #covid about my best friend getting it? Haven messaged me to check if I was okay, and we started talking, and then about a week later, her dad got it and she told me, I guess because I'm one of the few people she knows who's had someone get the virus?

I take a deep breath and force myself to calm down. Put like that, it makes sense, I suppose. It's not like what I'd feared—Haven reaching out to dish some dirt about me. Of course it isn't like that. That would be ridiculous. But even as I think that, I get a flashback of Haven and Dani and the other girls whispering to one another and shooting me dark looks as I watched from afar. No, it's not like that at all. Lisa is my friend. And we're grown women, for god's sake.

> **Fern:** I'm really sorry about your best friend. How is she doing now?
>
> **Lisa:** Thanks! She's doing fine. It never got bad, thank god, she said it felt like a really rough cold and she would get winded walking up the stairs, but other than that the symptoms were okay and she tested negative about two weeks later, so PHEW! I was just so scared when she first told me though
>
> **Jenna:** Oh, I bet! That's wild. I'm so glad she's okay

> **Lisa:** Yeah, and for a while we were really worried about her husband and kids getting it too; her 6yo has asthma, so that would've been really bad
>
> **Jenna:** Oh shit, yeah, totally

I sense the conversation about to slip into the realms of talking about children once more, and panic grabs me. Before I can stop myself, I type a new message.

> **Fern:** Wow, thank god they didn't get it! Hey so, how's Haven's dad doing? She had to move back in to take care of them?

The words "Lisa is typing . . ." appear and disappear. My heart sits snugly in my throat while I stare at the screen, unblinking. She types again.

> **Lisa:** Yeah. I don't feel comfortable revealing too much personal info about him, but she had good reason to worry about his health as well as her mom's health. So yeah, she's had to move back in to look after both of them, she's going through a pretty rough time

Somehow, I just can't imagine Haven Lee going through a "rough time." Someone like Haven glides through life effortlessly, with nothing sticking to her. Even after Dani's death, Haven bounced back just fine. All her Facebook posts about how much she missed Dani sounded so forced, and I heard through the grapevine that Haven spent that summer traveling through Italy with her parents. Right before she started at Stanford, where she was her usual shiny, brilliant self. I switch over to Instagram once more and look at her latest posts again. Nothing but upbeat, cheerful posts. The ones that include her parents showcase them smiling, laughing, and gazing at her with nothing but joy and affection. There is nothing here that implies a "rough time."

It's clear to me what's happening. Back in middle and high school, Haven excelled at playing the innocent victim. She reveled in casting herself as the underdog, a queen bee masquerading as a simple drone. I would often come across people saying things like, "Oh did you hear about poor Haven?" And the examples of her being downtrodden were generally things that were unverifiable by the rest of us students, such as her mom's visa getting denied and there being the possibility of her mom being deported. Very shocking and terrifying, sure, but nothing that us kids could've looked up and proved to be untrue, and in the meanwhile, Haven would receive all this attention and sympathy. I wouldn't have cared so much if she hadn't been so vile to me, but at the time, it felt like the worst kind of gaslighting, where only I saw the monster behind the curtains, and everyone else saw this perfect, harmless angel with soft, innocent doe eyes and a disposition that made them go "Awww!"

And now, here we are again, back at the exact place I thought I'd left for good. I want to grab Lisa and shout, "Haven isn't going through a rough time at all! She's probably made it all up about her dad getting COVID just to get to you!" Oh god. As soon as I think it, it becomes so painfully obvious. Yes, of course, this is why Haven's doing this. She knows that Lisa and Jenna are my only friends, and she's been scheming to get to them somehow, the way she did with Dani. Jenna is a little harder to get to because she's such a loyal friend, but when Lisa posted about her best friend getting COVID, Haven found her opening and got to her. My entire body aches at the thought of Haven sinking her claws into one of only two friends that I have. Why? Why is Haven so determined to take what little things I have away? She has more friends than I could possibly count, but no, it's still not enough. She needs to take, and take, until there's nothing left of me. God, I curse the day that I met Haven Lee.

And now, two paths fork before me. I could pretend to be just as clueless as everybody else about Haven and say sympathetic things. Or I could take the risk and tell Lisa that Haven is not to be trusted, that her dad seems totally fine and she's probably just made it all up.

There is nothing to gain from taking that risk, a small voice whispers. Keep your eyes on your own lane.

Then again, another voice pipes up, you decided on the first path back in middle school, and look where that got you. You listened to your parents. You put your head down and kept quiet, but you didn't manage to stay out of trouble, did you? She got you all the same. You curled up so tight you practically disappeared, but she found you anyway. She's set her sights on you. There's no point trying to hide. She sees you, Fern. You need to make a stand. You need to fight back.

I do. I need to fight back. I straighten my back and think of what to say. After a few moments, I type out my reply.

> **Fern:** That's so weird, because on Instagram she seems to be so happy and everything is going great for her. Her parents both look really healthy?

That's good, right? It's not too pointed. I'm merely making an observation, and I'm stopping short of making any judgments.

> **Lisa:** Umm, well I think people generally curate their social media posts, right? You know what they say, social media is just the highlight reel of our lives, and nobody sees the grisly details from behind the scenes.

> **Fern:** That's totally true, but IDK, just from everything I know about Haven, I feel like she tends to hmm, like, inflate a little?

Jenna: Do you mean like she makes stuff up?

Fern: I mean . . . I think she tends to add her own spice to the story, if that makes sense

Lisa: Huh. Really? It really didn't strike me as her making stuff up. She said some really specific things that I don't think you could make up . . .

I can't believe it's happening all over again. People choosing to believe Haven's word over mine. Me ending up feeling crazy, like I'm making things up about her. But I know what I went through. I know what Haven is really like. Lisa doesn't.

Fern: She can be really persuasive. Trust me, I know, I went through hell in middle and high school because of everything she did towards me.

Lisa: Oh gosh, yeah. I'm sorry, I remember you bringing that up now

Did Lisa really forget about that? How could she have? If she'd told me about her high school bully, I wouldn't have forgotten. I would remember it, and I would be a real friend, which means I would be on Team Lisa all the way and be predisposed to hating the other person. I'm not even asking Lisa to hate Haven right now; all I'm asking her to do is to take a step back and look at Haven objectively, without all the bullshit that Haven's been feeding her. Is that too much to ask for?

Lisa: What was it that Haven did to you again?

Fern: I don't really want to go into the gory details, but she basically turned everyone in middle school

> against me, including my best friend. And most of us ended up going to the same high school, so the bullying just carried on over all the way through high school. It was horrible.
>
> **Lisa:** Oh my gosh, that sounds horrific. I'm so sorry
>
> **Jenna:** I'm sorry you went through that too, Fern. Nobody deserves that

The sickening dark feeling abates a little, just enough so I feel like I can breathe again. I've said my piece and reminded Lisa and Jenna of the truth about Haven. I've warned them, and now I can go on and be at peace once more.

> **Lisa:** God, as much as I hate to say it though, I feel like people do change sometimes, and after everything Haven's told me, I think she's really changed! She's so different from what you describe. She even told me that she regrets a lot of things that happened back when she was younger. I bet she was referring to you! And you know what, just the other day when I was chatting with her, she mentioned that she admires how you were working as a photographer in New York. She thought it was really cool that you have such an artistic talent and she even said what a shame you couldn't continue doing photography!

The momentary peace I'd felt evaporates just like that, in the blink of an eye. I can't believe it. For a moment, I am an empty vessel, feeling nothing, sensing nothing. Then the rage comes, and when it does, it knocks me over, consuming me completely and utterly. My vision goes black, I have no awareness of what I'm doing—I have a vague sense that I've fallen back onto the bed and am tearing at my hair, literally just grabbing clumps of my hair and yanking. Somehow, a small part of me manages to cry out to be heard over the overwhelming waves of black rage. It surfaces onto conscious thought and pries my fingers open before I can rip out my own hair. Slowly, my clenched fists open up. I fight my arms down to my sides. I force myself to take an inhale and imagine the air filling up my lungs, and when I exhale, I imagine the darkness swirling out of my nostrils, filling the room with black smoke.

Haven knows that I was working for Annette back in New York. Annette, who fired me because of "numerous complaints" made about me. I remember scratching my head over those complaints when she first mentioned them, wondering what it was I could've possibly done to warrant a complaint. And not just one but several of them. I fleetingly suspected Haven, then scolded myself for being paranoid. But now, I know Haven was behind them. It's exactly the kind of thing she would do.

By the time I calm down enough to drag myself out of the spiral, it's clear what needs to happen. Haven is a poisonous snake. She's made me lose my job, and now she is reaching out to my allies and letting her lies and her charm poison them. I do not have the antidote for this powerful toxin; I see that now. I've tried talking sense into Lisa, but she's too far gone. She knows about Haven's past, and she doesn't care. She's bought into Haven's charm, Haven's irresistible persona, and I need to realize that I don't have what it takes to counter it, at least not like this. I cannot play Haven's games by Haven's rules. I need to change the game itself.

I need to play a different game.

Chapter 17

Age Twelve

Dani's been acting weird recently, and I don't understand it. Or rather, I understand it, but I don't want to. This morning, when I get to school, she's not waiting at the usual place for me like she always does. Instead, I find her already at homeroom, chatting so animatedly to Haven that neither of them notices me until I say "Hi." Then Dani says "Oh hey!" It's so awkward.

At lunchtime, the three of us walk together to the cafeteria, but maybe it's not right to call it "walking together" because they walk side by side while I find myself pushed to the back, trying to find a break in their conversation where I can insert myself. At one point, Dani says, "Oh my god, and pizza cake!" And they both burst out laughing.

"What's so funny?" I say, trying to hide my nervousness.

"Oh, Fern, you just have to have been there," Haven says.

I'm even more confused now. "Where?"

Dani and Haven share a look. It's a slightly guilty kind of look. "Oh, you know, just—" Dani says, waving her hands in that way that she does when she's nervous. "We were at my house last Saturday, and—"

"You guys hung out at your house? Without me?" Even I hear the slight whine in my voice. Ugh, I sound so babyish.

"It wasn't a big deal, it was only because Haven said she wanted to bake cookies, and I said—"

"I like baking!" I say, and it comes out so loud and so upset that they both stop moving and stare at me.

"Fern, it's not a big deal," Haven says, rolling her eyes. She shares another look with Dani, and this time, it's not a guilty one but an ugh-she's-tiresome one.

I look frantically between Dani and Haven, heat rising from my neck to my cheeks. I want to cry, but I know that if I did that, then everything would be over. Instead, I say, "Cool." And I run to the bathroom and lock myself inside before crying. I wash my face with cold water afterward, but my eyes are so puffy it's obvious that I've been crying. When I see Haven and Dani in class, they both look at me hesitantly, like they want to say something, but I duck my head and slide into my seat, and we don't talk for the rest of the day.

When I come home, Mom gives me banana slices with peanut butter on them, just the way I like it, but the peanut butter sticks to the back of my mouth and I feel like retching. Mom asks me if I'm okay, and I tell her what's happened. She says, "Oh, Fern. Friendships change all the time. You'll find new friends." As if it's so easy and I can just snap my fingers and conjure up a new Dani.

You don't understand, I want to say to her. I don't want a new friend. I only want Dani. Haven's got an entire school of kids she could be friends with; why did she have to choose my friend? If only Haven weren't here.

And I realize, then, that that's the answer. If I could make Haven go away, then Dani would be my best friend again. Haven moved here not too long ago, so maybe I can make her move away again. But how? Maybe I can send her a mean note telling her to move away? I sigh. We write mean notes to one another all the time, and no one's moved away because of it. It needs to be something bigger.

I have so much frantic, nervous energy inside me that I can't just sit here. I get up and decide to do a bit of baking. Before that, I go to the bathroom, and as I wash my hands after peeing, I look up and see the medicine cabinet. I don't know what it is, but something makes me open it, and there it is. Dad's laxatives. I take them out, and as I stare at them, something starts happening in my mind. I don't know how to explain it, but it feels like a new part of my brain has just been unlocked. Like there was always a part of me that I didn't even know existed, and now it's awakened, and it won't go back to sleep until I listen to it. A little bit will do, it says to me. A tiny bit, that's okay, right?

The cookies come out smelling beautiful. I eat one myself and give another to Mom, who calls me her sweet little baker. The rest I pack up into plastic containers, marking one of them with a little red dot. The one that contains the special one I've made for Haven.

The next day, when I bring them to school, everyone crowds around me, grabbing at them. I'm so worried that they might snatch up Haven's cookie before she gets here, so I set it aside, and when Haven finally gets to school, I hand it to her and say, "Here, I saved it for you."

"What? You did? Oh my god Fern, that's so sweet!" She reaches over and gives me a hug. "And I just wanna say, I'm sorry about yesterday. I feel bad about it. We won't hang out without you again."

I manage a smile. Why is she being nice now? My insides writhe with guilt, and I almost reach out and grab the cookie from her. Oh god, I feel awful. Why did I put laxatives in her cookie? Who does that? Only a monster would do such a thing. I wish I could take it back, but how can I now? If I took the cookie back, it's going to look so weird.

In the end, I say nothing. I'm too much of a coward to do anything.

Haven is out of school for a day. One beautiful, glorious day where Dani is my best friend again, and it's exactly like old times. But when Haven comes back to school, Dani immediately rushes to her side and says, "Oh my god, I've missed you so much!"

Then Haven's gaze lifts, and she meets my eye, and I see it on her face. She knows. She knows it was the cookie I gave her. Fear claws at my throat, and I have to fight to keep my face neutral. I force a smile and say, "I'm glad you're okay." She doesn't say anything to me.

Later, when school ends for the day, I walk my usual route home. I round a corner and find Haven there, just standing, looking at the ground. She looks up and says, "Hi, Fern."

"Hi." I have no idea what to say. I have no idea what she's doing here. This isn't in the direction of her place.

"I know what you did," she says.

My mouth goes dry. "Huh?"

"The cookie you saved for me."

"I don't know what you're talking about."

Haven steps closer to me, and I'm suddenly scared of her.

"I thought it was weird that you saved me a cookie. But I see why now. Do you know how gross it is to have diarrhea for a whole day?" I feel faint. But I only put a little bit in, I want to say. Instead, what comes out is "You can't prove it." I want to cry. I want to grab Haven and wail that I'm sorry, that I hadn't meant to actually hurt her. But I'm unable to get the words out.

Haven's face twists, turning ugly. "You are an evil freak. I've never known anyone as evil as you." She stabs a finger into my chest. "You need to stay away from me and Dani and everyone else. Stay away from me. I mean it." With that, she turns and walks off, her hand flying to her stomach like she might throw up.

I barely remember the walk back home. She knows. How did she find out? I guess it was obvious, like she said, because I saved her a cookie and she knew that I didn't like her. Stupid, stupid! How could I not have seen how obvious it was? What if she tells the police? Why hasn't she? I guess because she doesn't have any proof. And if she does, I can say that everyone else was fine, so it couldn't have been me who did it. What if she tells Dani? What if she tells others? Why did I do what I did? I feel so much disgust toward myself that I shudder thinking about it. I can't let that darkness out ever again. I need to really commit to being good from now on. Because I want to be good. I need to be good. The last thing I want is to turn into someone like Haven.

Chapter 18

I would so love to say that I wasn't in my right mind when I put on Mom's visor, sunglasses, and a mask and got back into my car. But the truth is, I was completely in my right mind. In fact, I would even go so far as to say that I can't remember the last time I had such clarity. Everything seems stark, all the edges around me sharpened into minute detail, and my mind is clean and undisturbed, like still water, all my thoughts focused into one single tiny pinprick of a thought: Stop Haven.

I call out to my parents, telling them that I'm going for a drive, and from the den where they are watching TV, Mom says, "All right." She doesn't bother asking me where I'm going at this hour of the night. It's nine now, and clearly I'm not going out to hang out with friends because (1) pandemic et cetera, and (2) I have no friends, but neither of my parents seems bothered by the fact that their single daughter is heading out at night while wearing a visor and sunglasses. I wonder how normal parents would behave. I wonder what it is that happened early in their lives that made my parents this way. And I think: I am not going to end up like them.

The moment I start up my car, I am transported back to my high school years. The truth is, I've done this so often that I can just sit back and let muscle memory take over. The number of times I drove to Haven's house back then, under the blanket of nightfall, and just sat in my car and watched her house. I don't know what I was hoping for back then. Part of me wanted to catch her doing something bad, I guess, but the other part of me became enamored of her home life, so different from mine. Her adoring parents. A home full of love and laughter, loud and bright.

The thing is, I used to have a habit of driving to Haven's and watching her. I never told anyone. And it wasn't out of control or anything. Eventually, I managed to break that habit. Nighttime would come and I would grapple with myself and manage to keep myself at home, manage to stop myself from climbing into my car and driving the now-familiar route over to Haven's. It was hard at first, but it got easier, and of course it became easier still once I graduated and was able to move to the East Coast. I healed myself. I did that. And now . . .

No. This time, it's different. I'm not just going to Haven's to watch her aimlessly. I'm going there with a purpose. I grip the wheel tightly as I drive. The houses around my parents' house in San Gabriel can't ever be accused of being extravagant, but they're nice enough. It's a safe neighborhood, and I've always liked the feel of it. But then I cross over to San Marino, and suddenly it's ostentatious mansions all around, with expansive front yards and elaborate Greek fountains, as though climate change weren't an actual thing. Focus, I tell myself. I go over the list of things I'm supposed to do when I get there.

Okay, so for one thing, I need to get evidence that Haven is full of shit. Back in school, Dani never quite believed me when I told her all the bad stuff Haven had done to me, and of course she didn't, because Haven always made sure to cover her tracks. It was on me to prove it, and look what happened when I failed. But I know better now. I'm going to find proof. And how do I do that? By proving that her dad's in perfect health and she made up all that stuff about him having COVID to gain sympathy.

That's a good plan, right? I can't even tell anymore.

For another, maybe I'll be able to get proof that Haven is a bad person some other way. Like if I could . . .

Nope, I'm drawing a blank on this one. All I can think of is if I stole in and grabbed her phone or something, but that is definitely over my head. They make it look so easy in movies, breaking into people's houses. Somehow, everyone in the movies knows how to pick locks, and every lock is a manual one that can be picked. Or everyone knows how to hack into phones and computers and do cool stuff like clone them. Well, I don't know how to do any of that, so I have no idea what I'd need to do to prove that Haven is lying. Maybe I'll get lucky and catch her doing something like kicking a stray cat or something. I snort at the thought. The sad thing is, I can totally envision Haven doing that.

I park my car down the street from Haven's house in case she recognizes it from school. It's been a relatively warm day, but nights in SoCal are always chilly, and this one's no exception. I'm wearing a hoodie, and I wrap my arms around myself as I walk down the street. Halfway down, I realize that wearing a visor and sunglasses at night will probably attract more attention, so I scurry back to my car and dump them in the back seat. Instead, I pull my hood over my head and hope that the mask I'm wearing will render me somewhat unrecognizable. I keep my head down as I walk, focusing on keeping my breathing even.

Haven's house is one of the smaller ones on this street, but it's still much bigger than mine, and much, much nicer. Despite the fact that we're in a pandemic and I'm sure no landscaper has been over here for months, the front lawn remains aggressively manicured. I slow down as I approach, my heart rate quickening. I feel painfully noticeable, sticking out in the silence. Why are these stupid streets so well lit? Back in San Gabriel, I can barely see where I'm walking at night, but here, the streetlamps are as bright as flood lights. I check my surroundings to make sure there's no one else around, then I duck into a gap in the hedges and walk closer still to Haven's house.

I've never been this close to the house before; back in high school, I always just sat in my car. But now that I have a clear goal, I know that I can't sit back passively, waiting for something to happen. I need to make it happen. I approach slowly, my breath roaring in my ears, so heavy that my mask moves with each inhale and exhale. I hate this stupid mask, the way it makes my face so warm and moist and makes me smell my own breath, but I'm also grateful for the way it hides my face.

I reach the side of the house. There's a gate that presumably leads to the backyard, and a few trash cans next to it. Now what? I retrace my steps, circling to the front of the house, and I've just reached a large picture window when I catch a figure moving inside the house, less than five feet away from me. I suck in a shocked gasp through my teeth, and if not for the pane of glass separating me and the other person, they would've heard me for sure. My instincts scream at me to duck down below the windowsill, but I make myself freeze instead, fearful that any slight movement might catch their eye.

It's Haven's dad. He's sitting on a lounge chair that is now familiar to me because I've seen it so many times in Haven's posts. It's his favorite reading chair. There are so many videos and photos of him sitting in it, looking out the window, or reading on it, or sipping a cup of coffee. And every single time, there's always a gentle smile playing on his lips, and he looks so at peace, a man who knows that he's been blessed with a good life and wants to savor every moment. I've seen comments referring to him as Asian Santa, and I have to agree. Mr. Lee looks—there's no other word for it—jolly.

But now, he's visibly diminished. His once rotund belly has shrunk; his barrel chest is thin. His sweater hangs loosely on him. His face was round on Haven's Instagram, but now it's gaunt, his chin pointy instead of soft. On any other man, the weight loss might have looked okay—good, even—but on Mr. Lee, it looks wrong, like someone's stabbed a straw into him and sucked out everything jolly about him. He looks tired and old, and every breath he takes seems labored. I have only seen him in person a handful of times, on parents' day at school or when Haven performed onstage, but because of Haven's Instagram, I feel like I know Mr. Lee, and the sight of him now, so greatly reduced in stature, physically hurts me to look at. I'm not a monster; my fight isn't against Mr. Lee. I don't want to see him like this.

And, I realize with a sinking feeling in my stomach, this proves that Haven was telling the truth about her dad getting COVID. Part of my mind tries to tell me that he might be sick with something else, that maybe it's the flu or something, but I know that it's just grasping at straws. And so what if it's a different disease and not COVID? He's still deserving of empathy.

As soon as I realize this, the rage descends once more. Why can't anything go my way, just once? I really needed this. I needed to prove that Haven is evil. Just this one time. And the universe can't even give that to me. I have nothing. No job, no prospects. I have one tiny book deal and no publicist now that I can't pay Sarah, which means my book will simply sink into obscurity, leaving me with truly nothing. And Haven, sweet, beautiful Haven, has been blessed with everything, and still, it isn't enough for her. Still, she wants to take from me. Why? She was the one who reached out and offered that olive branch, and I've stuck to my end of the bargain, haven't I? I've moved on, focused on other things, but still she keeps clawing me back into this abyss where we end up destroying each other.

What more do I have to do to get her out of my life?

The answer comes to me as clear as a bell, tinkling straight into the center of my brain. That's exactly it. I have to get her out of my life. And my life is mostly online right now. My real life is nonexistent, but online, I have everything—friends, a community, my publishing deal, my social media accounts, which are steadily growing. So what I need to do is to get rid of Haven from my online life. My gaze, previously locked on Mr. Lee, now travels back to the side of the house, where the trash can and recycling bin stand. I'd spotted something else there, stuck to the wall. I wait until Mr. Lee turns his head away from the window before ducking down and scampering back to the side of the house.

There it is. A white box with cables running out of it and into the ground. The fuse box? Or an internet box? Either way, without one or the other, Haven is not getting online. Well, she could use her phone to go online, but this will still put a damper on things.

Part of my mind, the part that's been raised by my parents to keep its head down and stay out of trouble, gibbers, This is crazy! Stop! Don't do it!

But it's overwhelmed by the other part of me. The part that's tired of rolling over and playing dead. I don't let myself hesitate before I grab the cables, then I give the cables a ruthless yank. They're tougher to rip out than I thought, requiring me to plant my feet firmly on the ground and give it two more tugs, but then there's a satisfying click as the cables detach from whatever's in the box, then a buzz of electricity, and for a moment, I wonder if I'm about to get myself killed, but I'm okay, I'm still here, and I'm holding a bunch of ripped-out cables in my hands. Voices are raised from inside the house. Confusion and alarm. I drop the cables, and without another look behind me, I turn toward the street and run as fast as I can.

I'm expecting to be caught, to hear Haven's voice shouting "I see you, Fern!" but nothing comes. No one even steps outside of the house. I'm out of earshot within a few seconds, so I have no idea what they're saying in there, and I don't stop running until I'm inside my car. I slam the door shut, the sound of my gasping, wheezing breath filling the small, enclosed space. Before long, my body heat and hard breathing fogs up my windows. I stay there for a long while, gripping the wheel tight, letting the fogged-up windows cocoon me from the rest of the world. I'm okay. I'm okay. I made it out.

When I finally catch my breath, I take out my phone and check Slack. I go through the channels one by one until I find Haven's name. Her last post was on the #celebrations channel, thanking everyone for congratulating her on the announcement about being a *Good Morning America* book club pick. That was sent just seven minutes ago. I estimate that I've been sitting in the car for about five minutes, so Haven posted this two minutes before I ripped out her cables. Excitement bubbles in my chest. Have I done it? Have I successfully gotten rid of Haven online, even if temporarily? I'm not delusional enough to think that this could be a permanent solution. I would be happy if it just means that Haven is even the slightest bit impeded from posting all the time. If she no longer has internet at home, she'll have to rely on her phone, and maybe she won't be so quick to respond to everything.

I wait a little longer in case Haven makes a new post in the next few minutes, but the channels are regularly getting updated by other members, with no Haven in sight. The dot next to her name remains gray. I've done it. I laugh out loud, the sound unabashedly happy in my car. I sound like a little kid getting an ice cream sundae. Time to get out of here. I turn on the engine and blast the heaters to unfog the windows, then I slowly drive down the street, keeping my headlights off. I watch Haven's house as I drive past, and it's shrouded in complete darkness. I guess what I ripped out was their electric cables and not just their internet cables after all.

Guilt stabs into my stomach. What if by doing that, I harm Mr. or Mrs. Lee?

But how would that harm anyone? Blackouts happen all the time. And if it were a true emergency, then they'd find help. Haven has so many friends and family members in the area. Surely she can turn to any of them for assistance. Unlike me, I think to myself with more than a little self-pity. I have no one to turn to in real life. It's why I need to take things into my own hands.

The adrenaline is still pumping through my veins when I get home. As soon as I get inside, I charge through the living room and rush up the stairs without even saying hi to my parents. I've only been gone for less than an hour, so they are still awake, watching TV in the den. If either of them wonders where I have been, they do not say anything. I lock myself in my bedroom and pace about the small space like a caged animal. I rip my mask off and take a few deep breaths. Did I really do what I just did, or have I imagined it all? Once again, I check the Slack group, and there is still no Haven in sight.

Holy shit. What a feeling. I really did just go out there and take matters into my own hands. I made it happen. I took her out. Another strange laugh burbles out of me. Game on, Haven, I think. How do you like it now? Now that the tables have turned. Is this what it's like to finally realize that you are not just prey at the bottom of the food chain? Learn at last that you, too, have teeth and claws that you can use to defend yourself? Well, it feels amazing.

Even though it is nowhere near my usual bedtime, as soon as the adrenaline drains from my system, I am suddenly left exhausted. I collapse onto my bed, my body covered in a cold sweat, shivering slightly. I think about checking Slack again, but my arms feel too heavy to even lift. I stare up at the ceiling, a small smile still on my lips, and in my mind's eye, I rip those cables out again and again and again. The popcorn ceiling swims above me, and slowly, my eyes drift shut, and I allow myself the sweet escape of sleep.

I wake up with a start, my heart going from a resting state to a sudden gallop, my mouth opening into a shocked O as I take in an aggressive gasp. For just a moment, I'm back in the bushes outside Haven's house, peeping into her front window at her sickly father. Then I blink, and I am back in my room, on my childhood bed, which is way too small for me. I will myself into calming down, doing my breathing exercises and looking around the room and making a mental note of the first five things that I see. These grounding exercises are such a lifesaver. My mouth is dry and fuzzy, as though my tongue has grown a carpet overnight, so before I let myself check my phone or do anything else, I pad into the bathroom and quickly wash up. Then I go back into my room, grab my phone, and go downstairs for some breakfast.

It is not yet 6:00 a.m., so Mom and Dad are still asleep. After last night's adventure, I am famished, so I pour myself a bowl of cereal before finally settling down and opening up the Slack group. I check the channels where Haven would have likely posted if she was able to. #Commiserations is full of the usual whining about publishing-related matters, but nothing about a blackout. #Celebrations is still hopping from Haven's news yesterday. People are still congratulating her. No one else has made an announcement since, and who could blame them? Who would want to go after an announcement as big as Haven's? The other channels are similarly Haven-free.

Victory dances inside me. This is the longest that Haven has been off the Slack group. But maybe it's too early for a victory lap just yet. I go on to Instagram and check her profile, and sure enough, there she is. She posted three stories last night. The first one is a video of her talking into the camera outside of her house.

"You guys won't believe what just happened," she says, clearly distraught. "We just had a blackout. We have a generator, but the reason why we have a blackout is because something—probably a raccoon or something—has ripped out our cables, so we can't get the generator hooked up onto the mains."

The story ends, and the next one begins. "As many of you know," she continues, "my dad is diabetic. And he has been through hell and back because he got COVID, and it was touch and go for a while back there. He is much better now, and he is home, thank god, but obviously he is still very fragile. I am worried to death because his insulin needs to be kept refrigerated, but now with no electricity we are in a bit of a bind. I do have relatives who live nearby, but they are all elderly, and we cannot risk passing COVID on to them. And with my dad having tested positive less than two weeks ago, I have no idea what we are going to do." Her voice breaks then, and she whispers, "Sorry guys, just—"

The cereal in my mouth turns to cement. What have I done? The last thing I wanted to do was to harm anyone, not even Haven. I just wanted to have a break from her online.

The third and final story starts. Haven is now in a well-lit room, beautifully furnished but small. "Thank you, thank you, thank you so much," she says, blinking back her tears. "You guys are magical. So for those of you who are asking me what's going on, a very kind soul has offered us their guesthouse to stay in. So I am here with my mom and dad—" At this, Haven swivels her phone around to show her parents sitting on a sofa in their pajamas. They smile and wave at the camera. "The three of us are going to share this one room, and you know what? It'll be kind of like camping when I was little, right, Mom and Pops?" Mr. and Mrs. Lee laugh and nod. Despite the scary time that they have had, they look peaceful and content, grateful for the way things have turned out in their time of need. And, above all, they are still gazing at Haven with that same adoration, with a confidence that says that they knew she would somehow save the day.

There is a knot in my throat that takes lot of effort for me to swallow down. Inside, my emotions are a maelstrom of anguish. Self-hatred wrestling with everything else that I feel toward Haven—envy, guilt, rage, and a lot of other things that I struggle to identify. How does she do this? How does she land on her feet every single time? If ever I needed a way to prove that Haven is unfairly blessed, then surely this is it. What are the chances that a random internet stranger would see her desperate Instagram posts and offer up their guesthouse to her and her parents, one of whom has tested positive for COVID? But even as I think that, relief courses through me that someone has come in and saved the day, because if something had happened to Mr. Lee because of the stunt I just pulled, how would I continue living with myself?

Even though I have only taken three bites of my cereal, I find that I have lost my appetite completely. I leave the bowl in the sink and go out into the backyard. I plump down onto a lawn chair and mindlessly scroll through Twitter, filling myself up on complete strangers' online rage. Maybe some part of me hoped that comparing my misery to others' might make me feel better, but it doesn't. Again and again, my mind goes back to last night, and my hands twitch with the tug of the electric cables. Shame burns me up from the inside. I need to do something to atone for what I have done. I am a good person, I know this. It is something Aliyah was so adamant I work on, because all Haven's words have carved a certain darkness into me that I hate. I refuse to let myself be defined by what Haven has done to me. Last night, I lost my way. But I will find myself again.

With that in mind, I open up the Slack app, and I create a new chat group. One with everyone on it except for Haven. Then I start composing my message.

Chapter 19

Fern: Hi everyone, I don't know if you have seen Haven's Instagram stories, but something terrible happened to Haven and her parents last night. They had a blackout, and since her dad is diabetic, they had to stay at someone else's house so he can keep his insulin injections refrigerated. They are very fortunate to have found a kind soul who is letting them stay at their guest house, but I am sure that it must be taking an emotional toll on them. I was thinking we could do something to cheer Haven up. What do you guys think?

The replies come in immediately.

Felicity: OMG yes I saw last night and I told Haven if I lived in SoCal, I would totally have opened my doors to them! Her poor dad!

Alicia: I saw that too. I can't even imagine how stressful it must have been to try and find a safe space to stay in especially when her dad has COVID.

Marissa: Seriously! Why does it seem like the worst things happen to the best people?

The familiar feelings of frustration threaten to rise up once more, but I beat them down. So what if everyone is reacting in this irritating exaggerated way? So what if Marissa is referring to Haven as "the best people"? I caused this, and now I need to make reparations.

Fern: Yeah, It's truly awful and so scary.

Felicity: 100%! What are you thinking we could do to cheer her up? I am totally down for anything!

Fern: How about we all pitch in a little money to buy her a really nice gift?

Felicity: I love that idea! She has always wanted a really nice espresso machine. Maybe we can all chip in and buy that for her?

Yuna: I would love to, but money is really tight for me right now, because my husband got laid off and I am only working part time.

Marissa: Yeah, I'm so sorry guys, I would love to join in on this, but we are literally counting every penny right now!

Despair claws at me. I need to do something to make things okay again.

Fern: What about if we all made something for her? Whatever we can do, I guess. Crafts or . . . well, I could probably bake something for her . . . stuff like that? Or a card? How about we get a giant card and we all sign it?

Felicity: Oh I love that idea! I think it might take a while for all of us to pass around a card though . . . there are so many of us

I'm about to give up when inspiration strikes.

Fern: How about this! I'll buy a giant card, and you can all send me a small Post-it note or something like that where you write some well wishes for her and sign it, and I'll paste all of it into the card so it's like a giant collage? And we can set a deadline, say in one week's time? And I'll send it off to her then.

Yuna: I love that idea! I'm in!

Felicity: Yasss me too!

Jenna: Fern! You are such a good person! I'm in

More people chime in to let me know that they're in, and every message that pops up gives me a little rush of endorphins. They all thank me for coming up with such a great idea, and you know what? It really is a great idea. I come away from the conversation feeling—well, not exactly good, but less awful than before. I'm being proactive, see?

I immediately go online to find a giant card. I find the nicest one I can afford and order it with express shipping, then I mull over what else I can do for Haven. After the ordeal she's been through, a card does seem kind of flimsy. I want to give her something more. Oh, right. Felicity mentioned that Haven has been wanting an espresso machine! I look them up online and despair at the cost of them, but then I look on eBay for secondhand ones and find one that's being sold for fifty dollars, so I order that. It looks like it's still in good shape, and the owner says it's less than a year old, so it should be decent.

With all that done, I go back inside and try to form some semblance of a healthy routine. Moving back in with my parents requires some adjustment. When I get inside, they're already up.

"Good morning," Dad says. "I see you've already had breakfast." He looks pointedly at the half-full cereal bowl in the sink. "Maybe pour yourself a smaller portion next time?"

My parents are the antithesis of the stereotypical Asian parents. While all my Asian friends—well, not friends, we've established that I don't have those. To be more accurate, my Asian classmates. While they all complained of super-strict parents who doled out punishments for everything from their weight to their grades to the way they talked, mine have always been the exact opposite. It's like I somehow ended up with repressed English parents or something. They never raise their voices at me. They generally leave me to my own devices. And I know the saying. The grass is greener on the other side, blah, blah, blah, and I should water my own lawn and appreciate what I have, but it's hard to do so when it feels like my side doesn't have anything to water. I just have concrete, stable and unchanging. It is possible that this analogy has gotten away from me.

I force a small smile and say, "Yeah, sorry about the cereal. I just . . ." Then I think, why not? Maybe if I open up a little bit to them, they'll do the same with me. "I just got some bad news when I was eating it, and it made me lose my appetite."

Mom is making some tea as I say this, and her head lifts abruptly, like a meerkat's. "Oh? What bad news?"

I can't possibly tell them that I stole up to Haven's house and ripped out her cables and created an emergency for her and her parents, so I scramble to think up something, and while my mind churns to come up with something, I see the concern on Mom's face begin to ebb.

They really don't give me much time at all before losing interest. "You remember Haven Lee?"

"Oh yes," Mom says. "Very nice girl."

I ignore the stab of jealousy. I wonder if Mom has ever referred to me as "a very nice girl." "Well, her house had a blackout last night, and her dad's insulin needs to be kept cold, so they were in a bit of a bind."

"Oh dear," Dad says, frowning.

"But it's all sorted now. Someone offered them a guesthouse to stay in while they get their power back on."

"Good," Dad says. Mom goes back to stirring her cup of tea. And just like that, the conversation is over. I nod to myself inwardly and grab a glass of water before going back up to my room. I don't know how long I can last here, in this house of ghosts. I can feel myself fading, too, just like my parents, and I need to fight it as much as I can. I don't want to become irrelevant like them. Is that a cruel thought to have about your own parents?

Over the next few days, I wait for the mail every afternoon. Our post usually gets in at around one, so after lunch, I perch myself on a chair in front of the window and scroll through social media while keeping an eye on the mailbox. The mailman arrives, masked, and delivers our mail. I wait for him to drive down the street and around the corner before coming out and taking the envelopes out. I separate out Mom and Dad's letters, put them on the coffee table, and hug the ones addressed to me to my chest before scampering up the stairs, taking the steps two at a time.

I know it's silly to feel the rush of endorphins as I open up the mail because none of it is for me, but I feel it anyway. The letters all contain Post-it Notes for Haven, and I take some pleasure in slicing the envelopes open and sliding the notes out carefully. I read every single one twice over at least, and some of the more heartfelt ones I read over and over, imprinting their words onto my memory. It feels like I'm getting a glimpse into the behind the scenes of Haven's life.

Take this one from Yuna, for example: "Dear Haven, you are so very much like your name, a safe space, a refuge from the madness that is publishing. I'm so grateful to be in your debut group. I'll never forget what you've done for me during those dark days."

I read that one six times over, wondering what the "dark days" Yuna mentioned could possibly be about. I do a search for Yuna's name in the Slack group and rifle through the search results, trying to find any mention of her going through a hard time, but it all seems like the usual publishing roller coaster that most of us go through. I come up with scenario after scenario, each one more imaginative than the last. Maybe she's been having health problems, or maybe it's her family, or oooh, maybe something to do with immigration? Whatever it is isn't actually important, I realize; what's important is the fact that she's somehow gotten close enough to Haven to turn to her for support. There are so many messages that are along the same line as Yuna's, alluding to Haven helping them out in their time of need. How does Haven do it? How is it possible for one person to form so many deep and meaningful relationships with so many people?

I read the notes the way an anthropologist might study ancient ciphers, trying to identify every hidden meaning, reveal every allusion. It feels like if I could just understand the roots of each of these relationships, then maybe I could begin to solve the endless puzzle that is Haven Lee. But I never come close. I paste each and every single message into the giant card, take a photo of the finished piece, and post it to the Slack channel.

Jenna: Oh Fern, it's beautiful! What an amazing idea.

In our private three-person group chat, Jenna says: Fern, I can't believe you did all this for your high school bully. I am so proud of you, girl! Look at you, taking the high road and everything. You are literally inspiring me to be a better person.

Lisa: Omg srsly, Fern! I can't believe you went to all that effort for someone who was mean to you in high school! You are a literal angel!

Their messages warm my heart, even though a small part of me riles at the part where Lisa describes what Haven did to me back at school as merely being "mean." But it's not the time or place for me to try to explain how Haven went out of her way to make life a living hell for me back at school. Like Jenna said, I'm taking the high road. It's good for my mental health to move on and accept that I can't change the past. The thought that I am embracing my future and not letting my bitterness color this time in my life is one I cherish. I may not be a perfect person, but I am working my ass off to become a better one.

The espresso machine arrives, and I have no idea what to expect from espresso machines, really, never having used one myself, but this one definitely looks secondhand. It's got scratches down the side, and the spout has some brown crud caked onto it. I open it up and find more dried-up smudges of coffee—well, I bloody well hope it's coffee. It takes me over half a day to take out the removable components and clean them as well as I can. When I'm done, it's sparkling clean but still looks secondhand. Well, it's the best I can come up with, given I have no income and practically no savings. I take a photo of it and send it to the group Slack.

Fern: I know we said no gifts, but I found a secondhand espresso machine online for really cheap, and I'm happy to gift this to Haven and sign it off as something from all of us

Yuna: WOW. That looks amazing, Fern! You're amazing!

Felicity: She is going to LOVE this!! I can't believe you did that!

Fern: It's nothing. I mean, it was so cheap. It was like fifty bucks, so I feel bad taking all the credit, lol!

Jenna: Nonsense! You should definitely take all the credit, you deserve it! And so what if it's fifty bucks now? I just googled it and the original price is one thousand and two hundred dollars. That's insane. You did well, friend! I'm so proud of you 🖤

Tears actually fill my eyes at this. I can't remember the last time someone told me they're proud of me. Oh wait, I can, actually. It was Aliyah, during our last session. She said to me, "Fern, you've come such a long way from the girl who walked in here a year ago. I'm so proud of all the work you've done to become the person you are today." That was about six years ago. I reread Jenna's message and memorize every word. I know I will remember this moment until I'm old and senile and I've forgotten everything else, including my own name, but I will still remember the moment my friend told me she's proud of me.

Fern: Thank you so much you guys. I couldn't have done this without all of your help. I'm going to bake some goodies for Haven as well and then tomorrow morning I will deliver everything to her house. I'm so excited for her to finally get this hamper!

Felicity: Ahh! I can't wait for her to get it! She's going to FLIP OUT!

Yuna: You're going to hand-deliver it to her? How do you know where she lives?

The joy that's been dancing in my chest stutters to a standstill, but only for a moment. I quickly recover.

> **Fern:** I do, yes. We actually went to the same high school and it's not a big school so everyone kind of knew each other.

> **Yuna:** Oh right! I forgot that you guys went to the same high school. That's so WILD!

I wish I could tell them all what it was really like going to the same high school as Haven, but it's not like I could say: Actually, she was my high school bully, lol!

> **Fern:** We were never close, but everyone knew Haven back at school. Anyway, her house isn't too far away from mine and I don't really want to go to the post office right now because pandemic etc, so yeah, I'll just drop it off tomorrow morning. It's not a big deal at all!

> **Jenna:** You are an ANGEL

> **Felicity:** Agreed!

Everyone else quickly chimes in, telling me how good I am and how lucky Haven is to have me as a friend. If I said I didn't enjoy all this attention, I would be lying. But of course part of me writhes with guilt. I don't have to be reminded that the whole reason I'm doing all this is to atone for my sins. But then I remind myself that the trouble is over now.

In the end, Haven and her parents only had to stay at that guesthouse for two days before their cables were fixed. And here, once more, it was her Instagram following that came to her rescue. There'd been a one-month-long wait list for an electrician, and she had despaired to her followers. Then one of them DMed her and told her that her brother's friend was an electrician and he was willing to drive all the way from Azusa to San Marino to try to fix it for her. He did so, and apparently refused any forms of financial compensation, merely telling Haven "I've been feeling so trapped and useless this entire pandemic. I'm happy I finally have the chance to help someone." And that is how, a mere two days after I ripped out Haven's electric cables, Haven and her parents were back home, safe and sound.

Thank god. I really couldn't have lived with myself had it taken any longer. I hadn't meant for it to cause them so much trouble, and I'm relieved that it's now fixed. And yet . . . A secret feeling worms its way deep in my guts. More envy that once again, Haven has managed to glide over the potholes of life. She needed a place to stay, and boom, one fell right into her lap. She needed an electrician, and once again, it simply fell like a ripe apple, warm and sweet, into her palm. As soon as this feeling crawls into existence, I squash it, feeling its insides squirt out as I flatten it ruthlessly. I can't afford to allow myself the luxury of envy. Look what happened the last time I did. No, I am determined to be good from now on. There is room only for clean thoughts in my head.

I spend the rest of the day baking up a storm. Doughlores happily devotes parts of herself to my creations, and I take pleasure in using her because I know that sourdough is especially good for diabetics. This is as much for Mr. Lee as it is for Haven. I bake whole-grain sourdough loaves, sourdough muffins sweetened with agave, sourdough bagels, and even sourdough cinnamon rolls. By the time I'm done, my back is stiff, and my legs are threatening to give out under me.

"Oh my," Dad says, "this is a lot of bread. How are we going to finish it all before it goes bad?"

"You don't have to worry about that. This is for Haven and her parents."

"Oh," Dad says, eyebrows raised with apparent surprise. I don't expect him to ask me anything else, but then he says, "Haven Lee? From school?"

"Yep." I put my head down and focus my gaze on the bagels, which I'm putting away into pretty cardboard containers I'd bought for this very purpose.

"Are things well?"

"Yeah. She's just gone through a bit of an ordeal, that's all. I told you about the blackout, right?"

"Of course. And you are baking all this to make her feel better," he says.

I'm not sure if that was said as a question or a statement, so I don't say anything.

"Can I have one?" he says.

"Yes, of course." I pick out a blueberry bagel and hand it to him.

He studies it carefully, holding it close enough to his face that his eyes cross a little bit.

"Dad, you are being so weird." I laugh.

"Mm. It smells wonderful."

"Tastes even better."

He takes a bite and chews methodically, and I wonder what it was that made our relationship so clinical. Why there is so little warmth in our family. The question coats my tongue, and I almost spit it out. But then he swallows, and the moment passes, and when he looks at me again, it's with that same bland expression that he always wears. The familiar disinterest takes over his expression, and I know that his walls have crashed back into place. "It's delicious," he says in the pleasant, removed tone of voice one might use to say "It's raining outside."

"Cool. I'm glad you like it." He turns and leaves the kitchen, still working his way through the bagel, and I shrug off our strange exchange and go back to packing everything up.

When all the goodies are packed up nicely, I place everything—the espresso machine and the food—into a big box I've ordered especially for this. Then I place the huge card on top of it, take several pictures of the whole thing, and tape the box shut. I go to sleep with a smile on my face that night. I've undertaken such a huge task, and now I'm in the home stretch.

Tomorrow, I will deliver it to Haven, and everything will be put right, and I won't have to live with this guilt slowly nibbling away at me anymore.

The whole time I drive to Haven's, I practice what I will say to her. "Hi, Haven. You look well. Here's something from all of us to you." "Hey. The other debuts and I put something together to show you how much we appreciate you." "Hi, here you go, I hope you enjoy it."

None of it feels quite right. The thing is, the thought of seeing Haven in person after all these years is making my entire body do very uncomfortable things. My palms are constantly sweaty no matter how many times I wipe them on my jeans, my mouth is dry despite the sips of water I continually take, and my heart jumps back and forth between a somewhat normal rate and a sudden sprint, which in turn is beginning to make my head pound. I get to Haven's street and park, then I sit in my car for a long while, just staring out at her house. I see myself again on that night, creeping along the side of her house, my hands wrapping around those cables, my entire body jerking back as I rip them out. The memory of it chokes me. I clear my throat and shake my head. Doesn't matter; what's done is done. The important thing is I'm putting things right.

"Come on, Fern. Be brave," I say out loud. I don't let myself wait another minute longer before I jump out of the car. I take the box out from the back seat. It's heavy, reminding me of the many days I had to struggle under the weight of Annette's photography equipment. I walk slowly across the street toward Haven's house, and every step I take, I swear my body fights back with increasing ferocity. Somehow, though, I manage to make it to Haven's front step. I so badly want to drop the box off and run away before anyone can see me, but instead, I ring the doorbell.

The one who opens it is Mrs. Lee. She says, "Oh! I forgot my mask! Hang on, dear." She shuts the door and reopens it a minute later, masked. "Sorry about that. I'm still not used to this." She laughs, the corners of her eyes crinkling, and despite the mask, I can sense the warmth of her smile, and it's so sweet I could just die.

"No, of course, no worries. Um, I'm here to deliver something for Haven. I'll just—"

"Oh! Well, you're in luck because she's right here." Before I can stop her, Mrs. Lee turns around and calls out loudly, "Haveyyy! There's someone here with a present for you." She winks at me and says, "I'm going to get you a snack." Again, she doesn't wait for a response before rushing back into the house.

I want to leave right now. If I just dropped the box on their doorstep and then ran, I could probably make it to the car before Haven gets to the—

"Fern?"

I look up, and there she is. My nemesis in the flesh. Haven Lee. Haven Lee, whom I haven't seen in person for so many years. Haven Lee, who manages to recognize me even though I have a mask on. I try to say a casual hello, but the word catches in my throat, refusing to come out, and I end up hacking and coughing. Haven takes a small step away from me, and I don't blame her. I mean, there's a pandemic for god's sake, and here I am, hacking up a lung like my entire system is overwhelmed by the virus. It's a wonder, in fact, that Haven doesn't just shut the door in my face. Instead, she says, "Are you okay?" and there is genuine concern in her voice. She turns her back on me and calls out, "Ma, can you get a glass of water, please?"

I shake my head desperately, trying to tell her it's fine, I'm okay, I don't have COVID, I just choked on my own words, that's all. But I'm still riddled with coughs. Mrs. Lee hurries to us, carrying a glass of water, and I set the box down and accept it gratefully. I turn slightly so they won't see me gulping down the water, and thank god, when I am done with the glass, the coughing fit has passed. I replace my mask before turning back to face them and handing the glass over to Mrs. Lee.

"I'm so sorry," I croak. After all that coughing, my voice now sounds like someone with a three-pack-a-day habit.

"Let me know if you need anything else," Mrs. Lee says, her face creased with genuine concern. Then she leaves, but as she does, I catch her giving Haven's arm an affectionate squeeze. It's something that's always struck me, the way Haven and her parents can't seem to stop touching each other. They're always patting each other on the shoulder or the arm. When they walk, Haven links her arm through her parents' like she is all of five years old, and it's a bond I want to roll my eyes at, but I know that deep down inside I would kill to have something approaching that with my own parents.

And now it's just me and Haven again. The sight of her, the nearness of her, makes everything rush back. Dani's presence, which I have pushed away for so long, comes back to haunt me. I can practically see Dani behind Haven, smiling, eager to tell Haven a funny story. I blink, and Dani's ghost is gone. "Um, thank you for—uh, the water," I say hoarsely.

"Of course," Haven says. She looks at me with a world of uncertainty in her eyes. "I didn't know you were back in LA. You moved to New York right after college, right?"

What a strange feeling, to find out that Haven Lee knows these things about me. "Yeah. I had to move back because . . ." The truth almost slips out of me like an eel. Because I got fired and I spent all my savings on a publicist so I can no longer afford rent. But I catch it just in time. I can't tell her the truth. Even now, after all this time, I don't want to look bad in front of Haven Lee. "Um, my mom caught COVID." The lie slips out of me like an eel, slimy and grotesque, and now it's too late to take it back.

Haven's eyes widen. "Oh no! How is she now? I'm so sorry to hear that."

"She's fine," I say quickly.

Haven places a palm on her chest and says, "Oh good. I'm so glad she's okay. I actually moved back for the same exact reason. My dad got COVID, too, and it was really scary." She takes a deep breath, hugging herself. "We thought we were going to lose him at one point. I'm glad both our parents pulled through."

I nod, wanting to end this as quickly as I can. I bend down and pick up the box. "Um, anyway, the other debuts and I heard about the thing with your electricity going out and how you guys had to look for a place to stay in the middle of the night and all that . . . and we wanted to put together something for you and your family." I hand the box to her, and for a moment, she hesitates, and I wonder if she's going to reject it. But then she gives me a small smile and takes it.

"Oh wow, it's heavy," she says.

"Yeah. Anyway, well, it's from all of us, so." There doesn't seem to be anything left to say, so I stuff my hands in my pockets. "Enjoy."

"Thank you for hand delivering it," Haven says. "You really didn't have to."

"It's fine. Don't think about it." I take a step back, give a quick wave, and leave her house. My breath comes out in one long whoosh. For the first few minutes, my emotions are a messy swirl in my mind. I'm not sure if I feel good or bad; mostly I just feel jittery and like I need a good laugh or a good cry or some way to release all this frenetic energy inside me. But as I drive away from Haven's, the tension uncoils, and I'm able to remind myself to breathe. I did it. I put the whole thing together from start to finish, and I personally saw to it that she received everything. I wanted to make amends, and I did. And now I can finally move on and pretend that this whole shit show never happened at all.

Chapter 20

The thing about obsessions is they rarely ever end when we want them to. I should've known that from all that time I spent in therapy. Aliyah often had to remind me, "Fern, healing is a marathon. It's not like flicking a light switch. Even with medication, we don't have a magic pill that you can take which will heal you quickly. Everything takes time, so be kind to yourself and take every day one step at a time."

When I drove away from Haven's house earlier this morning, I thought foolishly that that would be it. I'd closed the book, and I would be able to go on and mind my own business and live my own life. But the moment I walk back inside my parents' house, I see Mom and Dad sitting at the dining table eating. They're deep in conversation about something, but then they hear my footsteps, and abruptly, they stop talking. They turn to face me, and what strikes me is the complete lack of affection in their faces. Their coldness and sterility are made even more apparent now, after I've experienced Mrs. Lee's kindness a mere half hour ago.

"Fern," Mom says, "would you like some lunch?" Her voice is so even, like she's a waiter asking me what I'd like to order.

I open my mouth to say yes, I'm starving actually, but the thought of having to spend any time at the table with them and listen to the sounds of our mouths chewing in the tense silence is too much. "No." I turn around and go back outside. I feel strange, like everything around me has become fuzzy, almost unreal. Aliyah once observed that I have a habit of slipping through the cracks in reality and falling into a world of my own. She taught me to do grounding exercises to keep me firmly tethered in the present. I try to do them now, but still I feel my grasp on reality swimming away.

The next few moments are blips with time skips. Blip. I'm in my car. Blip. I'm driving. Blip. Haven's street comes into view. Blip. I've parked across the street, a few houses down, and I'm just gazing out of the window.

I give myself a small shake to bring me back to the present. What are you doing? I ask myself. Stop this.

Stop what? I'm not doing anything. I'm just sitting here. And it's different from the other night. I'm not upset at all. I'm not here to rip out her cables again, that's for sure. In fact, I'm the opposite of upset. I'm Zen. I'm a river of calm, floating peacefully by. I just wanted to come back and sit here and savor the aura of Haven's family, that's all. I'm not even going to come out of my car, I promise myself.

Having won the argument against myself, I take out my phone and open up Slack. Haven has posted in the #celebrations channel.

> **Haven:** OH MY GOSH YOU FOLKS ARE THE BEST!!!!!! 😭 I CAN'T BELIEVE YOU DID THIS!!! I DO NOT DESERVE YOU!!!

Underneath that is a photo of Haven and her parents posing with the giant card, the espresso machine, and the baked goods. People have already started replying.

> **Felicity:** Haven!! Don't be silly, of course you deserve this and more!! We wanted to cheer you guys up after the nightmare you've had to endure!

> **Lisa:** Yes, we're so glad you're all home and safe!!

Jenna: So glad you received it! Just FYI, Fern was the one who came up with the idea and put everything together. She even bought the espresso machine and baked everything. The rest of us just sent her the Post-It notes, lol!

Oh, Jenna. She can't help, even now, but to be on my side. She is a true friend, someone who goes out of her way to make me look good. Smiling, I chime in.

Fern: Felicity was the one who came up with the idea of getting you an espresso machine, so I can't take credit for it!

Felicity: Oh I only suggested it, Fern was the one who actually went and bought one. With her own money too. Fern you are so wonderful. I love this so much, women supporting other women!!

Haven: Oh wow, you really shouldn't have, Fern. Thank you so much! ❤ This is truly too wonderful for words. And all of the breads you baked smell sooo delicious. I'm actually toasting up a few slices right now to share with my mom and dad! They're so grateful too. THANK YOU AGAIN EVERYONE ❤

Pleasure courses through me like golden sunlight washing over me, warming me up from the core to the surface. It's so true what they say, that giving meaningful gifts to others is so much more rewarding than spending money on yourself. Look at me, I think. I wanted to be a good person, and so I became one. I feel so utterly at peace right now. With a happy sigh, I put my hand on the steering wheel and am about to start up the car when Haven's side door opens. I freeze, not wanting to make any movement that might attract attention. I'm parked far away enough that I'm pretty sure she wouldn't notice me, but I'm not taking any chances right now. I'm staying put until she's gone back inside.

Haven comes out with her arms full. I squint, craning my neck toward the window, and when I see what she's carrying, I actually go, "Huh?" out loud. Because she's carrying a bunch of familiar-looking cardboard boxes. Boxes that I ordered online and folded into shape with my own two hands. Boxes that are filled with my breads. As I watch, she opens up her trash and recycling bins, then empties the boxes one by one into the trash. When she's done, she stomps on the boxes, flattening them, and shoves them into the recycling. Then she wipes her hands on her pants and walks back into the house, closing the door tight behind her.

My hands strangle the steering wheel. Did I just imagine it? I must have, because what I have just seen makes no sense whatsoever. Why would Haven do this? She thanked me so warmly in person and so profusely online only to turn around and throw all my hard work in the literal trash can? No. It must be a mistake. The boxes I bought were plain brown boxes, so I could've easily mixed them up with some other nondescript brown boxes. Maybe she ordered stuff online, and it arrived spoiled or something. I sit there for a long while, tapping my fingernails against the steering wheel in a rapid staccato. I have to check. I have to know.

I get out of the car, and, after one quick look around me, I stride toward Haven's house. If she were to come out right now and see me, I'll just say that I came back because I'd mistakenly given her a box of bagels I'd baked for a different friend of mine. But no one comes out of the house. In fact, I notice that the front curtains are down, so I have no idea what's going on inside. I jog the rest of the way to the bins and lift the lid off the trash can. And sure enough, inside it, sitting atop plastic bags of trash, is a pile of freshly baked bread.

Even though I'd known that what Haven was throwing away had to have been my breads, seeing them now, sitting in a sad pile like this, is still a gut punch. Or a chest punch, maybe, because I feel winded. It takes a surprising amount of effort for me to draw breath. The bagels are there, and the sourdough loaf and the cinnamon rolls, which didn't survive their tumble and have fallen apart. For a moment, I have an out-of-body experience. I watch over my shoulder as I take out my phone and open the camera app. I take several photos of the breads, then I stalk off back to my car. I watch myself drive home at a sensible speed, my face betraying no emotion. I go up to my room after saying a cursory greeting to my parents, then I lie down on my bed and stare up at the popcorn ceiling again.

That's when I slam back into my body. I gasp out loud as the emotions come crashing over me. What a painfully familiar feeling this is. I was here before, years ago, as a kid, helpless as Haven wrenched the tray of cinnamon rolls I'd baked for the school's bake sale out of my hands and tipped the whole thing onto the floor. I simply stood there, frozen, not doing anything. She stomped one foot on a bun, then again and again, until no roll survived. Nothing but a mess of trampled maple frosting and crumbs. And she'd hissed, "No one wants to eat your food, you freak." Before shoving me with such vehemence that I fell on my ass. Then she whirled around and sauntered away, as though she couldn't even be bothered to make a quick getaway, as though it didn't matter to her whether she got caught or not, because even back then, Haven knew she was untouchable.

But this is different. That was for a bake sale. This was for Haven. An olive branch, just for her. Why would she throw it away? How is it possible for one person to hold on to all this hate toward me? Tears spring into my eyes, and I curl up into a fetal position, hiding my face from the light. I weep into my bed, muffling the sobs with my pillow. I sob for myself, for all those hours I just spent in the kitchen, baking for Haven. I sob for my past self, that harmless little kid who for whatever reason found herself within Haven's crosshairs.

When I'm done crying, I feel spent, like my insides have all been wrung out and there's nothing left. I take a long, hot shower, standing under the scalding spray and imagining the water washing all my troubles away. I feel slightly better afterward, but as I towel myself dry, I catch sight of my reflection, and I stop. I look closer, studying my features. I've never been accused of being beautiful. Not like Haven, that's for sure. At best, I can be described as nondescript. I wouldn't call myself ugly, but neither do I have any distinct features that would make me memorable. I should've been a spy. I would've made a great one. Nobody would even remember my presence. The thought is so ridiculous it makes me laugh, a strange, warped sound. I stop laughing abruptly and glare once more at my reflection. Stupid bitch, I think. Stupid cowardly bitch. Why did you have to roll over and expose your soft, vulnerable belly? Especially after all the shit she's done to you. Do you have so little regard for yourself? Have some fucking self-respect. Are you going to just sit there and let Haven trample over you like you did back in school? Did you forget how it ended? How Dani lost her life because of it?

"No," I whisper.

Good, my reflection says. Then you know what you need to do.

"Yes." I straighten up, pulling my shoulders back. My naked body is small but wiry. I was never built to be a fighter, but what I've just realized is I was built to be a skirmisher. Pop up quick, do some damage, and run away to live and fight another day. I'm no warrior, and that's okay. I finish drying myself off, wrap the towel around myself, and walk back into my bedroom. I lock the door and let the towel fall onto the floor. I stand in front of my mirror, naked, and stretch my lips into a smile. I may not be a looker, but I have a nice smile. Sincere and shy, it makes me look innocent.

I hold it there while I reach for my phone and open Slack. I go onto the channel that I'd created when I thought of doing something nice for Haven, the one that has everybody except for Haven in it. I scroll up for a while, skimming through our past messages. Now that the gift is done, the channel is pretty much dead. But maybe it's time to revive it.

No. It's too forward if it comes from me. Instead, I switch over to the private chat I have with Lisa and Jenna.

Fern: Hey guys? Can I just vent here for a second?

Lisa: Umm, ALWAYS! You don't have to ask!

Jenna: Yeah, what's up?

Fern: Sooo not long after I gave Haven that hamper, I was sitting in my car, you know, just preparing to drive home, when I noticed Haven coming outside of her house. She was carrying all these boxes that looked rly familiar to me so I kind of waited to see what she was doing with them. I thought maybe I'd given her too much baked goods and she was gonna give some to the neighbors . . .

Jenna: Oh no. Tell me she didn't do anything bad??

Fern: Well.

I attach the photos I took earlier of the breads in the trash and hold my breath as the pictures load. When they finally do, the reactions are as explosive as I'd hoped.

Jenna: WHAT THE FUCK???

Lisa: Is that the trash can??? Wait, what's going on???

Fern: Yeah. She threw away all of the bread that I'd baked for her. Literally, every single one of them. 😭

Jenna: WHAT!! Why the hell would she do that??

Lisa: That is so wrong, omg. I mean, especially considering how many people are struggling to make ends meet right now?? To throw away food like this is DISGUSTING.

Jenna: And let's not forget the amount of effort you've put into it. I mean, my god, you even made cinnamon rolls from scratch! That is so much bread you gave her, it must've taken you the entire day

Fern: It did, yeah. I spent all of yesterday on them. I used my sourdough starter because I read that sourdough is good for diabetics and I thought maybe her dad could enjoy them . . .

Lisa: This is crazy!! I don't understand it. Are you sure they're your breads, Fern? Could they be like, Haven had a lot of stale bread lying around and so when she got your gift she was like, "Oh, I should throw all this old stuff away to make room for Fern's stuff!"

Oh geez. Come on, Lisa, I groan inwardly. Can't you not switch back and forth between teams for once in your life? Have some loyalty, for god's sake.

Fern: No, these are the ones I made her. I recognize them. Hard not to when I spent the whole day making them

Jenna: Oh god. This is SO wrong! We should confront her about it

Fern: Yeah . . . IDK though, I'm scared of her. You know, after the whole thing back in school . . . you guys don't know how mean she can be. I watched her dump all this freshly baked bread into the trash bin and then stomp on the cardboard boxes like she was truly enraged. It was so disturbing. I don't think I want to confront her. It'll just blow up into a whole thing

Lisa: It feels so wrong not to say anything though

Jenna: Yeah!

Fern: I know. But for myself, it's enough knowing that you guys know the truth about Haven, at least. That I'm not just the crazy one making things up

Jenna: You are definitely not the crazy one! My god, Fern. She's really messed you up, hasn't she? Okay, how about this: we don't need to confront her because like you said, we have no idea what she might do, but we can't just keep this to ourselves. I'm going to tell Marissa. She and I DM quite a bit and I think she's trustworthy

Lisa: Ohhh that's a good idea! Yeah, spread it to the others over DMs so everyone knows the truth about Haven!

Fern: Hmm . . . I guess . . . but I don't want this to be just us gossiping about her. That doesn't feel right to me. I don't wanna gossip

Lisa: It's not gossiping! Omg Fern! It's more like warning people away from her because she is a freaking snake

Jenna: Lisa's right. I think we have a responsibility to tell the others the truth so that they can make an informed decision about whether they want to remain friendly with Haven or whatever. I mean, if the tables were turned and I were the rest of the group, I'd want to be told. I wouldn't want to continue interacting with Haven thinking she's a good person when there's actual hard evidence showing she's not

Fern: You're right. I'm just so scared about what she'll do to me

Lisa: Well, we don't have to tell them that you took the photos

Fern: Kind of obvious since I'm the one who lives nearby and I'm the one who delivered the box in person . . .

Lisa: Okay, how about we just tell them that we found out through some anonymous source that Haven threw out the gifts?

It seems obvious to me who the "anonymous source" would be (me), but I can't think of another way of telling everyone else what Haven did without outing me as the informant. I weigh out the pros and cons and decide that Haven has way more to lose than I do in this situation.

Fern: Okay. And I guess it's fine if they know I was the one who took the pictures. I'm not the one with anything to hide here

Jenna: YES, there you go, Fern! Now you're making sense! You have nothing to be afraid of! You're not the one who did terrible shit, she is! Okay, I'm gonna go tell people

Lisa: Me too. Big hugs, Fern! This is so shitty and none of it is your fault, okay??

As I watch my two friends go into battle for me, I feel a sense of security that I never felt before. They really do have my back, and what an incredible feeling that is. I sigh, dropping my phone onto my vanity, and finally root around in my closet for a pair of pajamas to wear. Once dressed, I wrap my arms around myself, feeling cocooned and safe. It's going to be okay. I have just made damn sure of it.

Chapter 21

Age Eighteen

You know what's funny? Public speaking. Even just the thought alone is enough to make my heart skip a couple of beats (and not in a good way). But I also, in a very weird way, am anticipating it. This morning, as I get dressed for school, I keep envisioning myself standing in front of my entire class, giving my presentation, and I am torn between horror and excitement. Which is really freaking weird, right? But the thing is, this presentation is special. About a month back, we were asked to prepare a presentation on any topic we were interested in. And I really mean any topic. Like, one boy decided to do a presentation on *World of Warcraft*. Actually, more than one boy did, I think. Anyway, doesn't matter. I decided to do a presentation on baking. I can't even count the number of hours I spent on my slideshow. I put in tons of photos of the things I've baked in the past, and I talked about food science and nutrition and how important they are. And as I polished my slideshow, I realized that I was actually proud of my work, and I couldn't wait to share this part of me with everyone else. To show them that there's more to me than just loser Fern.

Everyone else has put in a lot of effort too; I can tell because like me, they're all dressed extra nicely today. When the class begins, Ms. Lund brings her hands together and says, with a bright smile, "All right! I've been looking forward to this for weeks now. Who'd like to go first?"

To nobody's surprise, Haven raises her hand. I look down at my lap to avoid the temptation of rolling my eyes as she struts to the front of the classroom. When she announces that her topic of choice is Facebook, though, I can't hold back the eye roll. Luckily, my face is still lowered, so no one catches it. I think.

But as Haven goes into her presentation, I have to admit that I'm impressed. It's obvious that she's done a ton of research on the company and its history and all the twists and turns that it had to go through to become what it is today. She even goes into some shady things that the company has done to stay ahead of their competition. It's a much more complex talk than I expected, and when she finishes, everyone applauds and cheers like she's just scored a touchdown.

No way in hell I'm going to follow that, so I sink into my seat as Ms. Lund asks who'd like to go next. Aaron Lambert is next to volunteer, then Meera Patel, then another student, and another. I keep working myself up to raise my hand next, but each time Ms. Lund asks who'd like to go, my anxiety overcomes me, and my hand refuses to move. And now there's no one left to go next but me.

Everyone's eyes land on me. I can practically feel their gazes crawling across my skin like little insects.

"And last but not least," Ms. Lund says, gesturing at me to come up to the front.

As I make my way out of my seat and to the front of the classroom, my chest throbs with actual pain, that's how hard my heart is thumping. You've got this, I tell myself. You've worked so hard on it, and it's genuinely good.

With a trembling hand, I find my file on the class laptop and open it. I hit play and stand to face the sea of eyes. "Um, my topic is, uh, baking."

Take a deep breath, I tell myself. Then I launch into the introduction. My voice is wobbly to begin with, peppered with *um*s and *ah*s, but as I tell everyone how much I love baking and how my love for it has fueled my research into food science, I gain more confidence. Dani is giving me a small smile, and Ms. Lund is nodding at me, her eyes bright with encouragement, and most of the class seems to be genuinely interested in what I have to say. Warmth fills my chest. I'm doing it. I'm sharing part of me with them, and they're seeing me for the first time as something more than just a loser for them to make fun of.

As I click to slide number three, I say, "And here I am, making my very first cake."

There's a pause, then the entire room erupts into shrieking laughter. I stand there, gaping at them, my brain struggling to understand what's happening. Ms. Lund's expression has gone from kind encouragement to anger. I turn around and there, cast on the screen, instead of a photo of twelve-year-old me holding up a vanilla cupcake, is a photo of an elephant shitting.

All the blood drains from my head.

"Is this a joke?" Ms. Lund snaps, glaring at me.

"No!" I cry. "I didn't—it's not supposed to be—" My fingers scramble across the keyboard, hitting next, but it just gets worse. Instead of a photo of the basic ingredients needed to bake a muffin, the next slide shows a photo of a horse shitting. The class laughs harder. I click next frantically, and more photos of various animals shitting show up on the screen.

"You need to come to my office after school," Ms. Lund says to me.

By now, I'm openly sobbing, my nose running. I must look disgusting. I don't have any tissues, so I swipe at my nose with the back of my hand, and I can't help but notice how demurely Haven is giggling, covering her mouth with a manicured hand. It's too much. No heart is strong enough to withstand such humiliation. I don't even ask for permission before darting out of the classroom.

Thankfully, since we're in the middle of class, the bathroom is empty. I lean over the sink, still crying, and splash some cold water onto my face. I don't know how I can possibly survive this. Fantasies about moving away to some foreign country flit through my mind.

The door opens and I freeze, mid-sob. Why didn't I think to hide in one of the cubicles? I glance up in the mirror, and through the reflection, I see that it's Dani. She approaches me slowly, gnawing on her bottom lip as she does so.

"Hey," she says softly. "You okay?"

I can't help it. A bitter snort comes out of me. "No," I say.

"I'm sorry," Dani says. She looks down at her hands. "I didn't think . . ."

There's a strange note in her voice that catches my attention. It takes me a moment to recognize it. Guilt. Dani is guilty.

"Did you know she was going to do this?" I say, my voice hushed with disbelief.

"No!" Dani cries. "I just—well, she mentioned something, but I thought it was just her joking, messing around—"

"She never just messes around," I snap. "Not when it comes to me." The anger in my voice takes me aback, and it's only then that I realize how resentful I feel toward Dani. All these years, she's chosen Haven over me. She was my only friend, and she turned her back on me.

"I just wish you two could be friends," Dani says.

I can't even stomach the sight of her now. Her endless insistence that Haven and I could be friends, her refusal to accept the ugly truth. She only says that to alleviate her own guilt, not because she actually cares about me as a friend.

I pour all my venom into my response. Through gritted teeth, I hiss, "You know what a shit person Haven is, and you keep wanting me to be her friend. I may not have friends, but at least I still have my integrity."

Chapter 22

You know what I didn't see coming? I did not see Felicity being the one to take Haven down. But hey, I'm not complaining. There's a certain poetic justice in having Haven's bestie be the one who kneecaps her in the end. It all starts in the #celebrations channel later that evening.

> **Felicity:** Hey @Haven, did you have a chance to try the bread that we gave you yet?

I have to smile at the word *we*. As far as I know, Felicity, only one of us made the bread, but hey, I'm not one to split hairs.

> **Haven:** Oh, yes! I had a slice of the sourdough and split a cinnamon roll with my mom. My dad had the sourdough and about an hour later I caught him sneaking half a bagel. Deeelicious. Best things I've eaten in a long while. Fern, you should open a bakery!

> **Felicity:** Huh. That's so weird

> **Marissa:** Yeah, lol, I'd say

> **Haven:** What?

Felicity: Well, I thought maybe they tasted really bad or something, which is why you threw all of them away. But apparently you think they're the best pastries you've ever had, sooo IDK, haha!

Jenna: Yeah, it's confusing for sure, lol

Marissa: Maybe she threw it away because they were so delicious? I once made this banana chocolate cake that was so good I had to throw it away because otherwise I would eat the entire thing, not even exaggerating

Oh my god. These bitches are awful, and I love it. I can't take my eyes off their catty, sharply pointed messages. It's exhilarating to be sitting here, reading these mean messages and to know that for once, I am not the recipient here. I'm familiar with these kinds of messages, but usually they're aimed at me. There is nothing meaner than girls in middle school. They don't bully—they wage psychological warfare. And years of this type of insidious meanness have left me broken, warped. But now, I am realizing that when you're not on the receiving end, this is perfectly fine behavior. Fun, even. How do you like it, Haven, now that the tables have turned?

Haven: I don't understand

Felicity: What is it that you don't understand?

Oof, look at Felicity turning on her, no holds barred. I guess maybe she feels that as Haven's proclaimed bestie, she has to go the extra mile to prove that she wasn't in cahoots with her.

Haven: I mean, IDK, you guys are sounding pretty crazy

Felicity: Whoa, that is such an ableist term. You really shouldn't use "crazy" like that. Especially when we've got proof that you threw the bread away

Felicity then posts one of my photos, clearly showing my hard work in the bin.

Yuna: I'd say that's pretty hard evidence alright. Look, Haven, I don't like what's going on here. I don't like feeling like we're ganging up on you or whatever. It feels . . . not great. Can you just give us a reasonable explanation and we can move on from this?

Jenna: What the hell would count as a "reasonable explanation"?? There is so much wrong that happened here, I don't even know where to begin! I mean, she lied to all of us, for one thing. She disrespected Fern's hard work, for another. She wasted food when there's an actual pandemic going on and people out there dying from starvation because they got laid off?

Felicity: Yeah, I hate to say it, but I don't think there's any possible explanation for this. It's just bullshit. I think you owe all of us an apology, especially Fern

When is Haven going to reply? I wonder. I can almost see her sitting behind her computer screen, gnawing on her lower lip, her hands shaking—maybe every part of her body is shaking, why not—and her face would be white with fury at the realization that I, Fern Huang, was the one who caught her out. And with every moment that ticks by without an answer from Haven, more replies pour in. And they are all angry.

> **Marissa:** Yeah, I'm pretty freaking disappointed. I thought our batch would be the first one to be drama free, lol! I guess that was a pretty stupid thing to think, huh?
>
> **Alicia:** I mean, I think given we're all grown adults, it's not unreasonable to hope for a drama-free debut group. I didn't think it would be Haven, though. That's kind of a kick in the balls
>
> **Felicity:** Well, I was her friend, so I do feel pretty effin' stupid right now
>
> **Alicia:** Omg, Felicity, it's not on you at all! She had us all fooled!
>
> **Yuna:** Yeah.

Come on, Haven, ticktock, I think. Look at this, they're already talking about her like she's not even here. She really needs to come up with something good to salvage her name. But then, as I think that, Haven's name disappears from the members list. One second it was there, the next second, it's gone.

> **Lisa:** I think she just ragequit the Slack group
>
> **Jenna:** Good riddance! We don't need fake people like her in here. Publishing is stressful enough as it is

Felicity: Yeah. God, I really didn't know what she was like. I can't believe it. I feel awful. I'm sorry, Fern

Fern: Oh my gosh please don't blame yourself! This has nothing to do with you! She had us all fooled

Jenna: Well, I'm glad she's no longer here. It only takes one rotten egg to make the whole place stink. This group will be much healthier without someone like Haven in it

And just like that, I have defeated Haven Lee. At long last. I release my breath in an incredulous huff as more and more messages pop up, agreeing with Jenna that it was for the best. A couple of people even said that they'd gotten bad vibes from Haven all along. I narrow my eyes at them, wondering how real that is or if they're just jumping on the bandwagon now. I guess it's impossible to tell what's what.

When the messages start petering off and branching into other topics, I switch over to Twitter. I have a good feeling about this. Twitter is where publishing really takes its gloves off, and I wasn't wrong. Already, my fellow debuts are subtweeting the entire thing.

@FelicityLynn: You think you know someone and then next thing you know they turn out to be a pathological liar who's been gaslighting everyone in your debut group for ages. #LiveAndLearn

Twelve likes and two comments, both of them going, Omg what happened? 👀

@JennaWritesBooks: The thing about debut groups is, at the end of the day, it's just a bunch of strangers

> thrown together bc we happen to have the same debut year. #SnakeInTheGrass

Seventeen likes and three comments, again asking what happened.

There are more subtweets from the other debuts, but what's even more delicious is that I'm also seeing tweets from people who aren't in our debut group.

> **@ChaiLovesTea:** Waiting for someone to fill me in on what's going on with the 2020 debut group. #PublishingTwitter #PublishingDrama

> **@AaronPark:** Every year, it never fails to happen. Every debut group will have its own drama. And this year's drama according to the grapevine is a DAMN GOOD ONE. One might even go so far as to say it's DELICIOUS. #BookTwit #Publishing

I guess someone from the group has told @AaronPark what happened. I scroll through more subtweets that allude to the drama, then I finally find it. The one brave soul who's willing to pull back the curtains.

> **@JulesCesarRatesBooks:** Ok, I guess no one's willing to say it, but screw it, I'm done protecting your problematic favs. The author everyone is subtweeting is Haven Lee. If the name sounds familiar to you, it's cuz she's got a massive book deal and her book is being shoved down our throats everywhere we turn. Here ya go. #Publishing

Along with the tweet, @JulesCesarRatesBooks has posted Haven's book cover. Her post already has over a hundred likes and seventeen comments. I drink in the comments, reveling in the collective hate toward Haven.

> **@Chosaiseo:** OMG I got an ARC for this book and it was on my TBR list but I won't be reading it now!!
>
> **@Helelelelen:** I read an interview with this author once and I knew there was something off about her!
>
> **@CaileeChastnet:** Wait, can anyone tell me what she did?? I really wanted to read her book but if she's done something rly bad then obv I'm not going to support it . . .
>
> **@Supercutie103:** @CaileeChastnet Her debut group put together the most adorable gift for her and she threw it out.
>
> **@CaileeChastnet:** @Supercutie103 WHAT?? Why would she do that? Omg that is so mean, especially when they put in the effort to do something so sweet! I won't lie, I'm kind of a loner so hearing stories like these make my blood boil. I would love to have friends who cared abt me!! 😭

I hear you, @CaileeChastnet. I would love to have friends who cared about me enough to send me a care package too. But it's okay, I remind myself, because now I have friends who would go to battle for me. I wonder if I'll ever get used to that, to accepting that I'm no longer on my own. Well, I definitely won't get used to the fact that it's now Haven who's on her own for a while yet. I check on her Twitter profile and find that she's locked it. A thrill shivers through me. Would that be because she was getting so much hate? I go to her Instagram, and this one she hasn't locked yet.

Sure enough, when I open her most recent post, one where she's made mussels cooked in a garlic white wine sauce for her parents, along with homemade baguettes, the most recent comments are along the lines of Haven, do you throw out all of the food you make too, or just the ones that other people make for you? To more direct ones like You're such a hypocrite, you grew your content based on food but you waste food, that's so messed up.

I can't believe it. Have I really defeated Haven Lee? I don't see how she could possibly come back from this. Twitter will do its thing and spread the news to the rest of the publishing community. Then a small voice whispers: I wonder if Haven's book is going to get canceled over this.

It's a delicious thought to have, and I entertain it for a while. Sometimes when a book is deemed problematic, whether because of the content or the author's behavior, publishers have been known to postpone it. This is the most common outcome. Publishers will put out a statement saying they have listened to the protests over the book and are learning and will make the edits needed to make the book more palatable. But sometimes, the book, or its author, is so problematic that there is no saving face, and the only recourse for the publisher is to cancel it altogether. I don't know the logistics that go on behind the scenes when this happens: whether the author must give back the advance payments that have been made to them or if they get to keep the money that's been paid out but forfeit all other payments. Whether the publisher might even go so far as to sue the author for damages to their reputation, or whether the publisher is simply happy to cut their losses and call it quits.

For a while, I let myself revel in the daydream of Haven losing her book deal and being made to return money she's been paid. Publishing payments are usually doled out in thirds, or quarters if it's a major deal, which Haven's is. So assuming her book deal was for a million dollars, then she would've been paid two hundred fifty grand upon signing of the contract, and another two fifty when she's made the edits required and her editor formally accepts the manuscript. Now that we're mere months away from publication, Haven would've received at least two payments. I wonder if she's panicking right now, knowing she might need to pay $500,000 back to her publisher. It's not as easy as simply returning the money to them; when they make these payments, she would've had to take a third of it out for taxes, and 15 percent would've gone directly to her literary agent. Which means if Haven's publisher demands the payments to be returned to them, Haven will be in real trouble, unless she happens to have two hundred extra grand lying around. I suppose given her financial background, I can't dismiss the possibility of this, but it's unlikely.

So all in all, there is a good chance that Haven is going to be in financial ruin. The realization of this doesn't bring with it the sweetness of victory that I expected. Instead, I feel sad. Why did it have to come to this? Every step of the way, I have tried to take the high road, to mind my own business and stay out of trouble. But Haven has sought me out continually, rubbing her success in my face, making sly remarks with hidden jabs that she knows others won't recognize, but I will. And I did. Why did she have to disturb my peace? I was fine before she came roaring back into my life. Part of me does believe that she started writing to get at me somehow. Because after what I witnessed this morning, the way she stomped on those empty boxes, I know without a doubt that Haven Lee has a personal vendetta against me. Well, it doesn't matter anymore, because against all odds, I, the loser, the clown, the underdog, have won. And I may not be vindictive enough to celebrate this win, but I sure as hell am not going to hide from it.

Chapter 23

I am woken up by the strangest, most unfamiliar sound—a knock at my bedroom door, followed by Dad's voice.

"Fern, wake up." His voice is soft and reluctant, as though he is extremely uncomfortable at having to rouse me from my sleep, which he probably is because this is not a thing that has happened before. "Fern?" It is the uncertainty in his voice that fully wrenches me from my slumber. It sounds like he's unsure of who might be inside my bedroom, other than me, and the ridiculousness of it all makes me chuckle, which in turn wakes me up completely.

"What?" I call out.

"Your friend is here," he says, so softly that at first, I think I might have misheard him.

The next thought I have is: Did Jenna fly in from Boston to see me?

"Jenna?" I say.

"No. Your friend from school, Haven."

Haven? Then it sinks in with cold suddenness. Is here. Haven is in my house. Adrenaline surges through me and propels me out of bed. I rush to the door and yank it open, shocking my father. "Did I hear you right? Haven Lee is here?" I hiss in an urgent whisper.

Dad looks like he is tempted to run away and hide. "Y-yes. Should I tell her that you're not here?"

I want to laugh at him, at his cluelessness. By now, Haven would know that I am home. Our house is not big by any means, and sound travels with painful clarity throughout the small space. She would have heard our hushed whispers by now. I push past Dad and go into the bathroom, where I splash cold water onto my face in an effort to clear my scrambling thoughts. I brush my teeth viciously and rake a comb through my hair. Come on, I think to myself, you need to be fully awake for this. You need all your wits about you. I rush back to my room and yank off my pajamas before grabbing the shirt and jeans I'd left on the floor the night before. I nearly fall over in the rush to put them on, and by the time I'm done, I'm out of breath and I sure as hell do not look anywhere near presentable. But by now, Haven would have been waiting for fifteen minutes at least, and the thought of it makes me squirm. But then it hits me: So what if I keep her waiting? The tables have turned, and she is no longer the queen bee. I force myself to take a few deep breaths and straighten my hair out in the mirror. I dab on some lipstick and try out a smile, which ends up looking awkward as hell, but it's the best I can do for now.

My instinct is to rush down the stairs, but I make myself walk down at a sedate pace. Haven is sitting at the dining table, with my mom to her left and my dad to her right. They are both looking at her intently, as though they expect her to, at any moment, spontaneously combust, or do something else equally shocking.

"Ah, Fern," Mom says. "Haven is here." As though it weren't painfully obvious.

"I see that," I say. "Hi."

Haven smiles grimly at me. "Hello, Fern." Something in her voice reaches down into the depths of my survival instincts and tugs at an alarm bell. She sounds way too smug. My pores immediately start sweating. Why is she acting like she has the upper hand? "I thought you might want to talk."

Mom's and Dad's gazes ping-pong back and forth between Haven and me.

"Let's go out to the backyard," I say.

"Sure." Haven gets up, moving with that natural dancer's grace of hers. She looks back at my parents and says, "Thanks, Mr. and Mrs. Huang."

They smile and nod, and to my surprise, their smiles are genuine. Frustration boils in my belly. What is it about Haven that makes even my parents, who I've been pretty sure are dead inside, behave like normal people? I open the door to the backyard with more force than necessary, and from the corner of my eye I see the way my parents flinch. I almost regret doing it; it's childish and accomplishes nothing other than annoying my parents. I make a mental note to apologize to Mom and Dad later, when Haven's gone. None of this is their fault. It's all hers.

When we're both outside, I turn to face Haven. I'd planned on saying something badass, the kind of thing one might see on TV, like "Make it quick" or "You have some nerve showing up here." But the moment I see Haven standing right there, the real Haven, warm blooded, not virtual Haven reaching out to me over Slack messages, all my prepared words evaporate, leaving me with a blank mind. I really am not cut out for confrontation. I'm not that kind of animal. Once again, I am reminded of where I am on the food chain. Close to the bottom, if not right at the very bottom. A worm wriggling blindly in the dirt, eating only the remains of whatever the thing above it leaves behind.

Luckily, Haven fills the silence almost immediately. "I came here to show you something," she says, and there is a note of triumph in her voice that makes my senses prick up. She takes out her phone, taps at it, and brandishes the screen at me.

It's security camera footage, showing the Lees' front door and its surroundings. My mind short-circuits and starts to gibber with useless, frantic thoughts. How—what—but—

Part of me whooshes out of my body and watches the situation in a removed way. It laughs at my cluelessness. What do you mean, how? Isn't it self-explanatory? They have security cameras installed at their house.

I watch, frozen, as I appear on the screen, walking with my hands tucked in my hoodie pocket, my head down, my face half hidden by my surgical mask. It's clear from my gait that I'm about to do something shady. I walk to the side of Haven's house.

You have a really strange walk, ghost-me says. Also, you have really bad posture.

Video-me disappears from view as she rounds the corner of Haven's house, and I let out a small breath of relief. Thank god for small mercies. I don't know if I could stomach watching myself rip out Haven's cables. A few moments go by, and then the video suddenly goes black.

"That was when you ripped out the electrics," Haven says. "It killed the cam."

Once again, a hurricane goes off in my mind, too many thoughts barging in all at once, and they end up clogging my mouth. How does she know—does she have more evidence—does this prove—

Whatever horrified expression I have on my face must give me away, because Haven nods with satisfaction. "I knew it," she says. "And I wanted to ask why you did it, but I know why. Because after all these years, you're still the same little freak—"

Something catches in my throat. Even my heart stops beating for a second as I wait for Haven to say it. To mention Dani.

But she merely says, "You're the same little pathetic loser whose life is consumed by nothing but jealousy and evil thoughts."

She's chosen not to mention Dani, and I don't know how to feel about it. I want to scream at her, but when I open my mouth, what comes out is "I'm not. I'm a good person."

Haven barks with laughter. "Okay, Fern. Whatever you say."

Something breaks inside me. "You're evil," I hiss. "Did you forget what you did to Dani?"

"What I did?" Haven says, her eyes widening, as though she is truly shocked. "Are you serious right now?"

"None of it would've happened if you hadn't been so shitty towards me. If you hadn't bullied and gaslit me all the way through high school. Dani wouldn't have—she wouldn't—she'd still be alive right now."

Haven shakes her head slowly, looking at me with open disgust. "Don't you dare throw what happened to Dani in my face. You think you're so innocent. God, you're tiresome. Did you forget what you did to me back in middle school? You remember that fucking cookie?"

The memory of it slams into me, and I want to shrivel up with shame.

Haven continues to talk. "You know what, Fern? I was nice to you on Slack. I reached out, I tried to hand you an olive branch, and then you go and pull this shit? Fuck you."

"You were nice to me on Slack?" I echo in disbelief. "You ruined my life! You made me lose my job. You think I don't know that you were the one who sent emails to my boss complaining about me?"

For just a sliver of a second, guilt crosses Haven's face. It doesn't stay on for long, but it's enough to confirm my suspicions that Haven was the culprit behind those emails that Annette received about me. But any satisfaction I might've had for figuring out the truth is overshadowed by my own guilt.

"You can't prove anything," Haven says finally. "Unlike me, you don't have any evidence."

"I didn't—" I start to say, but even I can hear the flimsy lie in my voice. "I didn't do it," I say lamely.

"Let's let Book Twitter be the judge of that," Haven says, and with that, she turns and walks away.

Everything inside me recoils with horror. "Wait!" I gasp. "What? Book Twitter?"

Haven doesn't stop walking. She glances back at me over her shoulder, and her smile is pure malicious glee. "I guess you haven't been online, then. Bye, Fern. Be grateful that I didn't spill the beans about what you did to me when we were kids. Stay away from me and my family." She opens the back door and disappears inside my house, where my parents will no doubt flock to her and make sure she's okay, because that's the way the world works, isn't it?

I scramble for my phone and unlock it. My heart sinks as soon as I get to the page with my Twitter app, because on the right-hand corner of the app, there is a red dot and the number 20+. I haven't had over twenty notifications on Twitter since I made my book deal announcement. With shaking hands, I open the app and look at my notifications. And they're bad. They're worse than bad. Worse than I could've ever imagined.

> You bitch, you're literally insane . . .

> I've never come across anyone as evil as you.

> You deserve prison time!!

The tweets scream at me, bypassing my ears, going straight into the center of my brain like a dagger. I am so hated. Again. A feeling I am painfully familiar with. A feeling I'd managed to convince myself I would never have to deal with again, and yet here it is once more.

One of the notifications is a tweet from Jenna that someone else has tagged me in.

> **@JennaWritesBooks:** I feel some responsibility for all the hate that has been piled onto Haven Lee for the last few days, and I just want to say that I didn't know what Fern was rly like. I should have, and I fully take responsibility for trusting her lies. I want to make it clear that Fern and I are no longer friends and I want to vouch for everything Haven has posted in her Tweet thread. The screenshots below, taken from our private chats, will prove that Fern has had it

out for Haven from the moment she found out about Haven's book deal.

As promised, there are four screenshots attached to Jenna's tweets. Snippets of our conversations. My email to them: Hey guys, omg, the craziest thing just happened. My high school bully has a book deal and she's also going to debut in 2020. Even my chat with Yuna is somehow on there. Me saying: And also, I would be extra careful about any advice that Haven Lee gives . . . I just don't think she has other people's best interests at heart. Showcased this way, my private messages to other people, confiding in them about Haven, now look like a calculated move to sabotage her.

Why would Jenna betray me like this? She and Lisa were my two closest friends, and if anything, maybe this wouldn't have been so shocking if it had come from Lisa. Lisa, with her passive-aggressive way of questioning my judgment when it comes to Haven. Lisa, who has been talking privately with Haven behind my back. It should've been Lisa, but instead, it's Jenna who's ended up plunging the dagger into my flesh, and the fact that it was the friend I most trusted who did it kills me.

I go to Haven's profile and find the tweet thread she posted just over two hours ago. Through a blur of hot tears, I begin to read.

> **@HavenMLee:** Hi everyone, I have a statement to make. I know that many of you are upset at me, and I acknowledge and hold space for all of you. But I do need to explain why I did what I did.
>
> Fern Huang and I have a very long history. We first met back in middle school, where I thought she and I were perhaps friends. But I soon found out that Fern wasn't who I thought she was. Even as a child, she harbored many dark thoughts which are

harmful towards others. I spent the rest of my middle school years afraid of Fern, and I was dismayed when I found out she would be attending the same high school I was.

Throughout high school, I did my best to avoid Fern. I warned my friends about her as well, to protect them, and this resulted in Fern being ostracized, which was not at all my intent, but please trust me when I say it wasn't an ill-deserved outcome for someone like Fern. I don't expect any of you to take my word for it, so I won't go into too much detail about what happened back then. The reason I'm mentioning our past is because I want to put everything into context before I tell you what happened last week.

Many of you know by now that over a week ago, we had a blackout at my house in the middle of the night, and we had to scramble to find somewhere to stay because we needed to make sure my dad's insulin was kept refrigerated. It was a terrifying experience because he'd tested positive for COVID not long ago, so we couldn't stay in a hotel, nor could we stay at relatives' houses for fear of infecting them. I was so frightened and desperate. Thankfully, a kind stranger opened their guesthouse to us and saved us. I was so relieved. At the time, I had no idea what caused the blackout. I'd assumed that maybe a raccoon had chewed through our cables or that maybe bad wiring had caused some kind of failure. I found an electrician who came to fix the electrics, and afterwards, he took me aside and told me that our electric cable had been ripped out. I asked if he thought a raccoon or possum or something could've done it, and he said, "No. Critters would chew through cables, not pull them out. This was done by a person."

It was during this time that Fern Huang showed up at my door bearing bread that she had baked for me. I was surprised, because like I said, back at school, Fern was not a good person. I allayed my misgivings about her and accepted the gifts she'd brought with thanks, but after what had happened with the blackout and what the electrician told me, I was wary, especially since Fern and I, while cordial now, are not what I would call friends. So her overt gesture of kindness felt out of place. And that was why I decided that I couldn't risk our health. I chose to throw away all of the food she'd given me. I couldn't possibly tell the rest of my debut group what I'd done, and that was why I lied about eating it. I didn't want to dredge up the past and put Fern in the spotlight and turn her into an outcast once more. So I thought it best to keep quiet and simply chug along as per normal.

What I did not foresee was Fern coming back to my house, sneaking into my trash bin, and taking photos of it. I hope I don't need to explain what a violation of privacy this was, not to mention actual trespassing. I also did not foresee Fern sharing these photos with the rest of our debut group and turning me into a villain. Like I said, my plan had been to mind my own business. Fern's actions have rendered that impossible.

It was at this time that I remembered that my parents have a security camera installed at the house. I checked the footage, and this was what I found. You will see on the bottom of the screen the time stamp of the video; this was taken two minutes before we had the blackout. Unfortunately, the person in the video has on a baggy hoodie that's pulled low over her face, and is wearing a mask so to most people, she is unrecognizable. But I recognize her from her height and her gait and the features that are visible, and I strongly believe this person you see in the video is Fern Huang.

As you can see, she walks towards my parents' house and off to the side, where our fuse box is, and a minute later, the footage ends as the blackout struck. For legal reasons, I am not stating that Fern was definitively responsible for the blackout that put my father's health at risk, but you are free to make your own judgment based on all of the information I have shared.

I am in contact with legal counsel and will proceed as per their advice. I hope that this statement and the video help all of you understand why I chose not to eat the food that Fern gave me. I do not have an eating disorder, nor am I a pathological liar. I did it to protect myself and my family. I know this is a massive thread, so thank you for taking the time to read it.

"No," I croak. My legs give out under me, and I thump to the grass. I barely register the pain when I hit the ground. I'm completely numb, weightless. The back door opens, and footsteps run toward me.

"Fern?" Mom says. Her head appears in my vision. "Fern, are you okay? Dave! David!" she calls out as she crouches down and grabs my arm, shaking me.

My dad appears. "What is—Fern? What happened?"

"I don't know," Mom says. "Fern! I think we need to call an ambulance."

Her last sentence pierces through the shimmering fog in my head, and I manage to choke out a quick "Don't."

"Oh, Fern," Dad moans. "Let's get her up. Can you sit up?" He and Mom take me by the shoulders and push me into a sitting position.

I blink up at them. They look so worried. They're worried about me. It's nice having people who still care about me. I wonder, though, if they'd still care if they found out what I've done. I wonder if they'll go back to looking at me in that removed way they do. I should say something to them. Assure them that everything is all right. I open my mouth, but before I can speak, my phone rings. Poppy's name is on the screen.

"I have to take this," I hear myself say to Mom and Dad. "It's my literary agent."

They continue looking at me with creased faces.

"I need some privacy," I say, in a voice that sounds so formal.

Dad sighs. "All right, if you're sure you're okay."

I am about the furthest from okay I have been in a long time, but I can't say that, so I nod. Once they're both gone from the backyard, I take a bracing breath and answer the phone.

"Fern, I'm going to cut to the chase," Poppy says. She doesn't even bother with a greeting, nor does she give me any time to respond. Very New York of her. "Are you the person in that video?"

I swallow. Should I tell her the truth? Should I lie? I need more time, I want to say to her. I need time to work out the pros and cons of both paths.

At my silence, Poppy blows out a long breath and says, "I see. And were you responsible for cutting the power to Haven Lee's house?"

Again, I find no right answer to her question. I swallow once more, but the lump in my throat remains.

"Okay," Poppy says. "Then I'm sorry to say that effective immediately, I can no longer represent you as your agent. As per my responsibilities as a literary agent, I have notified Lindsay about what's going on online, and I will be updating her to let her know that we are no longer working with—"

I close my eyes. A single tear rolls down my cheek, and it is such a cliché—how does one even make just a single tear?—that I laugh. Poppy stops talking abruptly. The silence widens, and I can sense her uneasiness. Who the hell laughs at a time like this?

"I'm sorry," I blurt out. "I wasn't—it wasn't a laugh."

There is another moment of silence, then Poppy says, very carefully, "Fern, I am letting you go as my client. I wish you the best going forward. Have a good day." The call ends.

When I lower my phone from my ear, I see that there's an email waiting for me. It's from Lindsay. The notification screen shows me the subject, which is Re: Author Incident—Fern Huang, and the first few lines of the email, which goes: Dear Fern, It is with a heavy heart that I write to you. Unfortunately, due to recent events, we can no longer go forward . . .

And there it is. The worst thing I could've possibly imagined has happened. The only thing that's kept me going the past few years has been my hope of one day becoming a published author, and now, when I'm so close to reaching it, it's been wrenched out of my hands. I drop my phone, and the thud it makes as it bounces onto the grass is so anticlimactic. I wish it had broken. Shattered the way everything in my life has. I can't possibly face Mom and Dad right now, so I go out the side gate from the backyard. Fortunately, I forgot to take my car key out of my pocket yesterday. I get into the back seat of my car and lock the doors, then I bury my face in my hands and shriek.

The sound that comes out of me is barely human. It's animal rage and life-ending grief and anguish all rolled into one unearthly scream.

I feel it tearing apart my throat as it rips out of me, and I don't care, I wish I could scream so violently that it tears me to pieces and I could just stop existing. What is the point of my existence? What has my life amounted to? An endless roll of nothing. I am almost thirty, and I have nothing, not a single thing, to show. Nothing that, when I'm on my deathbed, I could look back on with a satisfied smile and say, "I did that. I achieved that. I was here, and I made my mark." I imagine myself dying, and the truth is, aside from Mom and Dad, no one would care. And even Mom and Dad would only care because I am their child, a product that came from them. Their love for me has always been obligatory and nothing more, and their grief for me would be similar. I wouldn't just fade into nothingness; if I were to die, what would happen is there would be a drama-filled storm of tweets which wouldn't even be about me—it would be more about what I had done to Haven and how I had tricked everyone into thinking I was a victim, and in the end, even my death would be centered around Haven before it was quickly forgotten.

At this realization, I burst into tears. Huge, body-shaking sobs that wrench out of me with so much force that I wonder if they might break my ribs. The sounds I make are so ugly that even though there's no one else around, I am embarrassed. I try to soften them, but it's no use. It's a dam breaking, and everything is pouring out, and there's no holding anything back. I have nothing. My book floats into my mind, and I wail even louder at the memory of it. I haven't even had a chance to hold it in my arms, to have that moment that every author dreams of. I'd been planning on doing an unboxing video when the copies finally arrived. I would open the box up with the care reserved for handling a newborn, because isn't that what this book is? My baby? And now it's been canceled from existence before it was even born, and the whole world is dancing on its grave.

"I have nothing," I sob, again and again, to no one. "I have nothing."

Eventually, my body runs out of tears and energy, and mid-sob, I slip into a deep sleep that I hope never to wake up from.

Chapter 24

I am awoken by Dad knocking at my window. My eyes open slowly. They're so dry it feels like my eyelids have sandpaper on the inside. I blink several times. My dad knocks again.

"Fern?" he calls out. "Are you okay? Mom and I are very worried about you. What's going on?"

I snort, sitting up, rubbing my face. It's not like I can talk to my parents about this. Not like I can talk to anyone about this. The thought strikes again: I have nothing. And just these three words are enough to make fresh tears spring into my eyes. I shake my head. Shake it off, Fern. It's fine. Hah. Well, actually, it's not fine. It's never going to be fine. But for now, I need to tell my dad whatever he needs to hear so he'll go away.

I climb out of the car, my shoulders rounded because I don't know what I'd do if Dad decided to hug me right now. We've never been big into physical affection. I can count on one hand the number of times my parents have hugged me, and every time has been painfully awkward for both parties. He doesn't, of course. His arms hang limply by his sides as he watches me with open concern.

"It's fine," I say.

Dad sighs. "I don't know what's happened between you and Haven, but I know it's not fine, Fern. Why don't you talk to me and Mom?"

Hearing Haven's name come out of his mouth eats into me, searing me like a branding iron. Why does everything have to be about Haven?

My bitterness multiplies until it spills out. "Don't pretend like you give a shit about me."

Dad's eyes widen. He doesn't hide the fact that he's shocked and hurt by this. "Fern, what do you mean? Of course we care about you. We've been so worried."

"You don't care about me," I snap. "You and Mom are so . . ." I gesture wildly for a bit, trying to find the right words. Damn it, I'm a writer. If there's one thing I should be able to do, it's to find the perfect words for every situation. "Sure, you've looked after me in the most basic way that a parent has to. You've fed me and clothed me and all that stuff to ensure I stay alive, but there's always been this distance between us. It's like you and Mom have been watching me behind a sheet of bulletproof glass, just observing me. You don't know anything about my life. You never ask. You don't care."

Dad's mouth opens and closes and opens again. He looks like a fish that's jumped up too high and landed accidentally on land. Finally, he says, "You're right. I—yes, we haven't been—I—"

I watch him struggle to form a coherent sentence. After a while, it becomes clear to me that he's not going to tell me anything of note. I scoff. "Yeah, you don't even know how to talk to me about this stuff. The real stuff, not just the polite crap like 'Have you eaten?' 'Did you sleep okay?' Forget it." I step around him and walk back into the house.

Inside, I find Mom standing in front of the window, where she's obviously been spying on me and Dad. Her eyes go wide when she sees me too. "Fern—"

"Later, Mom. Dad can fill you in. I don't really want to talk—" To my horror, my voice breaks then, because despite everything I've told myself about not needing my parents, about accepting that we're just massively different people and so on and so forth, at the end of the day, it breaks my heart to know that I don't have the kind of parents I can turn to at times like these. Parents like Haven's. And again, that thought reappears: I have nothing. It plays on a loop as I walk up the stairs, in time to my steps. I. Have. Nothing.

I go to my bedroom and take a moment to calm myself. I don't have the energy to cry again. What's the point of crying now? Crying serves one purpose: to let out one's emotions, to cleanse the soul and make room for new thoughts and feelings. I've done that, and I am all empty, and nothing has come to fill the void that now resides inside me. I have nothing.

And why do I have nothing? Most people don't have nothing. The average person, even the mediocre ones, has something. Most people my age are married with kids, have some semblance of a career, and have a solid social life. Why do I have none of those things? The odds were stacked in my favor—a stable home, responsible parents, good schools, all in all a decent upbringing. What was it about me that was so broken that despite everything I've been given in life, I am now pushing thirty with no prospects in sight?

The answer appears in glittering, stark brilliance. Haven.

Haven happened to me. Before Haven, everything was okay. I had friends. I had a best friend. My grades hovered between average and above average. I wasn't exactly brimming with confidence, but I wasn't a doormat either. I was a happy, average kid. Then Haven set her sights on me, and that was it. When she was done with me, I had turned into a shell of a person, a shaky, cowardly introvert who doesn't know how to handle social interactions, who is convinced that the entire world is full of people who hate her. And having my self-esteem shredded has had repercussions well into adulthood. I never was able to make friends in person. I never shone at any jobs because I was so bad at interpersonal relationships. I have never been on a single date, ever, because I didn't think I was worthy of love. The only thing I had was my writing, and this, too, has been torn apart by Haven. Everything has happened because of Haven. I have nothing.

That's right. I have nothing. And I realize, then, that having nothing comes with one upside: I have nothing, therefore I have nothing to lose.

The thought is thrilling. Liberating. I look at my reflection and see a pale, mousy woman. But there's a fire that's rekindling inside me.

I watch my jaw setting, my shoulders turning back. What can I do? Actually, the question should be, What can't I do? Now that I am free of the burden of having beautiful things like a book deal to give me hope, nothing. There's nothing I can't do.

And with this realization booming through my body, I pull out my chair and turn my laptop on. If I have nothing to lose, then what's stopping me from telling the whole world the truth? My truth, the one I've kept hidden for so long. And the answer is: nothing.

—

BuzzFeed Op-Ed

How I Turned from Bully Victim into the Bad Guy

by Fern Huang

BuzzFeed Contributor

I was twelve the first time I met Haven Lee. I didn't know it then, but Haven would end up being the most important person in my life, because with surgical precision and ruthless efficiency, she would eventually come to ruin it. People often say things like "So-and-so has ruined my life," but in this case, Haven has truly destroyed my career, my social life, and my reputation. Perhaps what hurt me the most is the last bit. Because all this time I have been Haven's quiet victim, tightening into a smaller ball whenever she decides to torment me, content to forever hide and never retaliate. But then I snapped, and one bad decision turned me from someone who has been bullied for years into, ironically, the villain.

Haven and I met in middle school. She joined us in the middle of the school year, and as the new kid, she was utterly enchanting. Everyone was enamored by her, including myself. And how could you not be? Even as a child, Haven was beautiful in a way that turned heads, and carried herself with a certain confidence and assurance that you would normally only find in grown adults. It was apparent from the very beginning that she was going to be our new queen bee. We all accepted it.

I was among the throng of people who crowded around her at recess, wanting to know more about her, wanting to be her friend. At the time I had Alana [name changed to protect privacy], someone I thought was my best friend. Alana and I talked about Haven excitedly at lunch, marveling over everything from Haven's hair to the bracelets that she wore to the way she talked. We hatched a plan to make Haven be our friend.

Over the course of the next couple of weeks, Alana and I would invite Haven to come sit with us at the cafeteria, or sit next to us in science lab, but it quickly became apparent to me that while Haven liked Alana enough, she had not taken a shining toward me. It hurt, of course, realizing that she had found me lacking in one way or another. But my disappointment then was nothing compared to the despair I felt when I noticed Haven starting to exclude me. By the end of the term, Haven and Alana were regularly spending time together without me. I was predictably upset, but I was twelve and there were plenty of other kids I was friendly with. And so I moved on.

Or so I thought.

The problem was, for Haven, stealing my best friend was not enough. She had identified me as a good target to have, and in this respect, she was absolutely correct, because as mentioned above, I am not one to retaliate. Over the next few months, I watched as one by one, the friends that I had made slowly froze me out. A couple of them told me it was because of what Haven had told them about me. I dared not imagine the things that Haven might have been telling people. And soon enough, I had no one left. This continued on throughout the rest of middle school, and then throughout high school.

You might be wondering why Haven did this, and honestly? I would love to know myself. She was and has always been at the top of her game, and I was a nobody. By rights, I should have been invisible to someone like her. Maybe she just liked an easy target. At the end of the day, the why doesn't matter. The mouse does not ask why the cat is after it; all that matters is that it is.

You know the story in which the scrawny, bullied kid gets a makeover and turns up at the prom looking more beautiful than the bully? This isn't one of those stories. In reality, by the time we graduated high school, I was a mess. After years of torment from Haven and the rest of my schoolmates, my self-esteem was nonexistent, replaced by a sense of self-hatred so strong that I believed I was deserving of nothing good in life. I had internalized all of their taunts, and the person I saw when I looked in the mirror was as worthless as they had told me. My grades had suffered, and the only place that I was accepted to as a result was a community college, where I spent the next two years of my life before transferring to a local college. I was aimless and, unlike most of my peers, I had no aspirations.

After college, I decided to leave my painful past behind and move to the East Coast, as far away as I could get from Haven. I went through therapy during this time, and slowly, painstakingly, my therapist helped me rebuild my core. In New York City, I carved out a quiet life for myself as a photographer's assistant. It was a small life, but it was peaceful, and exactly what I needed to continue healing.

I began to hope for a better life.

Back at school, the one thing that saved me from the endless vitriol was books. I kept numerous journals where I vented all of my sadness, and in doing so, I began to develop a love for writing.

[Pictured: One of Fern's journals from high school, open to a page on which is written: today, I opened my locker and four hissing cockroaches flew out at me. Oh God, I don't have the words to describe how disgusting, scary, and humiliating it was. One of the cockroaches landed on my chest, and another one landed on my neck. I can still feel their scratchy legs scrabbling across my skin as I write this. I did that dance that people do in these situations, jumping, slapping at my own body frantically, screaming the whole time. Teachers rushed out of nearby classrooms, and eventually one of them calmed me down enough to assure me that there were no more cockroaches. I guess they had all run away by then. I was in tears, and not like quiet tears, but like really ugly crying. And of course, the hallway was filled with curious students. I looked around me and all I saw were grinning faces. One of them was Haven's. But she wasn't just grinning, she was making a quiet noise under her breath. She was hissing, just like the cockroaches had been. And that was when I knew that she had been behind this.]

I started writing stories. I joined online forums for writers, and I integrated into the writing community. In this way, I slowly forged friendships. After a while, I had a little community of people who shared my love of writing. I wrote four manuscripts before one finally sold to a publishing house. It wasn't a huge deal, but it was my book deal, and I was so damn proud of it. It was the first and only time that I had done something worthwhile, and with this achievement under my belt, I found my self-confidence slowly returning. My book deal wasn't just a dream come true, it was the evidence I needed to prove to myself that I was worthy of a good life. I joined what is called a debut group, which is an online community of authors who are debuting in the same year. There, I made two friends, and we quickly became a close-knit trio, chatting with each other throughout the day, every day.

Imagine the horror and shock I felt upon finding out that Haven also had a book deal. I confided in my friends about my past with Haven, believing that it was a safe space for me to do so. Same as before, my natural instinct was to retreat to a corner and let Haven have the spotlight that she has always clearly loved. I had my own little book deal, and I was content.

Over time, though, I noticed Haven getting up to her old tricks. Undermining my chat messages, going out of her way to make me look bad in front of the others. I tried my best to ignore it, even as my anxiety grew and grew, threatening to overwhelm me. It was at this time that the pandemic became bad enough for the city to go into lockdown. I was laid off, and without my salary, I was forced to move back to my parents' house in LA. Without access to my usual healthy coping mechanisms, Haven's assault on my character bypassed whatever little defenses I had left and struck me in the soft underbelly. My fears grew unchecked. I knew that if I didn't do something, Haven would soon take me right back to high school. Because she is a predator, and all predators need prey.

After all of the work I had done in therapy, and all the effort I had put into restoring self-confidence, the thought of Haven tearing me down again for fun was unbearable. I wasn't sleeping, nor was I eating much. I was breaking down both mentally and physically. I'm not sharing this in the hopes that anyone might excuse what I did next, because there is no justification for my actions. I drove to Haven's house with the intention of confronting her and begging her to let me be. I should have known that this was a futile endeavor, because what kind of mouse would stop and turn around to face the cat and ask it nicely not to eat it? As soon as I arrived at Haven's house, what little courage I had disappeared, leaving me standing there bubbling with the familiar self-hatred and sense of despair. Only one thought remained: Stop her.

And stupidly, I thought that maybe if I could cut off Haven's access to the internet, just for a while, it would distract her enough to leave me alone. In hindsight, I realize never has a plan been more foolish. But that's the thing about prey: We are not used to fighting back, and when forced to do so, we will make the absolute worst choices possible. Like pulling out what I thought was an internet cable.

The whole world knows the story by now. The cable turned out to be an electricity cable, and when I pulled it out, it plunged Haven's house into complete darkness. When I realized what I had done, I let my fear overtake me and I ran. Later, I came to find out that what should have been a small prank had turned into an actual emergency. Because, as you might have heard by now, Haven's father has diabetes, and keeping his insulin refrigerated is a literal matter of life or death.

Trust me when I say there is no insult you can hurl at me that I haven't already stabbed myself with. You can hate me if you want, but I assure you that your hatred toward me pales to the hatred I have for myself for what I have put the Lees through. I felt such revulsion toward myself. To say that I was overwhelmed with guilt would be an understatement. I wished desperately to do something that might make up, just a little bit, for what I had done. And so I turned to the debut group, suggesting that we might put together a gift box for Haven. Unfortunately, though everyone loved the idea, many of us could not afford to pitch in due to financial constraints brought about by the pandemic. We decided on a card in which I would put together well-wishes from everyone, which is a heartfelt and wonderful gift but felt to me like it was nowhere near enough. I understand now that my guilt was so great that no gift would have been sufficient, but at the time, I felt that I had to try.

I bought a secondhand espresso machine, something that I had heard that Haven wanted, and given I had financial constraints of my own, I decided to fill the gift box with something else that was more affordable—homemade bread. I have always loved to bake. Anyone you talk to can attest to my baking prowess.

[Pictured: Fern posing with a sourdough starter, which she affectionately calls Doughlores.]

I hand delivered the gifts to Haven personally, wanting to make sure that nothing was damaged in transit. It was extremely strange to stand on Haven's doorstep, with all of this history behind us and the knowledge of what I had done a mere week ago. I handed the box to Haven and left the house in somewhat of a daze. I hadn't foreseen the maelstrom of emotions that seeing her in person would bring me. I wasn't in a state to drive, so I sat in my car for a while, trying to calm myself down enough to go back home. It was at this time that Haven's side door opened, and she came out carrying the bread that I had just given to her. I stared in confusion as she dumped all of it—the rustic sourdough loaves, the bagels, and the cinnamon rolls—into the trash.

Did I feel angry, seeing my hard work literally go to waste? Not really. What I felt above all else was fear. Because this was proof that Haven still hated me. It was hard evidence, something I had to document to assure myself that yes, this really happened, that I didn't just make it up. Because after all of those years of bullying and gaslighting, I no longer knew how to trust my own instincts. So I went up to Haven's trash can, lifted the lid, and took photos of the bread inside the bin.

Then I told my two close friends what had happened. They were understandably shocked, as was I, and they shared it with the rest of the debut group. And before I knew it, Haven was hated by everyone. It was never my intention for Haven to be excluded from the group, but when confronted about what she had done, Haven chose to leave the debut group. Once again, I found myself struggling with all of the contradicting emotions I was feeling. I knew that I wasn't innocent in all of this, but neither was Haven. And a not-so-small part of me was relieved now that everybody knew what Haven was really like. And, I consoled myself, after all, she still had a massive book deal and a career in publishing that was off to the most incredible start.

I should have foreseen Haven's retaliation. Shortly after I exposed her, she left the group. Haven then released a statement about me along with security camera footage of me coming to her house the night of the blackout. I deny nothing in the video. I was the one who pulled out the Lees' cables and created an emergency. I fully take responsibility for that. I was quickly fired by my literary agent, and my book deal has been canceled by my publisher, both of which are consequences that are appropriate for what I have done. But what broke me was reading Haven's statement where she painted me as the villain all those years throughout middle and high school. Seeing my history get rewritten under her pen.

And that is why I have written this op-ed. I may be a villain now, but I need to have my truth heard. I have nothing left, and I fully understand that I deserve this. It was no one else's fault but mine that landed me here, at age thirty, with no job, no book deal, and no friends. But I do not deserve to have my past be rewritten into something it was not. If you walk away from this hating me, don't hate me for what I haven't done, because what I have done is atrocious enough on its own.

Chapter 25

The op-ed I wrote goes viral. It is all over social media. On Twitter it gets over eighty thousand likes and over thirty thousand retweets, and the comments are at almost ten thousand and still going strong. And surprisingly, everyone is on my side. Well, not everyone. There are always exceptions to every rule. I still get some hate, but the comments are overwhelmingly, undeniably #TeamFern. Because the thing is, while some people may judge me for pulling out those electric cables, everyone has at some point in their life been the target of a bully. Everyone knows the way being bullied eats away at you from the inside, festering like an infected wound. It infects every part of you, including your sanity. Many people even support me losing my mind and ripping out those cables, because they get it. They understand and empathize with the primal fear that Haven had pushed me into feeling.

The days following the publication of my op-ed, I go to sleep clutching my phone and wake up with it still in my hand. I refresh Twitter over and over again, watching the numbers tick up, up, up. It is all over TikTok as well, where tons of people have posted videos of themselves summarizing everything that's happened between me and Haven.

I laugh when I watch one particularly animated user gesturing wildly at her camera and saying: "Y'all are not gonna believe the crazy shit that authors get up to behind the scenes! We all think of authors as nerdy little gremlins, hiding away in their dark caves typing away on their little keyboards, but these two bitches be crazy! I don't know which is the crazier of the two, but I know who is the more evil and calculating. It's Haaaven!"

The comments range from "Both of them are insane" to "I am totally on Fern's side. If I were her, I would've done the same, or worse. Haven had it coming." Even the ones that call me crazy or insane or unhinged generally agree that Haven is worse.

Reading all these comments from impartial strangers is a salve to my soul. I no longer feel as isolated. The bottomless hopelessness starts to abate, and I see a light at the end of the tunnel. I still don't have a job or a book deal, but it doesn't quite feel like the end of the world. I have shared my truth, and in doing so I have freed myself. I'm no longer hiding in a dark corner, waiting for Haven to pounce on me. Everyone knows now, and there is something so exhilarating about that.

Some people from the debut group reach out to me to apologize. Surprisingly, or maybe not surprisingly, none of them is Jenna. My closest buddy Jenna has remained staunchly silent. She took down the tweets she'd made about me, along with the screenshots of my private conversations, and based on that, I assume she's seen my op-ed and decided it's best for her to stay the hell out of this mess. Lisa, Yuna, and Felicity are the ones who reach out. Felicity is the most apologetic of them all, which is ironic.

Fern, she says over Twitter DM, I am so, so sorry for everything that Haven has put you through. I was bullied too back in high school, and reading that op-ed you wrote made me cry. My heart breaks for what you've been through. That journal entry about the hissing cockroaches? That . . . it's pure evil. I'm not saying you were justified in cutting Haven's electricity cables, but . . . I get it. When I was bullied, I often fantasized doing the most messed up shit to my bullies. I imagined running over them with my car! Of course I never did anything to harm them, but I just want to say I understand and I am so sorry that you lost your book deal over this. It's so unfair. The debut group misses you very much and if you ever want to come back into the Slack, you are always welcome to. Haven is blocked from there so it's a safe space for you.

I reply: Thank you so much, Felicity! I really appreciate your kind words. It means the world to me that people know the truth and understand where I'm coming from. I totally agree that what I did was despicable, and I am so ashamed of myself for doing it. I will never be able to make up for what I did. Thank you for inviting me back to the Slack, but given the inexcusable things I've done and also the fact that I'm no longer a debut author, I don't think I should come back there. I miss you guys very much, but we can chat over DMs! Please give my regards to everyone in the Slack group and tell them I wish everyone the best with their books.

I don't tell Felicity that the truth is, I've had enough of debut groups for now. Especially one that turned its back on me so swiftly. One where the friends I'd made plastered our private chats all over the internet. No, from now on, no more debut groups for me. Not that I have a choice, since I don't even have a book to debut with.

Haven has completely disappeared from social media. She's deleted her Twitter and Instagram. Completely wiped from the internet. Part of me, the old part that clings to bad habits, is tempted to take a drive down to her house to see what's going on with her. But it's a small part. Like I said, I'm healing, and seeing the words "@HavenMLee: This user does not exist" propels me onward in my healing journey. I stare at the screen for a long time, reveling in the delicious joy that these words bring me. She's gone. She had a business as an influencer, and she deleted it. That's huge. Earth shattering. And all because the world now knows the truth about her.

A week after the op-ed comes out, Haven's publisher releases a statement.

> We are canceling the publication of Haven M. Lee's book, *SHE ASKED FOR IT*, due to improper conduct by the author. Wallace Books has a firm stance on bullying, and does not condone the actions of Haven M. Lee.

When I read it, I actually gasp out loud so hard that Mom pops her head through the doorway. These days, I've started leaving my bedroom door open to signal to my parents that I'm up for a chat. It's part of my journey to recovery. I think they've sensed the change in me, because the suffocating tension that existed between us has eased up a little, and they're no longer as jumpy around me. They pop by my room once in a while, and each time, they will have a gift for me—a plate of freshly sliced apple, or my clothes, fresh out of the dryer, folded neatly. And I realize that for Mom and Dad, their love language may not be what I wanted, but it's been there all along. They show me their care and concern in myriad tiny gestures, like giving me the biggest piece of chicken at dinner, or switching from penne to linguini because they know I prefer it. They're still awkward most times, and they still speak in an overly formal way, but I remind myself to focus on the good stuff, and I think that overall, we're doing well.

But right now, Mom says, "Are you okay? What happened?" and when she says this, I see the old concern creeping back over her face.

"Oh, just some publishing drama." I hesitate, then I decide that actually, I would like my parents to know what just happened. I want to see my mother's face when she realizes that Haven isn't perfect. "You remember Haven from school?"

"Of course. She was here not long ago. The day that you, ah, fell."

"Yes. She has a book deal too. Well, she had. Her publisher just announced that they're canceling it." I'm careful not to sound too smug about this. I deliver the news in as neutral a voice as possible.

Now it's Mom's turn to gasp. "What? Why?"

"They said it's because of improper conduct."

Mom's hand flies to her mouth. "Oh my. What sort of improper conduct?"

"I don't . . ." I was about to say I don't know, but I don't want to lie to my parents. And anyway, they might find out about it; my op-ed is still being shared online. It's only a matter of time before one of their friends sees it and links it to them. "Bullying," I say. "But I don't want to get into it right now. Sorry." In my mind, Aliyah goes, "Good job setting boundaries, Fern."

Mom huffs and shakes her head in wonderment. "My goodness. Bullying. Who would've thought."

It takes everything inside me to not say "I would." I shrug, and Mom leaves the room, muttering to herself. I go back to Twitter and look up Haven's agent, and sure enough, there's a statement from her as well.

> With sadness, I am announcing that Haven Lee and I have parted ways. Rest assured, I am reading and listening to all of your messages and I am learning from them. We at Reed Literary cannot support any authors who take part in bullying or harassment of any kind.

"Wow," I whisper under my breath. The seven-figure book deal is no more. Without a doubt, all the different territories will also follow suit now that the US publisher has dropped Haven's book. How much would she have to return to them? Part of me recoils in horror as I make a quick calculation of how much Haven would owe them. Close to a million altogether, if not more. How much has she spent? Haven has always liked beautiful things. I'm sure she bought herself nice things as soon as she got the first check. Despite myself, I feel rather bad for Haven. This could spell the beginning of financial ruin for her, and though she's a horrible person, it never feels good to see anyone fall so hard.

My phone beeps with yet another new email. I've been getting so many. Most of them are from people reaching out to tell me their personal experience with bullies, and some have been from other news sites, asking me if I'd be interested in writing an op-ed for them. They're all emails I have loved receiving, so every time I hear the beep of an email, I get a little shot of endorphins. But now, the shot of endorphins is much bigger than the usual one. Because the email is from Haven's ex-agent.

> Dear Fern,
>
> Let me introduce myself. I'm Rachel. I used to represent Haven Lee. Since your op-ed came out, I have parted ways with Haven. I have been in long discussions with my colleagues. What you wrote was incredibly powerful. I really admire your courage in sharing your story as well as your unflinching honesty. You didn't hold back. You showed us everything, warts and all, and I think that's why the piece was so successful. You have a gift, and that gift is writing the truth. This op-ed deserves to be a book. It is going to change many lives, and that is not an exaggeration. Everyone has been treated badly at some point in their lives. Many people are currently going through abuse like this. This topic is timely and relevant and I have no doubt that your book will find a good home. You have an amazing voice for writing nonfiction, and I would love to be your champion who will take your book to publishers and negotiate the best possible deal on your behalf. Let's set up a Zoom call to chat. I look forward to hearing from you.
>
> Warmest regards,
>
> Rachel

For a while, the email leaves me speechless. Or rather, thoughtless? I merely sit there and try to digest what I've just read. I go back to

"Dear Fern" and start over. Oh my god. Is this real? Did Rachel Reed just offer to represent me? *The* Rachel Reed? The Rachel Reed whose client list includes actual celebrities and authors whose books have been on the *New York Times* bestseller list for years? I log on to Publishers Marketplace and look her up, and yep, she's made eleven deals this year alone, and not a single one was below six figures. In fact, only two of them are below "significant," and out of the remaining nine, four were for "major deals." In the previous year, she made fifteen deals, and again, they are all above six figures. This agent is nothing like Poppy. Rachel Reed is in the big leagues. And she wants to represent me.

I start drafting a reply immediately, though it takes me over an hour to settle on a message with what I deem the appropriate tone. As I delete and rewrite my message over and over again, I find myself thinking: I should go to the private chat and ask Lisa and Jenna to help me draft it! Then I remember that I am no longer in the Slack group. Oh well.

> Dear Rachel,
>
> Thank you so much for your email! I really appreciate your kind words. It means a lot to me that you understand where I'm coming from. I would love to talk to you over Zoom. Please let me know when you are available.
>
> Best wishes,
>
> Fern

Short and sweet. I send it off and flop back onto my bed, grinning wide. Never in a million years would I have ever thought that a superstar agent like Rachel would reach out to me to offer representation. Not me, quiet, mousy Fern Huang. But that's just it, isn't it? I am no longer quiet or mousy. I have made my voice heard, and I'm only now finding out that people like what I have to say.

I'm still deep in my thoughts when my phone beeps. When I tap on the email, I find a link to a Zoom meeting. Oh my god. She wants to talk right now. I jump up and hurry to the mirror. I check my teeth to make sure there's nothing stuck on them, then I quickly brush my hair. Fortunately, I'm wearing a plain black shirt, so I don't have to change out of it. Having made myself somewhat presentable, I click on the link and log on to the meeting.

"Hi, Fern!" Rachel says. To my relief, she's dressed casually as well, wearing a sweater with her hair tied up in a messy bun and reading glasses sitting atop her head. "I was hoping I could catch you right now. Sorry, I know I didn't give you much of a heads-up, but I am just so excited to speak to you."

Rachel Reed is excited to speak to me? "Oh, no worries!" I squeak. "I'm really excited too!" Okay, tone it down.

"Well, like I said in my email, you have such an amazing voice. It's so relatable, Fern, did anyone tell you that?"

"Um, a few people did, yes." I giggle. Oh my gosh, I can't believe I just giggled to Rachel Reed.

She doesn't seem to mind. "Well, I'm glad they did, because ah, your voice!" She kisses the tips of her fingers. "Let me tell you, nonfiction is a toughie. People think fiction is tough, but nonfiction is next to impossible to get just right. Well, that's my opinion, anyway," she adds. "So when I came across your op-ed, I just knew. You are that one-in-a-million writer that we're always dreaming of. Do you have any thoughts or plans to expand your piece into a book? Tell me your ideas."

Oh no. What ideas? I want to cry. I haven't had any time at all to prepare a pitch. And for a nonfiction book, no less. I'm a fiction writer, I wail inwardly. Then, just as I'm about to descend into a spiral, my mouth opens. "Well, to be honest with you, until you suggested it in your lovely email, I haven't thought of the possibility of turning it into a book, no. But," I add quickly, "as soon as I read your message, I was filled with so many ideas about how I could do so. I think there are so many themes to explore here, and obviously the main thrust of the book would be about mental health and my journey to learn how to accept myself."

"I love the sound of that," Rachel says. "Yes, mental health. That is so timely, especially with how bad it's become for so many people right now. I mean, we're all going crazy locked up in our homes." She chuckles, and I laugh along with her, and wow, I am having an actual conversation with Rachel Reed. "I love that. I presume you've saved all of your journals from school?"

"Yes," I say without hesitation.

"Amazing. I was thinking, you know what we could do? Maybe start each chapter with a photo of one of your journal entries. I mean, my god, that journal entry about the hissing cockroaches? Fern, my heart stopped when I read that. And it was even more visceral because it was handwritten in a teen's journal. I could almost see you writing it after that horrible thing happened, and I just wanted to reach out and give you the biggest hug. I think that was what won a lot of people over."

I can only manage a small nod. Hearing these words is so beautiful and so empowering.

"So each chapter will start with a journal entry, and hopefully we can come up with a theme for each one. I'm thinking the cockroach one can be about public humiliation maybe, or ooh, a form of gaslighting? We can brainstorm on the themes. Sorry, I was so excited to jump right in with your book that I forgot to tell you a little bit about myself and the agency."

For the next few minutes, I listen, enthralled, as Rachel tells me about her work experience and how their agency is run. It all sounds amazingly professional, and I can see why Rachel is always hitting her marks. She's incredibly well spoken and confident without being arrogant, and she's obviously knowledgeable and well connected. If I hadn't been convinced before, I certainly am now.

"So what I think we should do is we need to come up with a submission package for the book. Usually, for nonfiction books this is the first three chapters plus a chapter outline. But since you have the op-ed, we can use that instead of chapters, so all you need to work on right now is a chapter outline. Does that sound good to you?"

I nod firmly. "Yes, I'm so excited."

"Oh, I'm so glad to hear that! I'm so excited too. I haven't been this excited in a long time, I can tell you that much. I'll send along our agency agreement later today. Look it over, and if everything looks good, we'll make this partnership official." Rachel beams at me, and I grin back.

I actually skip around the room like a little kid when we end the call. I'm going to be represented by Rachel Reed! I'm going to have a nonfiction book! Okay, never mind, I know better by now than to count my chickens, et cetera, and I shouldn't celebrate the book before I sell it. But still, even though logically I know that, it's hard to keep my joy contained. What a turn of events. I have to believe that the universe is sending me a message at this point. I mean, to get not just an agent, but Haven's ex-agent? In a way, one could say that I took Haven's agent from her. The thought sends a shiver down my spine, and I can't decide if it's a good shiver or a bad one, because yes, part of me feels bad when I look at it that way, but part of me also feels really good about it.

Chapter 26

Over the next few days, I bury my head in work. After the mess I've gone through online, even though most people are on my side, I don't take the risk of announcing that I'm now represented by Rachel Reed. It hurts. I want so much to be able to scream about it, but people love an underdog, and I think I should stay the underdog for a while longer. Instead, I focus all my attention on coming up with a chapter outline. Just four days later, I send it off to Rachel, and she reads it and marks it up with comments that are both insightfully critical and yet supportive. I take a couple more days to make the changes she suggested and then send the revised version back to her. Again, she replies on the very same day, and this time, she only has minor tweaks to make. Her email says: Fantastic job! I think once you've made these minor changes, this will be good to go. I'll send it off to publishers first thing tomorrow morning.

And just like that, I am on submission, this time with a nonfiction book based on my life. How insane, how mind blowing, is that? And because she is the Rachel Reed, unlike my submission journey with Poppy, where weeks and weeks went by without a peep from publishers, with the rejections limping in after over a month, this time, we get answers just one day after the pitch is sent out. One day. Less than twenty-four hours. Rachel forwards the emails to me, and I tremble with joy as I read them.

> . . . brilliant voice, we are putting together an offer . . .
>
> . . . read this on BuzzFeed when it came out and was actually going to reach out to her myself so I'm glad this landed in my inbox . . .
>
> . . . our next acquisitions meeting is on Thursday and I will be bringing this . . .

"Oh my god," I say to Rachel when she calls. "Are we headed into an auction?"

She laughs. "Fern! We *are* at auction. The first offer just came in. It's from Salt Books, and it's for a hundred twenty, so obviously we're not taking that. But since we now officially have an offer, I have called for an auction."

I struggle to understand what she's saying. "Sorry, um, a hundred twenty? Like, a hundred and twenty dollars?"

"No, Fern!" Rachel laughs again. "A hundred and twenty *thousand* dollars!"

I feel my legs buckle, and I lower myself onto my bed. "Um. A hundred and twenty thousand? Wait, and we're turning it down?"

"Yes. And Salt Books knows it's a low offer. I have half a mind to tell them off, to be honest with you."

What world have I landed in that $120,000 is considered "low"? But I don't say it out loud. I merely nod and stay quiet as Rachel continues talking.

"They're one of the biggest publishers out there—they know that I know they have deep pockets. So. Don't worry, I have it all under control. Four other publishers have responded and said they will be taking part in the auction."

My mind is still reeling. I'm on auction? Holy shit. I'm on auction. When we end the call, I stare stupidly at the wall. My deal with Harvest had been for—what was it—$8,000? And I had cried with joy then.

And now here I am, turning down an offer for $120,000. What is this life I have landed in?

The auction is surprisingly swift. By the next morning, all participating publishers—eight of them—have made their official first offer. Salt Books, upon learning there is an actual auction, has put in a new offer. Rachel puts together all the offers into a list and sends it to me, and I nearly have a heart attack. The lowest number on there is $250,000—a significant deal—and the highest number is $400,000. When she calls me, I say, "So I guess we'll go with the highest bidder?"

Rachel gives me a quizzical look, then laughs again. "Oh! No! Auction's not over yet."

"It's not?" I breathe. My eyes must be perfect circles now, I'm so surprised by her answer.

"Nowhere near over. I've sent an email to them with rules for round two."

"Rules?" I knew, of course, that literary agents negotiate deals for authors, but I never knew the amount of tactics and strategy involved in these negotiations.

"Well, a good rule would be to set a floor bid—that means anyone who can't meet the floor bid will automatically drop out. I think four hundred is good for a floor. And the other rule is that the lowest two bidders will be cut from the auction. So we're lighting a fire under their butts." Rachel grins.

Who's ever heard of lighting a fire under a publisher's butt? I have never been in this position before. I've always been the one sitting on the fire, not the other way around. What if the publishers call our bluff and tell Rachel she's asking for too much? What if they're offended by the ridiculously high floor bid? A floor bid of $400,000? Who would've thought that was even possible?

"Don't worry, Fern," Rachel says, as though she's read my mind. "I know a good book when I see it, and this is it. And they know it, too, otherwise they wouldn't be publishers. I'll speak to you soon!"

I don't sleep the entire night. I lie in bed, facing one side, then the other. I check my email about fourteen times. I check my settings six times to make sure my phone isn't on silent mode, even though I know Rachel isn't going to email me at two in the morning. I open Twitter and look at the comments on tweets about my op-ed. They're still overwhelmingly positive. The number of likes has slowed down, but we are now at over one hundred thousand likes, and I can live with that. Eventually, I doze off, only to be jerked awake by a call at eight in the morning.

"Good morning!" Rachel says.

"Good morning," I say, rubbing my eyes.

"Did you see my email? Second-round bids are in."

"They are?" Belatedly, I remember that New York is three hours ahead of us, so it's nearly lunchtime there.

"I'll wait while you check," Rachel says with a coy smile in her voice.

I hurriedly open her email, and I almost drop the phone when I see the numbers. Five publishers now remain, with the lowest bid at four hundred fifty and the highest at—

"Is this real?" I say, blinking hard, trying to wake up fully. "Six hundred thousand?"

"Yes!" Rachel squeals. "And since we still have five houses in the running, I have called for one final round. A best-bids round."

"What?" I whisper. We're at $600,000, and the auction still isn't over? I can't process this.

"The deadline is four p.m. today, so by the end of the workday, you'll have a new publisher. How does that sound?"

I can only nod.

Rachel laughs again and says, "All right, I'll let you get back to sleep, and I'll speak to you in a few hours."

Like there's any chance in hell that I might get back to sleep after that. I get up and go about my morning routine. I try to speak normally to Mom and Dad because of course I haven't let them know about any of this for fear of jinxing it. Now that I have actually experienced the exquisite pain of having my book canceled, I am extremely paranoid about doing everything correctly so I don't mess this second chance up. And what a second chance it is. I know that it's the kind of chance that comes by less than once in a lifetime. Maybe not even once in several lifetimes. And I would do anything to protect it.

The day crawls by excruciatingly slowly. The slightest noise makes me pounce at my phone.

"Are you expecting a call from someone?" Dad says when I check my phone for the third time during lunch.

"Oh, yeah, just an old friend who wanted to catch up."

Mom and Dad exchange a glance, and I feel the old tension rising up between us, an old, grizzled beast raising its head slowly.

"Sorry," I say, "I can't tell you right now, but I will. I want to. Soon. I promise."

The tension eases a little. The beast goes back to sleep. The phone rings then, and I jump up so fast my chair falls backward. "Sorry!" I don't bother picking the chair up before running out to the backyard. "Hi!" I say as soon as the call connects.

"Hellooo!" Rachel crows. "Are you ready for the final bid numbers?"

"Yes," I say breathlessly.

"Okay." Rachel pauses dramatically, and I try my best not to scream at her to hurry. She's taking her time, enjoying this moment. "Let's start with the smallest bid. So, coming in at fifth place is Landmark with five hundred. Fourth place is Juniper Farr Books at five hundred and seventy-five. Third place—you listening?"

"Yes!"

"Okay, just checking I haven't lost you," she jokes. "Third is Sadie Small at seven hundred. Second place is Shields and Carey at seven hundred fifty, and at first place—drumroll please—we have Salt Books at eight hundred and thirty thousand dollars. Kind of a weird number, but we're not mad about it!"

Eight hundred and thirty thousand dollars? My mind short-circuits trying to envision this sum. This impossibly large sum. Life-changing money. Money that I could live off for the rest of my life.

"Fern? You okay?"

I blink. "Yes, I'm okay. I just—oh my god." And I burst into tears.

"Awww, sweetheart. You deserve this. You did this, don't forget that. You were so brave, and you wrote the raw truth for everyone to see. You faced down your bully in the most amazing way possible, and you deserve this."

I nod and blubber my thanks to her.

"So, shall I tell Salt Books that we're happy to accept their offer?"

"Yes. Yes!" I cry, laughing through my tears.

"Amazing. See, I told you they have deep pockets. They know I would never have accepted that first offer, but can't blame them for trying."

"You are amazing. Thank you," I say.

"No, you did this. This was your blood, sweat, and tears. All right, Fern. Congratulations! You have a major book deal! Go celebrate. Well, as much as you can celebrate in a pandemic, I guess. I'll speak to you soon."

I have a major book deal. A month ago, my life was in tatters, and three words had echoed over and over in my head: I have nothing. And now, somehow, I have a major book deal. And since the book is slated to come out in 2021, I will be able to join a new debut group. One that doesn't have Haven in it. Which means there will be zero drama on my end. I will be able to make new friends, and this time, I will be so incredibly careful with what I say to them, even when it's on a private channel. I will go in wiser and stronger than before, and I will come out of it as a published author.

I laugh out loud. My god. Life is wild. It's beautiful. I wipe my face dry and then go inside the house, where Mom and Dad look at me expectantly. I smile at them. "Mom, Dad, I need to tell you something."

The next few weeks fly by in a flurry. I'll sometimes be typing away at my keyboard and then I'll realize: Huh, I haven't thought of Haven at all today. Then, days later, I'll think: Oh, I haven't thought of Haven for multiple days now. And it requires no effort on my part to not think of her. How funny, to think that not very long ago, I was having mental wrestling matches with myself in an effort to stop obsessing over Haven. And now, I genuinely forget about her. What a gorgeous feeling it is. Of course, technically I am writing a book about bullying, so I do think of her, but when I do, I do so in a clinical way, removed of all emotion.

I am so busy these days. I have deadlines to meet and a book to write, and it's been a cathartic process, digging out my old journals and reading through them, identifying entries that might go well in the book and sending them to my new editor, Julia. Unlike Lindsay, I hear from Julia almost every day. She and I are working very closely on the book, and so far, she's so pleased with the chapters I am sending her way.

Oh, this chapter is heartbreaking! she'll say. Or she might say, Omg I laughed out loud reading this part. Your voice is both hilarious and poignant. I love it!

I think about my relationship with Annette and how bossy she was, how brusque and dominating, and I am filled with gratitude for this new working relationship. I keep a gratitude journal, which I write in every morning, to remind myself of how far I have come. It also serves to remind me of how much I have to lose now, and thus how very carefully I must step. Because what comes with having nice things in life is the fear that they might one day be taken away. But with Haven having disappeared from my radar, my fears are more easily kept at bay.

My book deal is announced in *E! News*.

> Julia Small at Salt Books has acquired Fern Huang's memoir, titled *I Didn't Mean to Do That*. Fern Huang is the author of the viral op-ed "How I Turned from

> Bully Victim into the Bad Guy." *I Didn't Mean to Do That* is an expansion of the op-ed, and has sold in a high-six-figure deal. Small describes the book as a heart-wrenching tell-all about the trauma of bullying and the invisible permanent scars it leaves behind. "I think just about everyone has read that op-ed and related really hard to the downward spiral that Fern experienced at the hands of her bully," Small says. "This memoir is so timely and important. I think it's going to mean the world for a lot of people. It's going to make people feel seen."

I post about it on Twitter and brace myself for the hate. But aside from the odd snarky remark here and there, what pours in is heartfelt congratulations.

> . . . so well-deserved!
>
> We love an underdog victory!!
>
> . . . so obsessed with the op-ed and I CANNOT wait to read this book!
>
> Is there a preorder link up??

My DMs fill up with fellow authors congratulating me. This time, I don't even need to apply to join the 2021 debut group—I get sent an invite to join their Slack group that very same afternoon. I do so and arrive in the Slack to yet more congratulatory messages. Most books have a lead-up of two years prior to publication, so everyone here knows everyone already, and I am a newcomer. But I don't feel intimidated. I've been part of a debut group before, and I have weathered the worst possible outcome that could ever happen to a writer and come out of it triumphant. I know all the pitfalls of being part of such a group, and I know how to avoid them. My posts in the various channels are measured; I never click Enter without checking my messages, asking myself every single time: If this were to be screenshotted and shared publicly, would I be okay? If the answer is anything aside from a confident yes, then I don't post it.

Two months later, I hand in the finished draft to Julia, who reads it in three days and sends me a three-page letter, two and half of which are her gushing over what an amazing job I've done. The changes she requests are nothing compared to what I went through with Lindsay, and I get to work with enthusiasm. Meanwhile, the marketing and publicity teams have already started working on my book. I am sent to a professional photographer for a full day of shooting, and they hire a hair and makeup team, as well as a costume person who puts me in a bright-yellow dress that ends just above my knees. The resulting photos make me look vulnerable, sincere, and hopelessly likable. After some back-and-forth, the team picks one photo and uses it as the cover. "I have a book cover, and the book cover has me on it," I write in my gratitude journal. When I show Mom and Dad, they actually get a little misty eyed. They don't go as far as crying, of course—this is still my parents we're talking about—but that's about as much emotion as I could've hoped for from them, and this, too, I jot down in my journal. There are so many things to be grateful for these days.

Six months before my book release, the publicity goes into full gear. My publicist has me booked for dozens of interviews, some of them for podcasts, some for radio, some even for local news channels, and others for magazines. I think of the external publicist I hired. She would never have been able to get half these things for me.

I am nervous at the first couple of interviews, but after that, I quickly get used to them, and I find that, to my surprise, I am actually good at talking about my book. It's one of many things I am learning about myself, that maybe I was never an introvert. Maybe I was always an extrovert, but years of trauma in Haven's hands turned me into an introvert, and now that I'm free of her, I can finally embrace my true nature. During these interviews, I joke easily with the hosts, and our chats are filled with easy laughter. When they ask me a question that's too tough, I say, "Oof, I don't think I'm equipped to answer that." I don't apologize; I don't give an explanation. I am comfortable with setting boundaries.

Then they tell me that they've booked me an interview with—my god—*Good Morning America*.

"Normally," Julia says, "they'd fly you to New York for the live interview, but since we're in a pandemic, it'll be done virtually. I hope that's okay with you?"

It takes me a moment to reply because my brain has short-circuited at the news. When I can finally speak again, I say, "Wait, what? With . . . the *Good Morning America*? The show? That everyone watches?"

Julia laughs. "Yes!"

"Oh my god!" I scream. "Yes! Of course, I'm okay with it! Oh my god!"

The morning of the interview, I wake up at 4:00 a.m. and begin getting ready, steadfastly curling my hair one lock at a time before applying my makeup with the care of a neurosurgeon. I log on a good hour before the interview is due to begin and sit there practicing my smile.

The interview is a lot easier than I'd expected. The hosts, Marie and Kevin, are warm and inviting. Their questions are friendly ones, nothing that makes me uncomfortable or wary, no gotcha moments.

Marie is in the middle of a question about my baking when she stops mid-sentence. Her gaze flicks to somewhere beyond the camera, and she says, "Uh, hold on, everyone, I'm just getting some breaking news." She presses on her earpiece and listens to it for a few moments.

My curiosity is building, but I don't feel nervous or anxious at all. I wonder if the breaking news is something COVID related. Maybe they've found a cure for it? That would be pretty cool.

But when Marie looks back up, it's obvious that what she's about to say isn't anything positive. She clears her throat, her expression somber. "I just received news that Haven M. Lee passed away last night."

The world falls away from me. Everything fades into a fuzzy background as I struggle to absorb what Marie has just said.

"Fern, are you all right? Fern?" Kevin says.

I blink, jerking my attention back to my laptop. "Uh," I manage to cough out.

"I am so sorry," Kevin says. "This must be such a hard thing for you to hear."

Marie shifts in her seat, and it's as though I can see her stance changing in that very second, going from a friendly show host to a hungry reporter who senses a good story. "Wow," she says, "yeah, you must be having a ton of emotions right now. Would you like to talk about them?"

My mouth opens, but no words come out. I'm still not quite grasping the reality of what's happening. Haven is dead? How? No, that doesn't matter right now. I need to focus. Haven is dead, and I am finding out on *live TV*. This is all my fault. No. It isn't. I merely wrote the truth. It's not my fault that Haven couldn't face the truth. She was a bully, and she got a taste of her own medicine, and it isn't my fault at all. Yes, it is. If I hadn't published that op-ed . . .

"Fern?" Marie presses. "We are here for you. Anything you'd like to share with us . . ."

I blink at the screen and grapple with my mind, trying to force it to pay attention to the interview. My instinctive reaction is to tell Marie I'm fine, but I manage not to do that somehow. Because I am not fine. I'm not. "I . . ." I say.

Marie leans forward, her eyes wide and expectant.

"I don't . . ." My voice trails away. What do I say? What should I say? "I'm sorry."

Marie makes an empathetic frown. "Oh, Fern, we're all very sorry for this loss. Haven Lee was . . . well, how would you describe her, Fern?"

Thankfully, Kevin reaches out and taps Marie on the arm. He leans toward her, covering his mic, and says something in a low voice. Marie sighs and nods.

"We apologize to everyone," Kevin says to the camera. "But Fern's publisher has requested to cut this interview. Thank you everyone for tuning in, and thank you, Fern, for talking to us about your upcoming book. The title is *I Didn't Mean to Do That*, and . . ."

I don't hear the rest of Kevin's words. I stare blankly as they wrap up the interview and log me off the call. The moment I'm off camera, I grab my phone and do a search on Haven.

And sure enough, the first hit is a news article with the headline DISGRACED AUTHOR FOUND DEAD IN APPARENT SUICIDE. A picture of Haven that I recognize as her author photo is published under it. I speed-read the article.

> Haven Michaela Lee, 30, was found dead in her parents' San Marino home yesterday. Officials believe it was suicide and are not looking into foul play. Lee was the author of the book *She Asked for It*, which had sold to Wallace Books in a seven-figure deal. However, an op-ed revealing Lee as a bully was released, and Lee was dropped by her publisher. Friends and family said she became depressed with suicidal ideation and chose to end her life.

There's a knock at my door, and Mom opens it. Her face is stricken, and when I look up at her, she grimaces. "You've heard?" she says. "About that poor girl?"

I nod. Behind her, Dad hovers like an anxious fly.

"Are you okay?" Mom says, looking at me like she thinks I might shatter like a precious vase.

"I . . ." I almost say I'm okay, but stop myself. "I'm kind of in shock. I think I just need a moment."

Mom comes into the room and places a hand over mine. She pats it lightly. It's her version of a hug. "If you need to talk, you know where to find us."

I nod, and she shuffles out of the room. Dad closes the door behind him.

This is bad. This is—I never meant for this to happen. "I'm a good person," I say. My voice comes out as a whimper. "I'm a good person," I say again. Who am I trying to convince? It's not just Haven's death that's scrambling my mind right now. It's Dani's too. Maybe both were my fault? I should've done things differently. I should've stood up to Haven back at school instead of airing everything out in that op-ed . . .

My thoughts go round and round in this way until I can't take it anymore. I sit at my desk and open up Twitter. Twitter has been good to me these days. I'll do a bit of doomscrolling to take my mind off Haven's death. My god, her literal death. I shake my head and begin to scroll. And that's when I realize the nightmare never ended; it merely took a break. And now it's back.

Chapter 27

Age Eighteen

"Why are we here again?" Haven says in a voice dripping with both boredom and derision.

If I had any guts, I would say "Yeah, why are we here again?" in an equally bitchy voice. But the truth is, when Dani called and asked me to meet up with her at our old hangout—a secret spot at Griffith Park that overlooks the city—I was so happy that I got teary eyed. And I do mean that literally. My eyes really did fill up with happy tears, and I rushed around my room, trying on various outfits, ranging from fabulous grown-up clothes to ones that screamed: "It's me! Your real best friend! Remember me?"

Of course, when I got there and saw not just Dani but Haven as well, my mood immediately soured. Then the dread set in. What if Haven thought up another mean prank to play on me, and this time, Dani is in on it? I don't think I would survive that. I'm pretty sure if that were to happen, I'd die of a literal heartbreak. And that is why I am standing there silently, staring at Dani with wide eyes. It's nighttime, sometime after nine, and it's surprisingly cold out here.

Dani looks somberly at both Haven and me. She's not smiling, and I guess it's a good sign because if she were in on a prank, she'd probably be giggling and looking shifty eyed. But her eyes aren't shifty; they're glaring straight at us.

"I asked you guys to come out here because I'm tired of whatever bullshit you've got going on between the two of you," she says.

"Excuse me?" Haven says, crossing her arms in front of her chest.

I can't stop myself from blurting, "She's the one who's been targeting me!"

Dani raises a hand. "Whatever. I don't care who started what. It's been going on since middle school, guys. It's gone on way too long. It's just pathetic now. We're about to go off to college—"

"You guys are off to college," I mutter. "I'm off to community college. Thanks to her." I throw a glare at Haven.

"Stop it!" Dani says. "Just stop! This whole thing has ruined my entire high school experience. It needs to stop!"

I gawp at her. I can't believe I'm hearing these words from my own best friend. Well, I guess technically she's no longer my best friend now, but Dani's one of the kindest people in the world, and I can't believe she's being so callous right now. It's ruining her high school experience? What about my high school experience? Is it my fault that Haven is a cruel person who has it out for me?

Haven looks equally outraged. Her beautiful, flawless face is frozen in an open-mouthed scowl. "I don't think so," she says finally.

Dani narrows her eyes at Haven. "I don't like this side of you, Haven. Everyone thinks you're this really nice person, and you are! I know you are. So stop doing mean shit to Fern. You're so much better than this."

Haven snorts. "Don't you remember what she did? She's such a freak, she—"

It's the f-word that undoes me. The word that Haven has branded me with, the word that has since defined my existence, thrown at me by everyone at school. *Freak. God, Fern, you're such a freak.*

Something overcomes me, and before I can stop myself, I lunge at Haven and shove her as hard as I can. My palms smack into her chest, and there is a surreal moment where my mind screams: Oh my god, what am I doing?

Haven stumbles backward, all the anger on her face replaced by pure shock, her eyes and mouth forming perfect circles. She lands on her butt on the grass with a loud "Oof!" It reminds me of the time I shoved her after she made me drop my cinnamon rolls for the school bake sale, and the moment is so ridiculous, the sight so surreal, that a shrill, cracked laugh barks out of me.

Dani's head snaps toward me when she hears the laugh, and I know I won't ever forget that look on her face. It's like she's seeing me for the first time, and she doesn't like what she sees.

"Crazy bitch!" Haven shouts, shoving herself off the ground and pouncing on me.

I've never been in a physical fight like this before. I don't see the force of it coming, the way my body suddenly feels weightless, the world tipping on its side before I can make sense of anything. I don't even register the fact that I'm falling until I hit the ground. All the air is thumped out of me, and I can't even catch a breath before Haven smacks me across the face. Pain explodes in my stomach, and I punch up, hitting something—I don't know what—I flail, I scream, or maybe someone else is screaming; I don't know anything anymore. The world has descended into a whirl of limbs and shouts and an animal instinct to lash out at anything within arm's length. I lash out, kicking as hard as I can.

Then there's a different kind of shriek. Not of anger, but of alarm. A sudden scrabbling of shoes trying to gain purchase, then nothing.

I push myself up, my mind whirling from adrenaline and pain and everything else, and it's only then that I realize how close I am to the cliff's edge. I scramble away from the cliff, still on my butt. God, that was way too close. I could've fallen.

"Did you see that?" I babble. "I could've fallen. I—"

I turn to my left. Haven is sitting next to me, her chest heaving, her face frozen in horror as she stares down the cliffside. "Dani," she whispers.

I look over my shoulder, expecting to see Dani there, but there's no one around. "Where did she go?" I say stupidly.

Haven's wide, terrified eyes meet mine. "She fell."

The wave of dread that rushes over me is so severe that I almost throw up. "What do you—how could she—" My mind flails, trying to piece together the last few moments. I was fighting Haven. Dimly, I register the memory of Dani screaming at us to stop. Then she dove in, trying to pry us apart, and—

"You pushed her," Haven says.

I gawk at her. "I didn't. I didn't even know she was there. I—" I remember kicking out, and my feet connecting with someone. Was it Dani? Did I kick her so hard that she lost her balance and tumbled over the edge? Fear grips my throat, choking me. I might have killed Dani. Why did I kick out like that? Without even looking where I was kicking and thrashing about?

"I don't think I pushed her. I don't know, I—" My voice cracks. Why the hell are we talking about this? "We need to get help. We need to—" I crawl as far to the edge as I dare and call out, "Dani!"

There's no answer. Around us, the city lights continue glimmering, and right below us, nothing but pitch black.

"Dani!" Haven shouts down. "Can you hear us?" Her voice is swallowed by the unforgiving darkness.

We look at each other, my panic mirrored in her face. "Do you think she's dead?" I whisper.

Haven shakes her head. "I don't know."

"We need to call nine-one—"

When she next speaks, the words that come out of her mouth are "I'm going to Stanford."

I want to laugh. Because isn't that just so Haven? "This isn't the time to show off about Stanford," I hiss.

Haven's gaze is laser focused on mine. "Which college are you going to?"

"I've told you, Haven." I shake my head bitterly. Of course Haven, who doesn't give a shit about me, can't remember a single thing I say. My life matters so little to her. "None, thanks to you. I didn't get accepted anywhere. I'm going to attend community college."

"Okay. Not great, but still way better than prison."

I blink. "What?"

"Where do you think we'll end up, Fern?" Haven says. "Prison, that's where."

"We didn't—she was—this wasn't—" Again, our fight replays in my mind. A complete mess. Haven was the one who pushed Dani, right? Or was it me? I don't know, and the not knowing kills me. "We can tell them the truth, that this was an accident."

Haven's face changes then, all traces of shock and fear suddenly melting away, replaced by a cold, unmoving calm. "Listen to me, Fern," she says, and even her voice is different. Gone is her earlier panic. Her voice is low but full of confidence. "Even if we don't end up in prison, no college is going to want either of us if this gets out. No company will ever employ us."

"But Dani—"

"It was a horrible accident. No point in it destroying our lives as well. She wouldn't have wanted that."

My mouth opens, but before I can say anything, Haven talks over me.

"I know what you're like," she says. "You can't help but be this . . . whatever this is. You want to rush home and tell Mommy and Daddy everything that happened tonight. But if you do that, you're the one who'll regret it. Trust me." She goes quiet for a moment, then all of a sudden, she bursts into tears, her beautiful face scrunching up as actual tears roll down her cheeks. "I didn't dare tell anyone because I was so scared of what Fern might do to me!"

I gape at her stupidly. "Wait, what—"

"Everyone knows how . . . odd she is," Haven continues, drawing in a shaky breath. "Dani tried to warn me. She told me that even when they were kids, she knew there was something wrong with Fern. I just didn't know she'd be capable of murder."

"Stop it," I beg. "Stop!"

Haven stops crying and smirks at me as she wipes at her cheeks daintily. "Meanwhile, you'll sit there and go, 'Buh-buh-but—' Who do you think they're going to believe? Me, the girl with a bright future ahead of her, or you, the school freak who's held a grudge against Dani for the last five years?"

"I never held a grudge against Dani!" I cry.

"Didn't you?" Haven says. "I think I could make a pretty good case to support that. You're always lurking around her, always watching her . . ."

Because she was my best friend! I want to scream, but I'm out of words. I'm caught in a nightmare I can't seem to wake up from.

"So," Haven says, "I'm giving you a chance here, okay? A chance for both of us to walk away from this. Or you could choose to go down in flames, which would be messy and ultimately result in you probably going to prison. I don't want that, Fern. I don't have the time nor the patience for it."

My mind feels like it's being ripped apart, one side reeling with horror from what's happened to Dani, and the other reeling with horror from the thought of my ruined future. Because Haven is absolutely right. Maybe she might be okay, with her affluent parents and her shiny personality, but I sure as hell won't ever be able to escape the shadow of tonight. Not if it ever got out that I was involved. It would definitely mean prison time, and that's much, much worse than community college. Not only that, but it would stay on my record for the rest of my life, making it impossible for me to find a good job. I'd thought that my life was miserable before, but the misery would be nothing compared to what's in store for me if they blamed me for tonight.

"Nobody can know that we were here," Haven says.

I feel my head nodding, as though of its own accord. "No one."

"Did you tell anyone you were coming out here to meet Dani?"

"No." Who would I tell? I want to say. I have no friends, and my parents don't give a shit about me. "You?"

"My parents are out of town," Haven says. "So I didn't tell them anything."

We stare at each other for another long moment, and though no words are spoken, it feels like a world of communication is being shared between us. Understanding settles over us, a silent promise twining itself around us, binding us forever to each other. If she talks, I talk, and vice versa. And neither of us will come out of this unscathed. Unless we stay silent and erase ourselves from Dani's death completely.

Now, as Haven and I sit in the principal's office, with two officers staring at us, I try my best not to think of last night.

"We're trying to determine the cause of death," the officer says. "Is there anything you can tell us that might help us understand how this happened?"

As usual, I am frozen, my mind both silent and also a cacophony of panicked thoughts. Nothing coalesces into a coherent thought. Again and again, the fight replays in my head, and still I can't discern who pushed Dani over the cliff.

It is Haven's voice that slices through the noise in my head. "Dani was struggling with a lot of stuff."

My head snaps up, my shocked gaze locking onto Haven's face. She pretends not to notice me staring as she continues speaking.

"She was always really hard on herself," Haven says. "She really wanted to get into Stanford, and she was devastated when she didn't get in. Maybe it all got too much for her."

My mouth is gaping. I can't believe how naturally Haven lies. If I hadn't been there myself last night, I would've believed every word coming out of Haven's mouth.

The officer notices my expression. "Fern, do you have something to say?"

I close my mouth abruptly. How could I possibly say anything now? If I did, Haven would tell them I'm a liar, and look what an incredible performer Haven is. Meanwhile, I have guilt wriggling through me like a worm. I can't see anyone believing me over her. And what would I say, anyway? That we were there last night, and Dani fell? They'd ask why we didn't call for help right away, then what? I look down at my hands. Dani is dead. And the cops believing one story over another changes nothing. She'll still be gone. And I don't have it in me to stand up to Haven. Not now. Probably not ever.

I shake my head. "No."

"You said Dani was your best friend," the cop says, leaning forward. "Is it true what Haven said about Dani being stressed out?"

Tears blur my vision as I nod. I hate myself so much. I wish I could trade my life for Dani's. I am weak. I have always been weak.

The officers thank us for our time, and Haven and I are dismissed. We leave in silence, and when she and I are alone in the hallway, our eyes meet.

"I hope I never see you again," I say, and I mean every single word.

"Me too," Haven says, her face hard and cold like a mask. She turns and walks ahead of me, and I, as always, am left staring at her retreating back, my insides coiling with self-hatred.

Chapter 28

The news about Haven's suicide is all over Twitter, and everyone seems to be incandescent with rage and grief, and they're all looking for somebody to blame. That somebody is, naturally, me. People say you should never read the comments, but there is not a chance in hell that I would be able to keep myself from reading them.

They are brutal. No one is holding back.

> . . . ironic that Fern Huang has bullied her bully into committing suicide . . .
>
> . . . fucked up how Fern Huang literally stole everything from Haven Lee??
>
> . . . wrote that disgusting article basically inciting the world to hate on Haven Lee . . .

My chest physically hurts. Breathing becomes harder and harder, to the point that I have to tear my eyes off the computer screen and focus on filling my lungs with air so I don't pass out. The whole time, I'm thinking: Oh god, it's happening again. I'm going to lose my book deal. It's like dying a million deaths, over and over again. Devastated doesn't even begin to describe it. I once read that heartbreak physically hurts because when the mind is in agony, the body creates more adrenaline, and the heart struggles to keep up with the sudden surge of it, which makes it hurt as it mimics the symptoms of a heart attack. That is exactly what I'm feeling right now. A series of heart attacks as I slump to the floor and envision a future where I lose a second book deal.

And, deeper still, beyond the surface-level panic of losing my career, is the unfathomable pain of knowing that a life was lost and I had something to do with it. A pain that is excruciating in its familiarity. Dani, and now, Haven. I may not have directly caused their deaths, but I am intrinsically tied to them. If not for me, neither one would be dead. The guilt threatens to crush me.

My phone rings. I squeeze my eyes shut, tears streaming down the sides of my face. I don't want to answer it. Please don't make me answer it. It continues ringing. I lift it and glance at the screen. It's Rachel FaceTiming me. I moan out loud. God, please no. Not again. I can't take this yet again. It will kill me. The thought makes me snort. What would truly be ironic is if I were to also kill myself right now. Why not? Now that once again, I am about to have nothing left to lose. I might as well lose the last thing I do have—my life.

Somehow, accepting that I once again have nothing revives me enough to accept the call. I don't bother getting up off the floor, though. Why make the effort when I'm just going to crumple back onto it once Rachel fires me?

When FaceTime loads, I find not just Rachel but Julia; Sophia, my publicist; Christine from Marketing; Louisa from Sales; someone else that I don't recognize; and, worst of all, Martin, the head of the publishing house, on the call. "Oh," I say, sitting up and frantically wiping away my tears. Are they about to fire me in front of my entire publishing team? This is a new level of cruelty that I was unprepared for. But I suppose I deserve it, and worse.

"Hi, Fern, how are you doing?" Rachel says. Her voice is full of sympathy, which is somewhat surprising.

"Um. Well, I just heard the news about Haven, and—" My voice cracks, and I wave at the screen. "Sorry! I'm fine. It's fine."

"Oh, Fern. It's unimaginably sad," Julia pipes up. "We all feel awful about what happened."

"Yeah." I pinch my thigh to keep the tears from falling. "It's all my fault."

There is a collective gasp. Rachel leans into her camera so her face fills the whole screen. "Fern, listen to me. It is NOT your fault. What happened is devastating, but it is not your fault."

Everyone else is nodding.

"Fern," Julia says, "I understand why you might blame yourself, but please, please trust us when we tell you that what Haven did is not your fault. You were doing what was right for you, and not only for you but for other bullying victims out there. You were writing your truth. Of course we hate that Haven felt like she had no other choice but to do what she did, but Fern, should you have stayed completely silent your whole life?"

"Exactly," Rachel says. "And nowhere did you ask people to attack Haven over what she did to you in school. You were only sharing your experience. The fault really lies on all those trolls who came after her."

I drink in their words with desperate gratitude. I want to believe them so badly. Maybe in time, I might. Right now, their kindness is almost painful, something I don't deserve. I want to end this call as quickly as I can so I can go back to curling up in my room and crying alone. "Thank you," I say. "Anyway, um. Look, I get why you're canceling my book. You don't have to explain it. I understand, and I will return all of the money." I move my finger to the Leave Call button, but before I can tap it, Rachel shouts, "*What?*"

I freeze. "Uh . . ."

They all stare at me with confused expressions, then Martin clears his throat and says, "I think there's been a misunderstanding. We're not calling to cancel your book."

"You're not?" My mind struggles to keep up.

"No," he says, "why would we?"

"Because everyone hates me? No one is going to buy my books."

"Who says everyone hates you?" Rachel says. "I mean, is there a bit of trolling going on? Sure. But trolls exist everywhere."

"On Twitter—"

"Let me stop you right there, Fern," Martin says. "We've got our social media expert on the call. Bree? Over to you."

The woman I didn't recognize before smiles and waves at the camera. "Hi, Fern, nice to meet you. My name is Bree, and I am the social media analyst at Salt Books. Now, because social media is so volatile, I hesitate to call myself an expert—thank you, Martin—but despite the volatility, there are patterns, and my job is to study these patterns and—"

Julia clears her throat meaningfully.

"Sorry," Bree says, "I tend to get carried away explaining my job. Basically, I'm here to help authors like you navigate the rough waters of social media when there is conflict. I have come up with a game plan. Let me just share my screen real quick . . . Here we go."

A slideshow appears. On it are the words *Social Media Damage Control.* The first slide shows a flowchart with the words *NEWS→BLAME→WHO→REFRAME.*

"Okay, Fern, so every time a publishing scandal breaks, people look for someone to place blame on. That's just human nature. In this case, the easiest target is you, because you are a primary player in this mess. It's nonsensical, because if the tables were turned and you had been the one to—I'm sorry for being insensitive—commit suicide, then Haven would have become the villain. When in reality, Haven's passing does not change what she did to you. Again, I apologize for being so direct. So, what we are going to do is we're going to pivot and reframe the discussion. The focus shouldn't be on who is to blame, because it's obvious who should be blamed."

I steel myself, but Bree says, "It's society! It's all aspects of human society—the social hierarchy in school, the way we've raised our kids to compete with one another, and of course, social media and how it encourages cruelty. You merely shared your story, and that's your right. You didn't ask anyone to hate on Haven—you didn't send her hate mail or death threats. Others did. People who didn't even know her. And why? Society. So, now that we have alternative targets, we need to reframe the conversation. Use this as a chance to focus on the importance of being kind. Of taking care of our mental health. These are all good conversations to have, especially since they are relevant to your book."

"Thank you, Bree," Julia says. "We think that's a really sound strategy, and we have scheduled you for more interviews—this story has blown up, and there's a lot more visibility with you and your book, which we think will work to our advantage. In fact, I'm so excited to share with you that we've booked you a live interview with Stephen Colbert!"

I'm so stunned that I can't speak. I gape like a fish at Julia. When I'm finally able to talk, I say, "Uh, Stephen Colbert is—"

"One of the most popular talk show hosts in the world? Yes! We don't want to overwhelm you, Fern, but this is a huge opportunity for your story to reach even more people. And it is such an important story, especially given the tragic outcome. We have so much to learn from it as a society. It's a chance for us to really have a conversation about all these themes you hit in your book—mental health, female friendships, healing from trauma. You have a chance to make a real difference in the world."

Everyone nods and makes "mm" noises as Julia speaks, and by the end of her speech, even I'm nearly convinced.

I want to believe everything they're telling me, but then I think of the comments I've seen on Twitter, and my resolve weakens. "But what about the hate? I don't know if—"

"You let us worry about that," Martin says. "Here at Salt Books, we've been very proactive ever since social media started becoming big in publishing. We have a robust influencer program where we work hand in hand with influencers who help us promote books and all that good stuff. And they will be able to help reframe the conversation around this topic."

It takes me a beat to understand what Martin is really saying, and when I do, I can hardly believe it. Salt Books has a network of influencers who can steer the conversation into a direction they want? "Is that ethical?" I say.

They all laugh. "Oh my gosh," Bree says. "Yes, of course it is! It's all very kosher. We're not manipulating anything—we're just helping to reframe the conversation into a more productive direction."

"If I can add something?" Sophia the publicist says. "Even with the help of our influencers, everything will shift very organically, so it's definitely ethical. Not everyone is going to agree with the reframing of the narrative, and that's okay! I think we should embrace it. What's so special about your story is that everyone can relate to it, so we should lean into that. I'm thinking interviews and op-eds with the headline 'You Hate Her. You *Are* Her.'"

"I love that," Julia says.

"This is why Sophia's on the team," Martin says. "She's the best publicist."

"Oh, stop it," Sophia says, laughing. "But I think that'll make you an even easier sell. You can love her or hate her, but you can't stop relating to her."

Everyone is being so cheerful on the call that it's infectious. Only minutes ago I'd literally been sprawled on the floor, wondering if I should just end it all, and all of a sudden I find out that I have an entire team of people wanting to save me. The thought is so overwhelming that before I know it, a choked sob burbles out of me.

"Aww, Fern," Rachel says. "I know. It's a lot to take in."

I shake my head, trying to blink away my tears. "It's not that. I mean, yes, it's a lot, but I'm just so grateful that you're not giving up on me."

"Oh my gosh," Julia says. "Give up on you? No. That didn't even cross our minds. Do not even worry about that."

I can only nod as I fight back the relieved sobs.

"Okay, so we have a plan, and I love it," Julia says.

"Fern, I will send you a shared doc with your itinerary on it," Sophia says. "You've got a ton of events lined up, and I will add to the document every time I get a new opportunity, and there will be a lot more opportunities to come, I know it."

"You're going to be busy, girl!" Julia says.

"And don't worry if you feel anxious or nervous," Rachel says. "I will be with you every step of the way, okay? I take care of my clients."

Is this what it's like to have an actual support system? To be able to fall with the confidence that a whole group of people will prop you up?

"Thank you," I say hoarsely.

"Thank *you* for having the courage to share your story," Julia says. "You and your book are going to be unstoppable."

And I find that despite everything, despite the crumbled mess of it all and the vitriol aimed at me online, despite the darkness that resides deep in my core and threatens at all times to burst through the surface and ruin everything, I believe her.

Six Months Later

My book debuts at number two on the *New York Times* bestseller list. I'm alone, visiting Dani's grave, when I get the call from Julia. Rachel had offered to be with me today, but I told her this was something I needed to do on my own.

When Julia tells me the news about the *NYT* list, I laugh through my tears. Unbelievable. I'm still crying when I get off the phone. I tap on the *NYT* app and see that Haven's book is number one on the fiction list. It's not a surprise to me. After Haven died, her parents sold her book to a different publisher. And all the publicity I've been doing in the past six months has done wonders for both of us. The nation is divided between Team Haven and Team Fern, and the ongoing controversy has created an endless stream of debates and arguments and even birthed its own spin-off drama—people have gotten into screaming fights over Haven and me. I've done all sorts of talk shows live, some of them gentler, others more aggressive, and though I was intimidated at first, my publishing team assures me over and over that even the less friendly talk shows end up selling more copies of my book. They're still driving hard at the "You can hate her, but you can't stop relating to her" angle, and it's working.

I look at the *NYT* list, with Haven's book at the top. *She Asked for It*, by Haven M. Lee. I wait for the bitterness to come, but instead, all I feel is a sense of peace. I have accepted that Haven will always be the queen bee. Even in death she can't help but outshine everyone. And there's something in knowing that I had a hand in it, that she couldn't have gotten here without me. I know that forevermore, whenever I am invited to speak at events or go on a talk show, or when I eventually write a second book, my story will always be intertwined with Haven's. She may be gone, but she and I will always be a part of each other's lives. And I can live with that. She has taught me so much, after all. She taught me that while I am prey, I am not harmless. She showed me that even under the thickest blankets of kindness, there can be a hidden sting. She was the one who made me realize that my generosity, my love for baking, can be put to good use, to humble the predators around me. It's only when I feel the claws closing in around me that I bare my own fangs in retaliation. And I don't think I would've even known that I had fangs if not for Haven's help.

"She always was special," I say to Dani's gravestone.

Around me, the cemetery is quiet, nothing breaking the stillness aside from my little hiccuping sobs. I take out a copy of my book from my bag and place it, along with a bouquet of lilies, on Dani's grave. Plucking a single lily from the bouquet, I flip open the book to the dedication page.

"To Dani, who deserved better."

I can never make up for what happened to Dani that night. And though part of me would like to blame Haven for everything, I know that I'm at fault too. That my cowardice and fear contributed to the series of events that ultimately led to Dani's death. And that by keeping quiet and letting everyone think that Dani had committed suicide, I was complicit in destroying the memory of her.

"I'm coming clean," I tell Dani. I had told Rachel in advance, as our relationship deepened from agent and client to true friends over the last few months. She said she'll come with me to the police station to file my report, which is a kindness I don't deserve. I don't know if the DA will want to press charges against me for keeping quiet all those years. Even if the DA doesn't, I wouldn't be surprised if Dani's family doesn't end up suing me in a civil lawsuit. And if they do, I won't fight it. I'll give them whatever they ask for.

As I straighten up, I reach out and gently touch Dani's headstone. "I miss you every day," I say. And as I walk away, I can hear her in my head, smiling and telling me, "I told you everything happens for a reason."

Acknowledgments

This book is a departure from the books I am known for. It is neither comedy nor thriller but a story that sits in the margins. And because it doesn't fit neatly into a single category, I am so grateful to those who took a chance on it. My agent Katelyn Detweiler, who is my tireless champion (and therapist), and everyone else at Jill Grinberg Literary Management. My editor Megha Parekh, who is sunshine in human form. I had the joy of meeting Megha in person at the LA Times Festival of Books, and it was one of the most fun, exciting, and delightful meetings of my life. I am so happy to have the chance to work with her.

I wrote this story to address both bullying and the multifaceted issues that belie social media. I am very fortunate that I did not have social media when I was younger, and while I appreciate the good it has brought, I am also slightly terrified of it. The way that anyone can be painted a hero or a villain, a victim or an instigator, sometimes both in the matter of a few hours. It is my hope that Fern and Haven's story leaves the reader satisfied but also uneasy, because it is messy and complex and sometimes, even the "good guys" do bad things.

Thank you for taking a chance on this book. Thank you for giving me space to write this story. And don't worry, there will still be more stories of meddlesome Chinese aunties to come. But for now, thank you for spending time with the quieter, darker side of me.

About the Author

Photo © 2022 Lovoto Photography

Jesse Q. Sutanto is the Edgar Award–winning, *USA Today* bestselling author of *Dial A for Aunties*, *The Obsession*, *Theo Tan and the Fox Spirit*, *Vera Wong's Unsolicited Advice for Murderers*, and *Well, That Was Unexpected*. The film rights to *Dial A for Aunties* were acquired by Netflix in a competitive bidding war, while the TV rights to *Vera Wong* were bought by Warner Bros. with Oprah Winfrey and Mindy Kaling attached to produce. Sutanto holds a master's degree in creative writing from the University of Oxford, though she hasn't found a way of saying that without sounding obnoxious. The author lives in Indonesia with her husband, two daughters, and a ridiculously large extended family.